THE CRIMSON SUMMER

TYLER NICHOLS

"THE CRIMSON SUMMER"

First Printing, 2016

ISBN-13 978-1530216970

www. zombievictim.com

tylernicholswrites@gmail.com

ACKNOWLEDGMENTS

It's weird to actually be writing this. Whenever I picked up a book and read the acknowledgments, I always wondered if I'd ever be able to complete a book, and would therefore need an acknowledgments section. Well here we are. I finally have my first book and I'm honored to thank all of the people that made it possible.

First off, my parents. Yes, that means all of you. I may not be able to get you all in the same room together, but dammit, I can put you in the same paragraph! Dad and Kim, you two always nurtured my love for horror and always supported me in my creative endeavors in school and in life. Those terrible DV horror films I made wouldn't have been possible without you. Mom and Ted, you supported me no matter what crazy idea I happened to have. You always believed in me and that means the world.

My brother, Marc, you made the writing of this book possible. You were always there for me to bounce ideas off of and whenever I needed words of encouragement. There are many people that, without their impact on me, this book would have never been conceivable, but in a more direct way, this book would have been a literal impossibility without your support. Thanks for being the best brother I could ask for.

My grandparents, Karen and Darrell. No matter what stupid things I've done in life, you two have always been there for me. When I told you I was releasing a book, your first reactions were "How can we help?" That kind of love and support is priceless in a world that constantly replies, "No." Now let's just hope you can get past all the sex, drugs, and violence in this book. I promise the next will be PG (Okay, maybe not).

To my fellow writer's that are always a source of great conversation as well as inspiration. Diego, Bea, and Todd, having other people with the same passion and drive is always a great source of inspiration and your opinions have helped shape my creative endeavors. Diego, you are pretty much my Yoda and without your guidance for the past decade, I'm not even sure which path I'd be on.

Andre, Sam, Max, Jason, Steve, Marybeth. You are a great group of friends who have always offered encouragement. Having your friends truly believe in you goes a long way.

Thank you to all of the Alpha readers. Your feedback was invaluable to where I proceeded to take the story. Without you, it wouldn't have become the animal that it is today. You affected which characters lived and died, and who would be the focus as the story went on.

It'd be kind of hard to make it through this without thanking the man who created the lovely cover art at the front, Álvaro De Cossio. I'm not sure if I would have been able to get others as excited about the book if not for that stellar art.

There are so many people have supported me throughout the years that it makes me truly feel blessed to finally be able to give them a written thank you. If I missed you, I am sorry and it is not malicious. I'm just a very forgetful person.

Most importantly, I'd like to thank YOU for reading this. If you hadn't picked yourself up a copy and gotten this far, then it all would have been for naught. I appreciate any words you have for me, good or bad, and truly hope that you enjoy the journey into Camp Watanka as much as I enjoyed writing it.

For everyone that loves the strange and unusual...

PART ONE

Chapter 1
Chase

CHASE COULDN'T GET THE IMAGE of frog guts out of his head. It wasn't exactly something he wanted to think about but no matter how hard he tried, the thought persisted. The guts as they smashed up against the rock, like a water balloon bursting. The sickening noise of *squish* and *crunch* that followed, ended any semblance the frog had to its original form. The ending mixture of green and red reminded Chase of the Christmas ribbon his school hung everywhere. Now the holidays made him queasy. It was all so visceral and unlike anything he had seen before. He could vividly remember the blue shirt, tattered grey jeans, and white Adidas he was wearing at the time. The way they all clung tightly to his body after his annual clothes shopping with his mom had been postponed yet again. He couldn't remember the clothes of the three other boys, just the look of glee that adorned their faces during the event itself.

The act of Tommy Tuscadero's brother, Ricky, smashing the frog against the rock had occurred nearly three years ago to the day, yet it still haunted Chase. The previous week had been particularly harsh as it had played through his head on the school bus, in the grocery store, at dinner—usually followed by said dinner not being eaten—and unfortunately even sometimes during brief moments when self-pleasuring. It's not like he ever wanted that to happen. Half a second would happen to slip in between Kate Upton and Jennifer Lawrence and before he knew it that expanded into some of the climax. *I have the worst fucking luck,* always popped into his head the moment one of those types of incidents happened. Chase wiped himself off in shame that night, equating it to accidentally thinking about his mom during climax. Eventually that thought haunted him enough to manifest itself during a session, a moment that Chase had long since erased from his memory bank. The frog however? Impossible for him to forget.

It wasn't that Ricky was a sadistic child. . . or at least Chase didn't think he was. In fact, in all other instances he had acted quite the opposite. He couldn't imagine hurting another creature on planet earth, especially not one that was so innocent. Which was ultimately Chase's big problem with it. What had a frog ever done to Ricky? Frogs were always put in a good light when he was growing up. They were busy either chatting it up with toads or kissing princesses so what could be they have possibly done to deserve such a fate? Ricky even seemed to have a vendetta against the amphibian, judging by the amount of hate he put behind every swing.

Chase's grasp on the effect of the frog smashing was certainly light. He had seen much worse things on the internet—and to actual human beings, not just frogs. Anywhere from a man shoving a dildo down his urethra to a person having glass jar break inside them, the internet put content in front of him without even asking for it. And Chase, being like any teenage boy with an internet connection, was there to test just how far his limits were. While those limits may have been pushed repeatedly, nothing affected him more than that damn frog. Even Tommy, a kid who would often pass out at the sight of his own blood, didn't seem affect by it. And yet Chase was considered the weird one.

No, Chase was as normal as anyone else, at least in his own eyes. Maybe the kids at school didn't agree but he hadn't seen any difference between himself and any of the other people that inhabited his high school. Sure, he hadn't done any sports in nearly a year and his group of friends seemed to diminish every Fall, with buddy after buddy moving to greener pastures but he made do. While he wasn't exactly a social pariah who wouldn't talk to anyone else, his social skills left a lot to be desired.

Even as he laid in bed, his mind wandered till finally landing on the question of whether or not anyone would even care that he would be gone that summer. Sure, some of his friends would be a little annoyed that they didn't have a fourth player for Halo nights or that suddenly splitting pizza was going to cost a little more but ultimately Chase doubted it would have much effect on them. That was what worried him the most. What if he was just simply forgotten after not being around for the summer? Chase had a really good friend in Elementary school that moved shortly after second grade and, no matter how close they were during those younger years, he found himself drawing a blank when it came to the kid's actual name. Eventually he'd either ask his mother or be reminded himself that it was Timothy but the fact that it didn't immediately come to mind was worrisome enough. He didn't want to be Timothy.

"Chase, hurry up, we're not gonna be late just because you're busy playing with yourself. Get a move on!" his mother yelled from downstairs and broke Chase's train of thought. Probably for the best.

Chase's mind raced. *Wait, does she really think I'm jerking off?* Immediately realizing how stupid that sounded, he attributed it to his mother making a joke, something she only seemed to do at his own expense.

"Yeah, I'll be down in a minute." Chase answered after a long and awkward silence, not really wanting to answer.

"Not a minute. *Now!*" his mom barked through the wall.

Chase shook his head. *Jesus mom, be more of a stereotype.* He slowly got up off of his bed and grabbed his large duffel bag. Something caught his eye from the corner of his room: a dark blue pouch, just small enough to fit a lunch in. Chase shook his head, debating whether or not to bring it. It could help him make friends. Or enemies with his luck. *At least they'll know me,* Chase thought as he grabbed the small pouch. He took one last look at his room, the various video game posters and massive gaming computer in the corner. He sighed, not wanting to leave. Chase was in his room more than anywhere else, although some of that could have easily been attributed to sleep. And he was almost always attached to technology. Now he was going to be without it all for five weeks. Resisting the urge to just lock himself in his room for the summer, he shut the door behind him, hauling his things across the hall and down the stairs, just in time to hear his mother shout, "I swear to god, if you take one more—"

"Mom, relax. I was just talking to Evan. Can I talk to my friends?" he asked with at least a little sincerity, despite the fact that he was lying through his teeth. Excuses were easier than telling her the truth. At least he learned something from his mother.

"I told you, 12:30. The bus leaves at 1:00 and it takes twenty-five minutes to get to Spaulding. So we now have. . ." his mother angrily checked her watch. ". . . Nineteen minutes to get there. And I am not taking you all the way to Camp Watanka. My car can't take that long of a drive and you know that. We're doing the bus for a reason."

"Yeah, I know," he said angrily. Why did his mom always have to state the obvious every time just to prove her point? It's not like Chase wasn't fully aware of her reasoning for not going. She wanted to meet up with that boyfriend of hers. Chase never understood why she couldn't just be honest with him. He was in High School; she should have been able to treat him like an adult. But she was too in her own world to worry about him. Her latest romantic escapade was more important.

They got into the car and his mother sped off, almost running over the neighbor's black calico that liked to hang out at the end of their driveway. Chase wondered how she would react if she were even later due to her lead foot.

"You need to stop acting like the world treats you so damn terribly. How're you ever going to make friends with an attitude like that?" she stressed harshly. She often claimed that she didn't mean to be so cruel, in spite of the tone she often took with him. She blamed it on her father, who took no bullshit, a trait she decided to carry into her own form of parenting. Chase didn't care what excuse she used though, it was just another way of her avoiding the reality of being a selfish mother.

"Yeah, because a smile is gonna do the trick," Chase replied with defeated sarcasm. It's not like Chase hadn't tried to fit in. He had gone through more haircuts and wardrobe changes than he could remember. Yet none of them really fit his personality and everyone seemed to know it wasn't his true self. The kids at school were like rabid dogs, smelling any sign of weakness. Chase's lack of personal identity made him more than a target: it made him a prisoner. No matter what he did, he was always seen as fake. The reputation seemed to follow him around.

He had to give his mother credit though, for as much as she moved from job to job, she still kept him in the same school system. After seeing so many friends leave, it was nice for him to have some kind of stability, even if they were switching houses every other month. They'd ultimately settled down in their current place but the streak was sure to be broken at any point, with his mom's current out-of-state boyfriend, Carter, making more and more appearances. She was already mentally packing.

"You need to just get over your whole 'fear of new places' thing. This is healthy for you. Helps you meet new people," she said with a southern drawl, not present before.

"Yeah, it's really fucking helped." Chase rolled his eyes. It was yet another case of his mother picking up a trait from her boyfriend. Just like the time she switched to cigars from cigarettes and ended up being sick all night. It was just another step in the process. Chase was used to it.

"Chase Daniel! Language! I am not your father. Do not think for one second that you can do that around me," she snorted.

Chase shook his head, knowing just how far from the truth that could ever be. His father was far more strict than his mother. It was so bad that he considered his mom to be the lesser of two evils, deciding to live with her instead—a decision that was likely to haunt his older self. Maybe a little guidance would have done him good. Maybe he could have really turned things around. Maybe he'd be going out to parties on the lake with his beautiful girlfriend and a huge circle of friends. But he couldn't just live his life in a world of maybes. No matter how much he thought of these things, nothing ever changed. Why would it? For effect there had to be a cause, and Chase just never seemed to be able to light the fuse.

"Look, I just want you to have a good time," his mother continued. "Last year your grandparents wouldn't stop calling me saying you were moping all around and not doing anything. Just sitting in that room playing games on your laptop. That's no way to properly live. We need to get you out and doing stuff. Having fun. That's what a boy your age should be doing. Being social and making bonds of friendship that can last the rest of your life."

"Sounds riveting."

"It's what people do, Chase."

"Yeah, well maybe you shouldn't just be sending me off to places away from home to try and get some free time for yourself," Chase quipped.

"You'll thank me for the experiences when you're older. Hell, I wish my parents did these types of things for me. I was lucky to be able to stick around town and work a part-time job. Maybe that's what you need, a part-time job. Make you have an appreciation for money. I'm sick of spending all this money to send you places—"

"No," Chase corrected. "You're spending *Dad's* money."

"Regardless," she responded, treating the situation as if he wasn't dead on. "There has been a lot of money spent on you in order for you to have good experiences. So please, I don't want to hear anything from you or from one of your counselors. I won't be picking you up within a day just because you decided to get yourself in trouble. And I won't be getting phone calls ruining *my* vacation. In fact, the number I left with the camp is your Aunt Jeannie's so if you want to leave, you're going to be spending the rest of the time with her, got it?"

Oh god. Not Aunt Jeannie, Chase thought, shaking his head at the suggestion. Aunt Jeannie had never married and spent most of her free time taking her cats to competitions. Her social life was practically non-existent, making her available at any time, whether it was as a babysitter or driver. Chase tried avoiding her at all costs but wasn't always successful.

"That's what I thought," his mother said with a pompous attitude. "Just remember, this is something that you're going to look back on years from now and *wish* you could go back to. It's once in a lifetime. You'll never forget it."

Like he could ever forget what she was forcing him to do that summer. For the first time, he would be attending summer camp and he had been dreading it for months.

And hoping like hell for no frogs.

Chapter 2

Carol

CAROL AWOKE WITH SUCH EXCITEMENT that it was nearly too much for her to handle. Endorphins pumped and her nerves were on edge. The day was finally here. The day she had waited for all year long. The day she thought about constantly as she sat at her boring university gig as a receptionist, twiddling her thumbs and just picturing all the great things that would start on this very important day. This was like Christmas to her. No, this was bigger than Christmas, this was the first day of summer camp.

It didn't matter what anyone thought about her excitement, she showed it without reserve. She had been at Watanka for several weeks helping to prep the camp with most of the other counselors and it was hard enough to get the smile off her face. And while she certainly enjoyed that—one of the only counselors that did—this trumped everything else. No one else understood the camp like she did. Except maybe Al, whose enthusiasm was more contained than her own. The campers' first arrival was the true beginning of all the fun for her.

Carol had spent the last few nights carefully preparing her daily routine. Every year she would follow a basic structure from day to day but there were always tweaks and areas to improve upon. It was an always-evolving process. In its current iteration, she'd wake up at 5:30 a.m., get out of bed and immediately wash her face with cold water, applying an organic cleanser, which she'd immediately wash it off. She would proceed to wipe her face with Stridex pads and allow the exfoliate to work its magic. This provided her with valuable time where she combed her hair, an essential part of her look. Getting all knots out of her mane transitioned smoothly into the ponytail she'd then put it into.

After making her way to the bathroom at 6 o'clock on the dot, she would take only a two-and-a-half-minute shower, as to not take all the hot water from everyone else. It was also her own way of avoiding the annoying shower plumbing which would sometimes go ice-cold out of nowhere. The longer in, the higher the chances were of getting iced. Simple fact of camp life that she'd describe to complaining campers as "charming." Carol tried to fix it once but, given that she had no experience in the subject whatsoever, she ended up doing more harm than good. Big Al certainly wasn't appreciative of the

$2,000 bill from the plumber. But it was the effort that mattered.

Spending twenty-two-and-a-half minutes adjusting her make-up, which looked shockingly similar to how she looked without the applied beauty products, she then put her hair into its signature ponytail and started the strangest part of her daily routine. She'd stare at the mirror for a good two minutes, pumping herself up, much like a coach would do to their players before a big game. Eye contact was key.

"This is the day that you change these kids' lives. You will do absolutely everything in your power to become the role model that each and every one of these camper's deserves. You will be the greatest counselor that has ever stepped on this green earth and help make this camp even better than it was last year. Big Al will be so impressed that he'll have no choice but to make you the head counselor. Because you are the only one that can do this. You are the only one that can help save these kids. You are a champion."

She did that every morning, no matter how she was feeling. The pump-up was an essential cap-off to her personal routine. But those were all just primers for the start of her real day. After all the "dolling up", then came the fun stuff: her counselor routine.

First, Carol would embark upon her campers' bunk at precisely 7:30 a.m., waking them up with the rapid clanging of the bell, hung outside of C1 (Cabin 1). They'd wake up on the grouchy side, but nothing Carol couldn't fix with a massive smile and interesting fact, usually regarding sleep and often more opinion than fact. Her go-to on the first morning was always,

"The natural human sleep cycle follows the sun, and the more *you* do too, the more likely you'll grow up to be big and bright."

They may have been *mostly* opinion.

After shuffling the campers off to the showers—an activity she allotted 45 minutes of time for—she'd calmly read her school books in front of her cabin. This gave her a clear view of both bathrooms and allowed her to keep an eye on all the hormones. Sometimes she'd peek in on the girls and tell them to hurry up, just to keep them in line and maybe hear some choice gossip. This was her favorite time because the day ahead had limitless potential. Plus, she really loved reading.

Once the campers were all showered and dressed, it was time for the meeting at the flag. Every group would stand in line and say the pledge of allegiance as the American flag was risen high in the sky. They used to have a prayer at the end but that changed in the 1990's to a moment of silence, then finally in the 2000's, it was dropped completely.

The Camp Watanka song would follow. Carol, accompanying on the guitar and easily the loudest voice at the camp, would stand near the front and sway back and forth, like she was on a stage in front of thousands upon thousands. She really liked that song.

With the campers' stomachs rumbling, it was time for breakfast. This would usually happen at 8:30 but given Al's looseness with scheduling, it would sometime go over or under by several minutes. No matter though, Carol always kept a spare hacky sack on her when she needed to fill time and build bonds of friendship in her group.

Giving a helping hand to Marjory, the camp cook and a staple of Camp Watanka since 1973, Carol would stand behind the counter and serve food. It was her way of making sure every camper had their meal for the day and no one went hungry. Carol had read long ago that an easy way to avoid a grouchy teenager was to give them plenty of fuel for the day ahead, something she treated like it wasn't common knowledge to society. It was.

It took almost thirty minutes to get all of the kids through the line, then an additional thirty minutes for them to eat—thirty-five if it was omelet day. This meant that by the time they were ready to separate into groups and begin the day's activities, it was already 9:30 a.m. Carol repeatedly told Al that the kids were slow and should be faster so that they could start the activities by 8:30 a.m. but Al just wouldn't budge. He claimed that "The kids needed their sleep and don't need to be rushed everywhere" or something stupid, at least Carol thought so. She had far too much to do to have such a late start.

Once the campers were separated into their groups, that was when the day really began. It was when all her hard planning paid off. See, she didn't treat the day's activities like most other counselors— an unfortunate fact given the amount of time Carol spent lobbying for her system to be implemented camp-wide—no, she took it upon herself to have the most well-rounded program around.

From health books on physical fitness for youths, to psychology books about mental stimulation through problem solving, each book was a vital tool in her overall plan to make these kids, at the end of the 36-day period, better in every way possible. These were the minds of tomorrow, and Carol needed to do everything she could to nourish them and let them flourish. She even tried explaining just what a benefit it would be to the counselor's themselves but they wouldn't listen. Eventually Al convinced her to drop it.

For some reason the other counselors found her odd.

The three-hour period of activities before lunch ranged from scavenger hunts, hide and seek, and word association games, eventually culminating in a trust fall for each of the group members. This was Carol's favorite activity with her group because it showed how close everyone was getting in such a short amount of time.

Then at 12:30 p.m., lunch would follow a similar structure to breakfast, with Carol assisting Marge with food. Some days when Marge wasn't feeling well, Carol would serve the entire meal. She always strived to be as useful as possible. Given that the campers were more awake from all the physical activity, Carol would bust out her guitar and sing upbeat poppy music. Sometimes she'd even seen certain campers bobbing along to the tune. That was enough for her to consider her job well done. She figured that not every genius was appreciated in their time and the others would catch on eventually.

After lunch at precisely 1:30 p.m., all of the groups would remain as one and participate in a massive activity. This would range from rock climbing to volleyball to basketball to capture the flag, all depending on the day. Marion would usually take the reins here but Carol would end up taking over naturally throughout the course of the session. For some reason, Marion would often look at Carol, annoyed as she yelled out commands.

Some people just don't understand how to have fun, Carol thought.

Next came a completely useless time of the day: swimming at the beach. Year after year Carol tried to get rid of it, considering it was nothing other than hormonal fraternizing and nonsense, but Al and Marion insisted on it staying. The entire camp would venture to the lake and enjoy the water and sunshine. But Carol saw it for what it really was: nothing more than a chance for the boys to oogle the girls, who themselves were being inappropriate by wearing such scantily clad clothing to lure the boys in. And with the threat of skin cancer, its inclusion in their schedule felt downright dangerous. But everyone still refused to listen to her. Marion's case for socialization and cooling the campers off in the blistering heat always seemed to win out. Carol just ignored it and knew in her heart that if anyone were to get pregnant, the blame would be solely upon Al and Marion. Carol would do her best to watch over them on top of the lifeguard stand, with her custom made one-piece bathing suit; a design adoring it having been popular in the 1950's, and absolutely caked in sunscreen. It was all she could do to protect the campers from themselves.

At 4:30 p.m. the groups would separate into whatever specialty class they wanted to take. These classes included kayaking, pottery, rock climbing, as well as a new one, archery. Carol taught pottery and her attendance numbers were well below the average for the other groups. Al always told Carol she needed to come up with a different one. "Kids just aren't that into spinning clay" he once said. Carol scoffed at the notion, refusing to believe such an art-form would go unappreciated. It just gave a cause to her pottery class. Last year she had two campers sign up, a win in her eyes.

Dinner time would spring up around 6:30 p.m. and the groups would converge much like lunch and breakfast. This time, however, Carol would not join Marge to pass out food. Since dinner had a much looser feel given the lack of planned activities afterwards, Al told Carol it was unnecessary for her to help out. Carol repeatedly refused, but when Al said that dinner was valuable bonding time for the counselors, she shut up and did as told. So instead of being a useful employee for Al, she just sat stoically at the counselors' table, trying her hand at bonding with her coworkers. It usually resulted in silence while she judged whatever the others were talking about. But could anyone blame her?

It wasn't her fault that the other counselors discussed such vile things. Louie would always be talking about some kind of drug he had done at college, Diane carrying on about her sorority at school and all the boys she'd no doubt slept with, Barry listing off the different sexual positions he'd tried that year and Marion just sitting there, allowing it all to happen. In Carol's eyes, she was the worst offender of them all. Of all the counselors, Keith seemed like a nice guy or at least he refrained from speaking about inappropriate things at dinner. Either way, Carol appreciated it. Keith was so sweet.

Once dinner finished, it was considered "free-time." Just how much they were free depended greatly on age. The older campers were allowed to either go to the campfire pits, stay in the mess hall for board games, or return to their cabins. Most would split their time between the fires and the cabins, wanting to get away from authority. The younger kids would be forced to stay in the mess hall. Carol remained in the hall and played board games with those that stayed.

Once 9 o'clock hit, Carol would close up shop in the mess hall, sending the campers back to their cabins in order to keep the 9:30 p.m. curfew. Usually she'd have some difficulty getting some of the older kids to leave the campfire, but then Marion would come along and sort it out. Carol resented the position Marion had, but she was at least thankful for the respect she commanded. It was always something that Carol strove for. If only Big Al would implement some of her ideas, she imagined her own authority would have been even greater. An intimidating figure even.

At precisely 9:35 p.m. Carol would enter the cabin she shared with Marion who, unless she was suffering from an illness or invested in a really good book, would not return to the cabin for several hours. She'd be off gallivanting with the other counselors from times ranging anywhere from midnight to 3:37 a.m. Once Marion didn't even come back to the cabin. Carol was shocked at Marion's pure disregard for her own mental health and hated her unpredictability. It was no wonder most of the counselors had such a difficult time getting up in the morning.

After a fairly quick routine of removing her makeup and brushing her teeth, Carol would rest her head down on her pillow and drift away, no later than 10:00 p.m. If it was her turn for patrol, then she had two different alarms set in order to walk the perimeter during the course of the night. It was usually uneventful, with most things happening on her off night. She had a theory that the campers avoided doing things on her nights out of fear of being busted. At least she liked to think so.

These were her days. This was her routine. This was the only way she knew how to live at the camp. It may have made her predictable but that's how Carol liked it. Old reliable Carol.

The 16x16 structure that Carol called home during her time at Watanka had become more of a home to her than even the one from her childhood. It was a place where she actually enjoyed spending her time. A place that always seemed to represent something better. At least that's what Carol would often tell herself when she was away from it. It wasn't like her cabin was anything special. She shared it with Marion, a person Carol both looked up to and despised, depending on the day, so space was always tight. And outside of beds, they had to share everything else. That meant even drawers, which sometimes lead to unfortunate mishaps of the wearing of each other's clothes. Marion didn't care much about it but Carol sure did. Still, the cabin had a comfort to it that she just couldn't seem to replicate anywhere else. She loved her cabin.

Carol's appearance completely encapsulated her personality: her strawberry blonde locks almost too perfect and full of volume. Her flawless skin glowed in the most doll-like of ways. Carol clearly took good care of herself in every way. In fact, she may have even drawn in some boys if she ever actually dressed the part. Instead her look could only be described as "layered." She felt that anyone who would fall in love with someone for their looks would not be the person for her anyway, so she made sure to send avoid putting out anything that could be misconstrued as promiscuous.

In the bunk next to her own, Marion stirred awake, immediately grabbing the small cartridge next to her bed and taking a small puff. *Those damn electronic cigarettes*, Carol thought to herself, being a person that despised all forms of smoking. She couldn't imagine why anyone would want to do that to themselves. Especially someone as smart as Marion.

Eyes still closed, Marion exhaled deeply, opening them to see Carol, her own eyes already meeting Marion's gaze. Those wide, blue, doll-like eyes.

"You have to stop doing that. One of these days, one of two things will happen: I'm either gonna have a heart attack or you're gonna *accidentally* get socked in the face. Either, or. Just sayin'." Marion covered up her mouth to yawn.

"Well wake up, boss." Carol smiled so big her face hurt.

"I don't know how you do it," Marion said, barely getting the words out through another yawn. "5:00 a.m. and you're as chipper as ever. Old reliable Carol. No alarm clock even. Totally normal."

"You don't have an alarm clock either."

"You are my alarm clock, Carol," Marion sighed, clearly not impressed with the situation, which would repeat itself for the next month, much to Carol's amusement.

"Well, you're welcome then," Carol responded with an even bigger smile.

"Yeah, waking up to Princess Peach staring at me is a wonderful way to start my day. Not terrifying in the least." Marion laid the sarcasm on thick.

"Oh come on! Don't be a sour puss. The kids arrive in just a few short hours! We're about to change lives," Carol said playfully. Her voice was light and flowing, taking cadences from nearly every Disney princess, forming a unique and somewhat ridiculous speech pattern. Carol could tell that Marion was just going to ignore her, having many years of practice.

"Yeah and I have paperwork to file for two last minute applicants, a phone call I need to make to Steve to figure out what's wrong with payroll since currently no one is being paid and I can't really corral a bunch of irresponsible college kids to work without reward," Marion said, catching her breath. "That's all *prior* to when a hundred kids join us, where they need to be separated into bunks, hopefully ones that don't cause problems but you know how that goes, it's pretty much just luck. Then we have to set up the whole spiel about what to expect and sing that stuuuupid song. God I hate that fucking song."

"I love that song," Carol slipped right into it before Marion could even react.

"Ohhhh IIIIIII love Camp Watankaaaa
It's the best camp in the whole United Staaaates.
There's no sad place, on our campers' face
Come on and join the fun and join the craze
And brace yourself for thirty days!

> Cause there's no place quite like
> thiiiiisss greeaatt plaace,
> Camp Watanka!"

Marion was out of the cabin before Carol even finished her rendition.

Chapter 3
Liz

ANOTHER YEAR. The thought repeated in Liz's head over and over as she boarded the bus for another journey into an oddly familiar alien world. It was all so polarizing. Another year spent listening to Big Al tell stupid jokes, Carol act overly excited for anything going on in the camp, and the stupid baseball fields that they never used. *I hate all of it,* Liz thought. She walked down the cramped bus aisle and laughed at the flaking and chipped off yellow paint that covered every surface. The bus driver always claimed, "He'd get to it after he dropped them off at camp." It never happened. Liz had surmised that the driver was just lazy and it'd never get done. Not a surprise given that he was just a local that Al had hired for two days of the year. Liz was surprised he actually knew how to drive.

Even with the chipping paint, Liz probably would have been disappointed had there been a fresh coat of paint present. For nostalgia's sake, it was all part of the package and the predictable nature of it all. Summer camp was just such a routine in and of itself that even the things she used to hate about going became things she looked forward to. She just had to go through fits of annoyance with the process to get there. Going to Watanka had become such a big part of Liz's life that she stopped complaining to her parents about it long ago. It didn't matter what she said anyway. They were sending her and that was that. Oddly enough she couldn't help but be a little grateful about the whole ordeal. The idea of staying around her parents was more torture than 36 days at Camp Watanka could ever be.

Taking her seat, her eyes scanned the crowd on Bus 2, trying to see if she spotted any familiar faces. Was that the cute boy from Louie's group last summer? No, he said his family was moving back to Arizona. Oh wait, Liz thought, that's definitely Molly Austin near the back. Her hand quickly rose to greet her but stopped the moment the realization came to her that Molly had a very distinct mole on her left cheek. This girl had no mole. Fuck. That girl always would sneak in top shelf whiskey. So much for that. Liz sighed. Her eyes continued to scan, trying to figure out if this would be another summer she had to completely start over with friends. Before being dropped off, she had made a promise to herself to try and make at least one decent friend that summer. Even if it meant actually getting close with someone like Alice, she'd bring herself to do it. As a last resort, of course.

It wouldn't be the first time that she had to start anew. Outside of the Belar Twins, Liz was the only consistent camper that Camp Watanka had. And that was probably for good reason. Summer camps had their hey-day in the 1980's and had casually fallen off ever since. Nowadays, the only kids that went were those that either A) wanted to try it out once or B) their parents wanted them out of the house so they were going to be leaving for the summer no matter how much protest there was. Didn't exactly leave the ripest friends for the picking but Liz always made the best of it.

No, what scared her more than the prospect of new friends were the counselors treating her like she was the teacher's pet again. Given that the camp only had three consistent campers, it was hard to not be labeled as such and it hadn't helped that she was on a first name basis with every counselor there, including the big boss. Early on, Liz had even begged her parents to let her just go to a different camp. Anywhere that would help out her social standing. They refused, despite intense whining and rebellion on Liz's part. None of it mattered to them. They didn't want to suddenly have to parent during summers.

Another year she tried to convince her parents to sign her up under a different name, and surprisingly she succeeded. Her new wardrobe, haircut, and voice lasted all of two seconds; the illusion shattering the moment she stepped off the bus. Crazy Carol was able to sniff her out in a heartbeat, making an even bigger deal about her appearance and odd trickery. She didn't make a single friend that summer. In fact, that summer was easily the worst in all of her years at Watanka.

Having not learned her lesson the first time, two years prior Liz made a scene during the opening speech, cussing out Al in front of the entire camp. It wasn't Liz's finest moment but she thought it would prove a point. Instead, Al took it upon himself to treat her as a pet project, like she was some juvenile delinquent that he would help reform. His grand plan was to make Liz fall in love with the camp and all it offered, just like Carol did. He had her do all sorts of things: set up game nights and arts and crafts for other campers, serve food during all three meals, and lead the campfire songs, most of which consisted of non-participation and one person singing—usually Carol, and often very loudly. Liz just saw it as Al training her to be the next Carol, something any sane camper would want to avoid. If anything she would have the laidback demeanor of Marion, not the overenthusiastic, dictator-like approach of Carol. It was an insult for Al to think otherwise.

While that wasn't the end result, it did help Liz gain an apathetic approach to her feelings on the camp. Instead of hating everything about Watanka on the outside, she learned to look at the camp with softer eyes. Just because everything wasn't how she wanted it to be, didn't mean she had to have a bad time while she was there. Liz figured if she didn't at least have a positive outlook going into it, there was no way she was going to end up having a good time. At the very least, it was an extended vacation from her parents.

Liz found an empty seat near the middle of the bus that wasn't completely falling apart or covered in old gum. She sat down on it with a grunt, bringing up a cloud of dust that joined the mixture of body odor and "country air" that was already prominent. Other kids, ranging anywhere from nine to eighteen, congregated towards the back, which prompted an "I've got my eyes on you back there" from the bus driver. Staring out the window, Liz looked through the crowd of parents, searching for her own mother and that ridiculously large hat of hers. Nowhere to be found. *How the hell can I not see her in that*—just when she was going to give up the search, she spotted her mother's car as it sped off down the road, blowing up dust behind her. The other parents looked at the car, then at each other, clearly disapproving of the driver and their actions. Liz just shook her head.

You don't know the half of it.

Hearing more ruckus down the road, Liz looked out, seeing another vehicle. It drove equally fast as her mom had, and was driving directly at the bus. The car skidded to a halt, some of the parents backing away a little, as a disheveled teenage boy stepped out of the passenger's side. The driver didn't even get out, yelling something out that Liz could only catch part of: "Jeannie." *Odd name for a boy*, Liz pondered, wondering if she even heard it right.

Just as quickly as it had arrived, the car sped away, leaving the boy and his bag of luggage behind. *Okay those parents may suck more than mine. Maybe.* The boy made his way onto the bus, his eyes looking down at the floor. He looked close to Liz's age, so that was a plus, and his messy brown hair, parted to the side, reminded her of that cute boy from a couple years back. Liz scanned the seats around her, mostly full already. Those with a free seat had a bag next to them, sending a clear message of "Don't sit here." Liz, on the other hand, had her bag snugly between her legs, and plenty of room on the seat next to her.

It didn't even seem like the boy was paying attention when he plopped down in the seat next to Liz. She greeted him with a smile but his eyes darted right down to his lap, holding tightly onto the phone in his grasp. She had already stowed hers away and shut it off, not wanting to give it up to the front office.

"I doubt you're really gonna to need that," said Liz. The boy's eyes darted up at her, defensive before he had even gotten a word out.

"What?" he looked around, completely lost and miles away in thought.

"They don't allow cellphones really," she explained. "Al started that policy a couple years ago. I think some kid got his MacBook dropped in a lake or something. The parents sued, and the camp almost went under. Now they just don't let people bring expensive electronics. So they just put them all in the main office till the end of summer. Part of me thinks that Al just really hates technology and doesn't want a camp full of zombies on their phones. I guess being in the main office, he could also use them, but I doubt he'd even be able to power them on. He and Carol both are super tech-challenged. Two years ago this girl brought a vibrator and Carol thought it was a massager so she just kept it locked up with the laptops and the iPhones. Yeah. . . Al wasn't too impressed when he found that."

"Uh. . ." before the boy could even answer, Liz was at it again.

"Oh sorry, yeah, of course you don't know names. Marion is head counselor and Al is the owner. You'll randomly see him out and about all the time. He's cool though. Just likes to get drunk and hit on the older counselors. Typical lonely bachelor stuff but he's really harmless. And Marion is pretty much the coolest person on the planet. She's the big sister you always wish you had—do you have a sister?—Doesn't really matter, she still fits that role. She's super cool. As long as you don't do something too stupid, she'll be your best friend. One summer when I had a boyfriend back home, she let me sneak off and text him at night. Seems kind of silly now but it was a pretty big deal for me then. That lasted until Carol tailed me and tried to get me kicked out but hey, what're ya gonna do? Though sometimes I wish I had just let her. Oh and—" Liz stopped, realizing just how much she had been going on about stuff that was clearly, judging by the blank look on the boy's face, of no interest to him. She tried to make up for it with a "Sorry, I talk a lot" but the boy still just stared blankly at her.

This wasn't a good start to her whole "make new friends" initiative, but Liz hoped he may find her awkwardness charming. Trying to avoid any second more of silence, she said quickly, "I'm Liz. In case you couldn't tell, I'm kind of a veteran of the camp."

"Yeah, that's what I figured what with the rundown you gave me. I think that may have been more useful information than the entire website," the boy squeamishly said.

"Oh god, I'm pretty sure Al hasn't updated that website since 1999. It's covered in that awful 'Geocities' shit. Gotta love it. Okay, so I told you my name, are you gonna help me out with yours?" she asked, not knowing whether she'd even get a straight response. Everything about his body language was uninviting.

"Oh, sorry. Chase! My name is Chase. Chase is. . . yeah, that's my name." He was uncomfortable and stumbled over his words. Liz couldn't help but be drawn to it, as she could relate to the awkwardness. Liz was usually weird and uncomfortable but she took the route of never stopping her mouth. It was a nervous tick that always kicked in with new people. Chase seemed to be the opposite.

"You sure about that?" she smiled.

"Yeah, sorry. I guess I just don't know what to expect from this whole thing. Never been to a summer camp before."

"Nothing to be nervous about." She barely held back her own anxiety as she noticed just how engaged Chase's eyes were with her own. "You're about to go to the most unexciting summer camp and have the most mediocre summer of your life." Liz was only half-joking.

"Well I revel in mediocrity so I'm sure it'll suit me well." Chase loosened the death grip on his phone and his posture relaxed.

"You and I are gonna get along all right," Liz smiled. Maybe her "make new friends" initiative wasn't doing so bad.

The rest of the drive was spent with little to no interaction from the boy while Liz made sure to keep the "conversation" going, telling him enough of her life story to bore just about anyone. But not Chase. He sat there, nodding his head, occasionally a big smile would spread across his face and he'd be completely engaged in whatever she was saying. It was nice for

Liz to actually have someone listen to her for a change.

She was rounding out her experiences from the previous year of high school when she looked out of the bus window and noticed a familiar sign next to the road:

"Welcome to Camp Watanka The best camp in the whole United States!"

It always made Liz chuckle when she saw the decaying wooden slab, just barely clutching onto the pole in which it was nailed. What was once a beautiful painting of the lake, with a hint of the camp in the background, was now just chipped away ink that made no discernable picture. The only aspect of the sign still legible was the writing, which Al made sure to repaint yearly. It made sense for him to want to repaint the camp's only welcome sign but continuing to push the slogan "Best camp in the whole United States" was just desperate. Maybe it was true once, but those days were long gone. Liz doubted the camp was even top 100.

The bus made its way down the winding road, with miles of forest on either side. Despite it being the middle of the day, the trees swallowed up nearly all of the sunlight in the forest bed, an eerie contrast to the bright light setting down upon the bus. Somewhere in the trees to the west was the softball field, but Liz knew there was no way she'd be able to see it. Still she tried, hoping they had finally cleaned it up a little and at least given them another activity to take part in.

After several minutes the bus finally came to a clearing and grass appeared on either side as the forest expanded outward but never fully disappeared. They drove further down the dirt road, the camp becoming more and more visible. The mess hall and main office were first in her sight, with the cabins off in the distance behind them, everything looking old and worn. To the west was one of her favorite spots: the rock wall. The bus rolled up to the flag pole and Liz couldn't help but get a little excited as she spotted all of the counselors. Marion stood near the front, with Louie, Diane, and Keith standing behind her. And there was Carol with a giant, almost creepy grin on her face. She didn't spot Al, but figured he was trying to make some grand entrance to try and look like a big shot.

"This place looks straight up out of a horror movie," said Chase, almost startling Liz after his prolonged silence.

"Just wait. . ."

"What's that supposed to mean?" Chase leaned forward in his seat, almost devious.

"That's all I'm saying. Just wait. . ." Liz looked away, a smile on her face.

He'll find out eventually.

Chapter 4

Marion

MARION HOPED IT WOULD BE A DECENT GROUP of kids this year. Every summer was a bit of a gamble and after the prior year, where she had eight kids that she had to send home for inappropriate behavior, she wanted this group to actually stick around. Nearly all of the expulsion involved some form of sexual activity. "It happens at camp" she had said, but that made no difference to Al, who had implemented a strict "zero tolerance policy" against any kind of sexual activities. The biggest drama came when two of the discovered lovers were both boys. While Marion did a good job to keep news from spreading throughout the camp—in an attempt to save the boys from any harassment—their father's wiped all of that away in barrage of swear words as they exited office cabin. Neither boy came back and Marion shuddered to think of the things they had to go through with their homophobic fathers.

Assholes.

Fortunately for the counselors, the no sex rule was in effect for campers only. If Al had the same rule for counselors, he'd have been without workers by summer's end. Marion once had a "camp boyfriend" (definition: a standard boyfriend type who existed only during the month of summer camp attendance) several years before she took up the head counselor position but that ended in heartbreak when she found him in bed with one of the older campers. It was their second summer together and she still hadn't had sex with him. Sure, they had made out a lot and she blew him a couple times near the end of the previous summer, but it never ended in sex. . . or climax. She just didn't ever really feel like doing it with him. He was nice but the spark was never there. Every sexual act felt tedious and uninviting. And she made it clear that one night stands weren't really her thing. Apparently they were Jake's.

The kids coming off the buses looked well-behaved, but with today's youth, it was certainly a different definition from generation's past. Getting them corralled was easy enough once they were actually off the bus but Marion attributed that more to Carol darting all over the place, trying to put everyone in a specific spot than the campers actually being calm and orderly. As big of a pain as she was, Carol was never one to give less than 110%. Once everyone settled into their lines next to the flag pole, Marion stepped to the front of them, the six other counselors taking places behind her, and everyone seemed to know it was time to shut up. Maybe this year wouldn't be so bad.

"I know that you're all anxious to get into your groups and start today's activities. But unfortunately we have a looooot of the boring stuff to go over first," Marion announced, trying her best to make her voice carry with authority.

"I think you mean uber fun stuff there, Marion," Carol chimed in and even tried to give Marion a playful elbow to her arm which Marion ignored. Carol wouldn't be escaping her label of "total camp suck up" anytime soon. Marion, on the other hand, had an easygoing demeanor that allowed for the kids to connect with her. She treated them like peers and didn't care if things weren't perfect; it was just a job. That was one of the many reasons that Al chose her as head counselor four years back. The kids respected her and would actually listen when she had something to say, a trait even Al lacked.

"Okay, we have to do roll call. If I butcher your names, I'm sorry but some of you have names that are next to impossible for me to pronounce. That's just a fact of life as I'm sure you've found out every time you've had a substitute teacher. Don't worry, I'll avoid anything that sounds like it could be turned into a bad nickname," Marion began, making some of the kids laugh and snicker to themselves. "We're pretty group-oriented here so that means all your daily activities will be taking place with these people. Which means you better play nice. And you'll be reporting to your assigned counselor for everything. So be sure to pay attention when I call your name because you'll be assigned your cabin as well. Okay, let's give the end of the alphabet a chance to be first for once. . . Santiago Villalobos?"

Marion looked down at her sheet and still couldn't believe the number of blue checks next to so many of the names. The blue check meant they were court ordered and usually consisted of troublemakers. But looking at Santiago, it didn't seem so bad. Sure, he was seventeen-years-old with a dozen tattoos, but he certainly didn't look any worse than the other delinquents she had seen throughout the years. His file made him out to be a gangbanger but, outside of the glares at Carol, he seemed sweet enough. In fact, he looked overjoyed to be there.

"You'll be in C-2 which means you get to go with Louie over here," she said to Santiago before turning back to her list. "Now let's see. . . Elizabeth Thompson!"

Marion was relieved to see Liz, her favorite recurring camper. There weren't many carryovers from year to year so it was hard to not grow attached to those that did. Her brown hair and often punk-rock clothing, reminded Marion a lot of herself from only a few years prior. It was likely the reason they bonded as much as they did. They would casually text during the offseason even. Liz came up and visited her at school once, which ended in a frat party where Liz almost beat the crap out of the school's starting shooting guard. She was never one to let someone take advantage of her.

Uncharacteristically she was giggling and talking to some boy off to the side. She wondered if this would finally be the year Liz would be "too cool" to hang out with Marion and would just be off canoodling with the boys instead. She really hoped not as Liz was the closest thing Marion had to a best friend at the camp. She was practically a sister.

Their true bonding moment came when Marion caught Liz smoking a joint off near the shore of the lake. It was nearly midnight when she noticed the spark of the lighter and, given the camp's early schedule, the counselors would surely be fast asleep. It had to be a camper. The moon provided just enough light, but still made it difficult to see in the distance— it was her only advantage. Had it been brighter, Marion was positive she would have been spotted long before being able to sneak up on the unsuspecting smoker. Had any other counselor been on duty, Liz would have had little to worry about; unbeknownst to her though, Marion also liked to smoke at this particular spot on the lake. They even shared the exact same tree, tucked on the southern part of the camp, on a small hill next to the woods. Liz almost hadn't noticed when Marion took a seat on the ground next to her, the joint already almost down to a roach.

"You know, smoking is bad for you," Marion had said, almost laughing at her own voice.

"Don't worry, it's not cigarettes," Liz shot back. *This one is quick*, she remembered thinking.

"Oh I'm sure I'd be about thirty seconds into a heartfelt lecture if that were the case," corrected Marion.

"What?"

"Cigarettes are bad news bears. I'd be very disappointed in you since I took you for such a forward thinker. Although, smoking weed at this age isn't the best for you either. Can really screw up your short-term memory if you do it too much during those precious developmental years. Maybe even until twenty-five—I can't remember—but short term memory can just completely go to shit. Then you can't remember where you put your keys for the rest of your life," Marion said before quickly correcting herself. "Oh wait—cellphones. That's what I meant. Much more relatable, am I right?"

"So I guess you're just out here trying to catch campers smoking and then bore them to death with lecture?" Liz asked and seemed somewhat surprised by Marion's immediate eruption into laughter.

"Probably under my job description *somewhere* but no ma'am. That would be giving me far too much credit." Marion thought for a moment about whether she wanted to give too much away, but Liz seemed to be in need of a friend, not a guardian.

"Midnight stroll?" Liz asked, still curious and hoping to somehow get out of trouble.

"I guess you could say that," Marion said, pulling out a joint of her own and resting it between her lips.

"You've got to be fucking kidding me."

In a moment that could have gotten her fired, she lit the joint and took a massive drag, handing it over to Liz afterward. This resulted in Marion playing several songs off her cracked iPod from Pink Floyd, The Residents and Velvet Underground. It was a bonding moment they hoped to share every year after, but with Marion receiving her head counselor promotion the next year, those hopes were dashed.

Being that this was Liz's last year, there was a certain bitterness to her presence. She was going to be gone in no time, and that was just the way it went. Unless they carried over into counselor roles, the campers were gone just as they were getting more relatable. And as much as Al wanted to recruit Liz as a counselor, it was the last thing Marion wanted for her. *Who in their right mind would stay here that long?* Marion would think but then a mental image of Carol would always pop into her head. Old reliable Carol would, that's who. Although, she wondered how many more years it'd be till she took over that role. The time was ticking.

It took nearly 20 minutes to get through the hundred campers, mostly due to Carol and her excited squeal every time she'd get a new kid for her group. Seemed by the end that every child that wasn't called yet was just hoping to be placed in any group besides Carol's. This was typical but Marion still found it infinitely amusing. Carol just never could seem to shut it off, and made the majority of campers want to avoid her. Those that ended up with her looked at the other groups with immense envy.

Marion's group seemed well behaved, but she wasn't the best at reading people at first. Having Liz around certainly guaranteed that she would still at least enjoy some aspect of the activities that summer. Plus, Diane and Barry were taking the kids under 13, making it so Marion's resentful days of what she referred to as "babysitting duties" were long over.

Marion was relieved to have everyone finally split into their groups because that meant it was time for Carol to step in and go over the stuff that Marion tried to avoid. This also meant she was able to tune out for a good half hour. Which was precisely what she did for the seemingly endless speech that Carol gave, where she alternated between happy-go-lucky and harsh dictator in a single sentence. While Carol droned on, going over her complete daily routine as if it would be their own, Marion stared off, thinking about the fireside beers the counselors would be sharing later. She really needed it at that moment.

"Okay, I'm sure all of you are antsy to start all of the crazy fun but first we have the most important part of the day! Let's give a big round of applause to all those wonderful counselors of yours!!! And now the man you all came here to see." Carol stopped for a moment to laugh at her own joke. "The magnificent Big Al!"

Makes him sound like a magician, Marion thought. *Or a pornstar.*

A large man stepped out from the front door of the office, Al Bundy-like in his characteristics; an irony not lost among the counselors and a couple campers who understood the reference. The most obvious of these traits was the gut that protruded from his shirt in an almost cartoon-like way and the hairline that reached around to the back of his head. He was trying to retain the last memories of happiness from his childhood, before they disappeared and all he was left with was the present. Al took pride in the fact that his introduction was almost verbatim what his father would start camp off with in the 80's, with a few phrases updated from personal perspective.

"Hello Campers!" Al said enthusiastically but rehearsed. "Are you ready to have some fun?"

The response from the campers was mostly groans, with Carol's excited squeals piercing through it to make it at least seem like more people were all about the fun. The other counselors just stood behind Al, their interest even less than the campers, having had listened to this routine several times before. Marion hoped she didn't have to repeat any of the important changes he'd been stressing this year because as much as she loved her counselors, they weren't always the most motivated.

"Now I'm sure you all are wanting to set foot in the cabins that you'll be spending the rest of summer in but unfortunately that's gonna have to wait a couple hours."

Groans echoed throughout the camp as the idea of getting to lay down in a somewhat comfortable cot anytime soon were vanquished. Marion couldn't blame them, usually the cabins were open right away, but Al's procrastination with the paint of the bed frames meant the fumes wouldn't be completely clear until after dinner; a huge inconvenience for Marion's counselors.

"That just means you get to enjoy our lovely facilities a little more. And you know, this camp is a part of my being as much as the blood in my veins. My great-great-grandfather opened up this place in 1912 with just the money he had saved up while building houses all along the great town of Reynolds, New York—that's the town you passed on the way in, ladies and gents. Anyway, it started off small, just maybe half a dozen campers at first. Then every year there'd be more and more, they'd come from far and wide. So he built more cabins and more boats. Finally, he had built all the great things you see here today; with a little help from my father and myself, of course. 'Vital cogs in the ol' wheel,' as my Father used to say. And we've been providing nonstop excitement and thrills all the way since 1912, a fact I'm quite proud—"

"What about '91?" an excited shout resonated from someone in the back. Al ignored it and plastered a big fake smile on his face, the effects of the outburst very evident beneath the facade. Marion couldn't believe someone actually said it. It had been years since the event was mentioned in a public manner. It had been relegated to campfire fodder. Al's reaction was sure to settle any doubt when the story made the rounds. The mere mention made that almost certain. Marion caught Liz's line of vision and they exchanged a look of concern. It was going to be one of "those" summers.

"We've had thousands of campers enjoy the facilities and make life long bonds, be it with your peers, your counselors, or even your ole camp owner— hey, don't laugh. It has happened," Al said with a belly laugh. Marion could hear the nervousness in his voice. He put on a good show, but it was painfully obvious just how much the question got to him.

1991 was not a year that Al wanted to discuss.

Chapter 5
Al

"THESE KIDS ARE GOING TO be the fucking death of me," Al remarked just moments after having to punish some juvenile for fighting with Carol. "Not even a full day and I already have one of these brats getting sent to me. I told you we should have stopped taking these juvie kids. Nothin' but problems, the lot of 'em."

"Yeah, well let's see if you still have that opinion when the government checks stop coming. Can't stay afloat without 'em. That's what happens when you have non-competitive pricing," said Marion. She sat across from him at the desk, helping him sort through the chaos, as she always did. But no matter how much sorting she did, she never understood the basics of what it took to run the camp.

"Non-competitive? We're competing with everyone. The internet gives out everything for free these days. People aren't wanting to spend. It's just 'free, free, free!' We raise the prices anymore and we'd have half the kids. Then we have even less money. Life just don't work how you seem to think it should, Marion. That's just the way it is," Al said matter-of-factly. What didn't kids these days understand about economics? The solution couldn't always just be raising the price. Al figured that was why the country was in the toilet.

"Yeah, I'm well aware. I just think you need to remind yourself of that when you threaten to pull the only funding we get." This was the third summer in a row that they'd had a similar conversation. At this point, it was just another item to mark off on the conversation checklist. While Marion had good ideas, those ideas often took more money to implement and their usual problem would rear its ugly head.

"Oh come on, Marion, you know I'm just frustrated. That little shit wouldn't even look me in the eye. Kids today just have no fucking respect," said Al, for what felt like the millionth time in his life.

"So what do you want to do with him?" asked Marion.

"What do you mean? He's with old reliable Carol, she'll whip him into shape eventually."

"Or he'll attempt to set her cabin on fire."

"Two birds with one stone! Heh," he laughed.

"AKA *my* cabin," Marion said, and Al pictured the flames, an angry camper dancing in front of it, and a can of gasoline in hand.

"Just keep an eye on him. If he becomes too much of a problem, we'll send him packing. . . after two weeks of course," said Al, always budget conscious. The courts weren't able to retract their funding if the juvenile was there for half the time. As ignorant as Al was when it came to most financial aspects of the business, that was one part he was always on point with.

"Eventually they're going to start noticing that you send home half of them at the two-week mark and then we're going to lose them all," Marion said, trying to be the voice of reason. Al knew she was right, but if there was one thing he hated, it was disrespectful campers. Unfortunately, that meant most of the juveniles fell under that umbrella.

"Fine, if he has any more issues, he's your problem." Al looked down on the mounds of paperwork on his desk with a grumble. It was his usual routine of freaking out about the many campers—a number that kept lowering with every passing year. His stomach would turn and his muscles would tighten yet this was still his routine and he wasn't sure if he would be able to run the camp the rest of the summer without it. Even mundane, Al was a man of routine.

"How is it that this gets more and more complicated every year? Isn't it supposed to be easier the more years under my belt?"

"That's the theory but there's a reason it's not a fact." Marion wrote furiously into the ledger.

"You fucking said it," said Al, moving over to the other side of the office. He opened up one of the filing cabinets, sticking some more papers into the mass of previous documents. "God dammit. I think I need to get another filing cabinet. Think we have it in the budget?" A seemingly ridiculous question, given the small price of cabinets but. . .

"No! Not even a little. I can't believe you'd even ask that after the hell I just went through with Jared. I've stretched this budget as far it as it'll go. I'm not adding one more expense; I don't care if it's paperclips," Marion stressed.

"Tell me again why the boss has to ask his head counselor for permission to do things in his own camp?"

"Because without his head counselor, the boss wouldn't have the reliable counselors he has now, not to mention the countless number of hours your lovely head counselor spends on the phone with parents, collecting money, and general babysitting. Not an easy task," Marion pointed out, too busy to look up from her paperwork. "And don't even bring up my raise as a counterpoint. I earned that and wouldn't be here still without it."

It was like she was reading his mind.

"I think you may be the closest thing I've had to a wife. I also think I get why I've never been married," Al joked. Looking at the office space around him, he should have known they didn't have the money for it. The wooden walls were just days away from rotting. Every window had at least a tiny crack in it, with some being full on shattered and replaced with wood planks. It was far from paradise.

"Why don't you just get rid of the older papers? All they do is take up space," Marion pointed out, her head buried in the accounting books, trying to figure out the final billing for all the campers.

"I can't do that. What if they come back? How else am I going to remember them? The ol' memory ain't what it used to be." Al knew it was sad that he even thought like that but it was a hard one to let go.

Back when his father ran the camp, people returned constantly. Watanka was the place to be during summers in the entire tristate area. Past campers would even bring their kids, wanting them to embark on the same great experience that they had as youths. Nowadays, he was lucky enough to have three regulars, a far cry from his father's 75% return rate, a number he often boasted. It seemed like his father did just about everything right when it came to the camp while Al felt his head was barely above water most of the time.

Al desperately wanted to return the camp to its former glory but he just didn't have the money to do so. Watanka already had a reputation that was hard to outgrow. The camp was falling apart—even the sign out front had trouble staying on its hinges. Two of the cabins had succumbed to termites, although the lack of campers may have made that a blessing. And the chairs were breaking left and right, mostly being composed of other chair parts, and shoddily put together with nails and super glue. The greatest problem of all was that kids just weren't going to camp like they used to; something the bank was sure to point out when declining Al's request for another loan. Whenever Al tried to turn the camp around, the world always had different plans. He learned to live with it.

"You know that's not gonna happen," she said, unenthusiastic at the prospect of returning campers. Marion was always the voice of reason, even when Al didn't want her to be. She would tell him what he needed to hear and not what he wanted to hear, a rarity in his life.

"A man can dream."

Al's mind wandered off, heading into the glory days of the camp. He could remember so vividly the remodeled cabins, hundreds upon hundreds of kids and the man at the center of it all: his father Abe. The kids loved him, the counselors respected him, and the parents envied his status with everyone. There was nothing that brought a smile to his father's face more than the operating hours of the camp. He even refused hiring a maintenance man, deciding he would fix any problem himself. The camp was like his child, and he treated it with the utmost care.

One huge difference in operations was just how long his father was able to keep the camp open in the 80's. There was such an influx of kids that it would stay operational for two months, rather than the current system of just one. By the end the kids were begging to stay, exclaiming how they couldn't wait to be back the next year. And they weren't lying either. They'd be back in spades, sometimes even bringing friends with them. Abe had to turn kids away, not having enough room to house them all, a problem Al could only dream of having.

Now the only reason they could even last one month was due to parents wanting a break from their kids. It was no longer about sending their children off to better themselves, it was simply another reason to get them out of the house so they could fuck in peace. If the kids had their way, they wouldn't even be at the camp. Most hated it and just wanted to be behind their computers and video games, wasting their lives away. He had even stopped asking the campers who had plans to come back the next year as he was tired of having all the kids lie right to his face. It was disheartening. Al loathed the current generation. Not to mention their insistence on pre-marital sex.

Outside of a few rare occurrences, Al's father didn't really have a problem with sex at the camp. If it was happening, it was happening out of view, making sure none of the adults were aware. Girls weren't getting pregnant, or if they were, they were having the decency to not let it be known while at the happy camp. They had respect for their elders. Nowadays Al was lucky if he didn't have a girl step off the bus pregnant, not to mention a disgusting same-sex hookup that would occasionally pop up during the summer. The world was going to shit and all of the horny millennials were taking it with them.

"So do you think we're gonna have any issues this year with the counselors?" Al asked, knowing Marion always had a better perspective when it came to those things.

"Al, I told you, sex is gonna happen. You just have to accept that. College kids like to fuck. It's a simple fact of life," she said, finally closing out one of the books in front of her.

"They have ten months to do that, why can't they just be respectable citizens for the short time that they're here?"

"Either we have a bunch of counselors fucking or a lot of counselors masturbating. At least one's more social."

He knew hormones did crazy things to people but Al still felt it was all disrespectful. He hadn't had sex in eight years, so it had just become another thing in life that he wasn't getting. He wasn't sure if he held resentment towards that fact or not.

"I would just like to go an entire summer without walking in on two of my counselors three fingers deep. Can't even respect me enough to hide it." Al shook his head in disgust.

"Most of our lives are spent hiding sex. When we're teens it's hiding it from our parents. When we're adults it's hiding it from our kids. This is just the time in life where people can fuck without hiding it. It's the beauty of the college years."

"I just wish—"

"That it was 1982? I think you're gonna have to start giving up on that dream," Marion laughed.

"Yeah, yeah, yeah. You say what you want, but I'm convinced those fuckers do it just to spite me."

"Now you just sound like a bitter old man. No one is out to get you, Al. They're just living their own lives. Watanka just happens to be a pit stop." Marion sounded sincere but the words still stung.

"Is that what this place is to you? A pit stop?" Al asked, really only hoping for one specific answer.

"Absolutely. And if you think otherwise then that's how I know you're getting too fucking nostalgic. I hate this place almost as much as you do," Marion said. The exact words Al needed to hear.

"Every year I just tell myself 'one more year. Then you'll finally be done with this place.' And yet every year, I'm back. What does that say about me?" Al asked, genuinely wanting an answer most would have just deemed rhetorical.

"It says you're in a routine. It happens to the best of us. Just look at Louie, he was supposed to be off at film school—"

"Please do not compare me to *Louis*. Ever." Al didn't like being compared to the idiot jester he somehow hired as a counselor. Marion claimed he was good at his job but Al never saw any proof.

"Fine, then compare yourself to me. I hate this place. I tell myself every year that I'm not coming back. But I just keep coming back. Why? Because it's easy and I know what I'm doing. It can be a lot of work, but nothing I can't handle. I probably could have gotten several different jobs—better paying ones at that—while I'm going to school. But sometimes when you live in a crazy world, all you want is familiarity." Her words sat with Al for a moment, as he stared forward, face drooping downward.

"You're right. Maybe this is the year I do it. Hell, Carol is just chomping at the bit to take this place over. Some days I wonder if I should just do it and get it over with."

"Ha! You do that then you'll need to find yourself a new head counselor," Marion trailed off towards the end, already thinking what Al was about to say.

"Oh silly Marion. You actually think that she wouldn't just appoint herself?" Al joked.

"The thought certainly entered my head but I wanted to hold out a little hope for her own humility."

"If she weren't so damn extreme I'd happily put her in charge. No offense to you, dear, but she's definitely the most committed counselor I've ever had. No one loves his place more than her."

"Please don't tell her that. It'd destroy the image she has of you in her head where you spend all off-season thinking about this place. Not to mention the mental breakdown that would follow."

She was right. Al put on a show for everyone except Marion, the only person he'd trusted since his dad's passing. He couldn't help putting on the façade. He wanted everyone to view him in the same light as his father. It was hard though, and each passing year was just making it more and more difficult. Especially when he used to hate the camp so much. But he had to keep putting on a show.

No one would even know of that reality if it weren't for a drunken confession to Marion during her second year. He regretted it at first but grew to appreciate having a person to turn to in dark times. It made the decision to make her head counselor in her third year an easy one. While Carol wasn't pleased, she respected Al's decision. He certainly knew that Carol would make a tremendous head counselor—she was undoubtedly the best worker he had—but he just couldn't imagine giving her that kind of power. It would surely to go to her head. When he finally decided he was done with the camp? When he'd move down to Florida and never think of camps or campers every again? That's when he'd let her run the madhouse.

Until then it was his own personal playground.

Chapter 6

Chase

CHAOS. THAT'S WHAT THIS WAS, PURE CHAOS. It was like all the campers went right back into school mode on cue: being as loud as possible, launching spit-balls across the room and lacking all respect for authority. The dining hall, if it could even be classified as such, was an absolute mess. Over a hundred kids crammed into an area that should have only sat fifty. Given his slight claustrophobia, Chase wasn't looking forward to the next month of meals. That was before even seeing the food itself, for which his expectations were already low.

"This place is always such a fucking madhouse," a familiar girl's voice resonated from behind. He turned to see Liz, the cute girl he sat next to on the bus. He had been looking for her since they'd all been herded into the dining hall but had no luck until that very moment. He was relieved to have someone to talk to.

"I feel like I'm going to be touched inappropriately just by taking my seat," Chase jested.

"Just pray it's a camper and not Al and you'll be golden," Liz said, Chase hoped jokingly.

"I don't think there's even any place to—"

Before he even knew it, the decision of where to sit was made for him as Liz grabbed his arm and led him towards a spot away from the counselors, who were stationed at the head of the chaos. There just happened to be a handful of spots here, clearly out of view of the others furiously searching for any possible place to sit and having no luck.

"Is this place usually so cramped? Did they forget to open the other dining hall or something," Chase asked, hoping for any kind of reasonable answer. There had to be some kind of explanation for this. Chase wasn't even sure if this was legal while Liz just laughed at his sorrow.

"You may need to drop those expectations a little bit. Watanka is definitely no five-star resort."

"Well, yeah, I get that. But. . . do you seriously see this?" Chase asked, pointing around at the overcrowding.

"It'll settle eventually. Especially since the cabins aren't open till after dinner. Once everyone drops into their routine it won't be nearly as crazy. Hell, I usually just eat out by the lake. And don't forget that some of these kids were on a bus for nine hours to get to this lovely paradise," Liz said it all rather calmly, but the news shocked Chase. *I wouldn't spend nine hours to come to this shithole.*

"You're seriously fucking blowing my mind right now. How in the hell is that even possible? Jesus, why are people coming from all over to this shitty place?" Chase asked, not understanding how the camp could even drum up the business it did.

"Not many summer camps left nowadays. Especially not many that take your kids for a whole month. That right there is good business for any parent. . . those not wanting to be actual parents, that is—which I think is most. So I guess you could say that's the charm," said Liz as she peeked up at the line, seeing if it was getting shorter. It wasn't. They were likely to be there at least another ten minutes. Chase sighed and ignored his grumbling stomach.

"You know, some parents actually like being around their children. In fact, I'm pretty sure that a select few even have them *on purpose.*"

"Oh, those poor, confused people. Just not understanding what they're getting themselves into," Liz said with a big smile.

"I take it you weren't hugged much as a child?"

Even if Liz was right about why parents sent their kids there, Chase still couldn't believe they got away with such conditions. His mother made Watanka out to be much nicer than it actually was. The pictures on the website were clearly from a late 80's remodel that hadn't been touched up in the years following. He would have loved to have visited to the place that the website claimed it to be, and maybe had been thirty years prior. He was now certain that place didn't exist and hadn't for quite some time.

Waiting five more minutes for the line to go down, Liz and Chase finally went up to get food. Chase grabbed a tray, bringing with it another dish attached to the bottom. He pulled them apart to reveal something sticky connecting the two together. Gum? Chase wasn't sure if he even wanted to know. Liz just looked at it with a gag then a smirk, taking a different tray instead. They moved towards the counter where Carol and the lunch-lady, her nametag reading Marjory, served the meals.

"Spaghetti or Chicken?" said Marjory.

"Chicken?" said Chase, not entirely sure which he should choose or if it was even real chicken.

"Hey, Marge. Got any vegetarians left?" Liz asked with smile.

"Of course I do. You're the only one that actually eats them. Damn vegan and your morals," said Marge. Taking some bread and a chocolate milk—Chase quickly doing the same—Liz walked over to their spot near the back, which had now been taken over. Entering the search again, their eyes scanned, looking for an available spot. Liz appeared to see one as she guided him over to a table with two fraternal twins. Before reaching the available seats, she whispered back at him, "The brunette is Nancy and the blonde is Alice. Just a warning, they can be a tad. . . bitchy. Don't take it personal."

"I thought for sure we wouldn't see you again," Nancy said on cue.

"Can we sit?" Liz asked, trying to ignore her rude tone.

"Sure, who's the boy toy? Very unlike you to pull a Pattie Nelson." Alice may have been the nicer of the two, but not by much. Chase quickly introduced himself as he and Liz tried to squeeze onto the bench. There was hardly enough room for one person, let alone two. They barely managed to get situated at the table, with Chase immediately apologizing to the hunched up guy next to him, but finally it was time to eat.

"You two fucking wish," Liz shot at the twins, pissed they'd even accuse her of such a thing.

Liz had a history with the twins but Chase was having trouble finding where the friendship part actually began. Their reunion in the camp felt more like they were feeling sorry for each other for having to come back for yet another year, and not genuine joy for seeing long lost friends. Being the nostalgic person he was, this astounded Chase.

How could they not be at least a little happy to see each other? They must be holding it in.

"So what's the deal? Thought you had some lifeguard thing lined up to get you out of this?" questioned Alice. *Lifeguard thing?* Chase thought. *She made it seem like she never had a choice.*

"You know how things go. Just didn't work out," she responded, evidently annoyed she was reminded of her failed summer plans. Chase couldn't blame her. Getting paid to sit poolside all day didn't seem so bad.

"And you fucking love this place," Nancy cackled, her voice reeking of sarcasm.

"Oh you know I'm just glutton for punishment. Figured spending the hottest summer on record at a place with no AC would be an ideal way to spend my precious summer. Plus, I heard that after seven years I get an eighth year for free." Liz was quick with her words. "So you know I just couldn't pass up that kind of savings."

"Oh damn. Looks like we're gonna have to miss out on our free year," Alice said through perfect pearly whites.

"Boohoo, what a tragedy." Nancy's sarcasm almost outdid her sister's as she slapped on another layer of blueberry chapstick.

"Wait, you're seriously not coming back next year either? What happened to the parental ruling? I thought you two would be counselors and all that jazz?" asked Liz.

"Daddy left. Went with some Oncologist to California to live on the beach," Nancy started.

"Mom's devastated and all that. Wants to go spend dad's money seeing the world—Europe, actually," Alice continued, almost uninterested.

"We'll be joining her in a couple months so right around the time that this lovely hell-hole opens up next year, we're gonna be sipping daiquiris on the beach in France."

"Wait, so she's already gone? She didn't take you with her?" Liz asked, somewhat amused by their parent's neglect.

"She's a dumb whore," Nancy spat out, clearly at annoyed at their mother's decision not to take them with her immediately.

"She wanted to find a place," Alice tried to reason. "Plus she already had the camp paid for."

"Paid for camp or wants to get plowed by half of Western Europe? You decide."

"Ignore her she's just sour. Always was daddy's little girl," Alice's words stung Nancy who glared daggers at her.

"He's your father too."

"Here we go. . ." Liz whispered to Chase.

"Yeah and it doesn't mean I need to blame either of them." Alice said matter-of-factly. "Divorce happens. People fall out of love all the time—if those were ever in that category to begin with. Everyone we know has divorced parents or if they are still married they're sleeping with half the country club. It's life. Quit being a child."

"God, you're just like mom." This was the worst thing Nancy could have said to Alice, who erupted into a fit of obscenities. The two argued, with Liz interjecting occasionally, seemingly very amused by the happenings.

Maybe they were friends and this was just how their dynamic worked?

Chase wasn't sure but found the situation extremely uneasy. Never mind the fact that the physical position he was in had been putting his arm slowly to sleep. Pulling his left arm back, his shoulders angled more, he was able to get more space, breathing a sigh of relief but was awkwardly turned to the boy next to him.

The girls continued to argue at his left so he looked to the people to his right, some of whom were watching the twins with voyeuristic amusement. The boy sitting directly next to Chase was keeping to himself, eating his food in silence. Chase wasn't sure if he wanted to engage in conversation but knew he needed to fight those first instincts. He needed to socialize. Be normal. Besides, he was already facing the kid.

"So how's your relationship with your parents? Think we can outdo these girls?" quipped Chase, just loud enough that the twins couldn't hear him.

"Heh. Yeah," the boy said, clearly in his own little world and not picking up on Chase's sense of humor.

"So either I'm really unfunny or you're more the dark and brooding type. I think you may be well on your way to success because, don't tell anyone, but the girls down the table may have a daddy issue or two."

"I agree with the first one," Liz said out of nowhere, apparently paying attention to both conversations. Chase playfully nudged her.

"Sorry, just nervous. Lots of new people," the boy said meekly.

"I hear ya. I'm Chase. That's Liz next to me, who may or may not be spying on our conversation." Right on cue Liz nudged Chase, acknowledging that she was, in fact, listening.

"I'm James. It's nice to meet you Chase." James lit up a bit more. Chase was the clearly the first person to initiate a conversation with him.

"I'm hoping you're like me and have no idea what to expect from this place?" asked Chase.

"Actually both my sisters went here so I have a decent idea of what's going on. At least they tried to prep me," James responded.

"I can only imagine what that consisted of. So wait, your sisters were regulars? Wonder if Liz—"

"What are their names?" Liz interjected.

"Well I wouldn't call them regulars. We go to one secular summer camp before we're 18. Helps open our eyes to non-religious folk," said James.

"Oh so you're religious?" Chase asked, somewhat skeptical. It wasn't that he hated religion. No, Chase always found it intriguing and was respectful of it. He just didn't understand how anyone could put such blind faith into anything. He needed proof. Something tangible. He needed science. He needed some kind of logic. Still, Chase was just hoping for less evangelical and more modern.

"I believe in God, yes. My father is a traveling minister and my mom homeschooled all of us," said James, loosening up while Chase became more tense.

"How many in the family?" asked Liz, even though Chase could have sworn she had just responded to something Nancy had said. *How did she do that?*

"Eight total. Five girls. Three boys." James replied.

"Oh wow, that's a big family. And all homeschooled. . ." Chase pondered just how loony the education had to have been. *I wonder if he's ever even heard the word 'evolution.'*

"Yes, my mother was quite the saint. Certainly wasn't an easy task. Us kids certainly can get into some trouble but she raised us right. So in the end it all worked out."

"Yeah, I can only imagine. . ." his thoughts trailed off as he heard Alice whisper. "Can you believe that someone mentioned '91?'"

Before he could even ask, Liz leaned into Chase and whispered, "Only five more minutes till we get to leave this place. Power through that delicious meal of yours."

"It can't come quick enough." Chase adjusted in his cramped seat. He slowly realized his left arm had casually rested right behind Liz's back. *Oh shit!* Chase thought, and pulled it away as quick as possible. They had known each other all of six hours and he was already going to scare her off. Had she even noticed? Was Chase just worrying about something that wasn't even a problem? Apparently more time had passed than he'd thought because before he knew it, Liz had stood up and was ready to go.

"Let's go, cuddlebug," Liz joked, making Chase cringe at her acknowledgement.

Chase and Liz left the twins to their arguing and strolled out of the dining hall, as other waited around, not really knowing what to do. Most just wanted to go back to their cabins and go to sleep, but unfortunately they still weren't open and most were too timid to go exploring the camp on their own. Not Chase and Liz, who strolled out of the dining hall, ready to go on a little adventure. At least that's how Liz put it. Chase had his doubts that anything in this camp could be considered an "adventure."

But nighttime had brought a certain charm to the camp. At least in the odd way that Chase found appreciation in the scary. He had always been a fan of the strange and unusual but he wasn't sure how many others in the camp shared his opinion. The moon shone bright enough that the entire camp was illuminated and the dinginess felt all but erased. The old rotting cabins, ancient rock-climbing wall, and hobbled together archery range. *This is what they should be advertising on the website,* Chase thought, truly believing it'd drive sales. He could even imagine adults wanting to stay there to take advantage of living out all their horror movie related dreams. But what did he know?

Chase was especially intrigued when Liz mentioned a baseball field that was on the other side of the woods, across from the archery range. Chase liked baseball a decent amount, but seeing it under this moonlight seemed worth the trip through all the bugs and dark and creepy forest that separated the two.

"Not saying it's the worst idea ever, but going into the scary woods to go to a baseball diamond definitely seems like something that'd be scribbled down on that list," said Liz, unimpressed with the notion, before adding. "That's like a two-mile hike, one way."

That was all she needed to say for Chase to lose any interest in making it over to the baseball field. With that in mind, it didn't seem likely he was going to see much time there. Besides, the many signs that read 'Trespassers will be shot' were enough to quell too much interest in entering the forest.

His favorite part of the tour, that lasted all of ten minutes given the camp's size, was the lake. The light fog that started to develop over its surface. The way the moonlight bounced off it and illuminated the area around it. It was all so mesmerizing. He liked it so much that he asked Liz if she wanted to sit on the beach until the cabins opened, to which she quickly accepted.

"So what do you think?" she asked, half-joking.

"You know, you're gonna think I'm crazy for saying this but I actually don't think it's too bad. The dining hall was a little terrifying but the rest of this place is. . . unique. And not in such a bad way. As I said, crazy. Though I guess that would mean that maybe you're crazy too since you keep coming back here."

"That's certainly one way to look at it."

"I take it that means you don't?" Chase asked, wondering if he had read her wrong. She seemed to have a bit of glint in her eyes as she showed him around the premises.

"Depends on the day," she responded with an exasperated sigh.

"I think I hate the world on most days so this is a nice change of pace."

"Hating the world is a lot of work."

"So is loving it."

"No it's not, emo boy. If you love it, then it shouldn't be considered work. Work is for something negative."

"Tell that to Carol," Chase said immediately.

"Okay, Carol is not from the planet earth so I don't think that's exactly fair."

That was true. Carol didn't act like anyone else he'd ever met. She seemed to both genuinely enjoy her job while simultaneously hating everyone else for not doing their jobs "correctly." Maybe it was all because she cared too much.

"You have to appreciate how much she loves her job at least."

"Yeah, I guess when I first saw it. Then it enters sadness territory around day five or so."

"Really? I think it's great that she cares that much about anything, let alone the job she's going to have to do no matter what. Both of my parents have jobs they hate so that means more than you think." It was the truth too. Being around his parents made him decide one thing in life: he'd make his career something he loved, not something he had to do to survive. His parents taught him a lot but that lesson always felt the most valuable.

"Yeah, I guess that's true. My parents always were a bit more artistic in their endeavors." Liz leaned her head back onto the ground, staring up at the stars that peeked out in the darkening sky.

"Which were?"

"Art. They painted and all that."

"And they actually made a decent living?" Chase had genuinely never known anyone who made money artistically. His life was full of blue-collar-workers.

"Well, I didn't exactly say that," Liz laughed. "They did alright at times. Had to get jobs teaching eventually. At least my dad did. Mom kept on keeping on. Real commendable for a while."

"Probably a stupid question but. . . were they any good?" He wasn't sure how she would respond to the question given the position of hostility some people would take from one of that nature. It's not like he was trying to offend, he had just. . . he was doing it again. Overthinking every minor detail. What was this girl doing to him?

"Yeah, they were good. . . I think. But what do I know about art?"

"Still, pretty impressive." Chase settled into the grass next to Liz, staring up at what he thought was Perseus but, having done terribly in astronomy, he wasn't sure.

"So Mr. Watson, what is it you want in life?" Liz asked out of the blue. It was the last question Chase was expecting and one he'd never been asked before. He could feel his arms start to shake, his nerves getting to him. The question bounced around his head for several moments, trying to find the right answer.

"That's kind of a deep question isn't it?" Chase deflected it entirely. He wasn't so sure he even wanted to respond to the question. Hell, he wasn't even sure if he had an answer.

"Sure. But that's the point. My grandma used to ask me that all the time. I'd see her once every year— either Christmas or Thanksgiving depending on the rotation—and that question would always come up," said Liz, staring forward at the lake, mind clearly back in the past.

"Yeah, that's a really deep question for a little kid. I'm sure the response certainly. . . evolved over the years," he said, wondering what he even would have said at six-years-old. *Probably a Power Ranger.*

"That was the fun of it all. Every single year she'd ask me and every year it'd be different. She used to write it down in this little purple journal of hers. It started at toys, then graduated to jewelry and eventually landed at plain ol' money. Everything I chose just seemed to be materialistic and stupid in hindsight. But back then? Then it was all that mattered to me. And yet every year she'd meet me with the same response: 'That's nice, dear' as she wrote it down in that purple, leather bounded journal. She was the sweetest lady in the world but for some reason, those words always stung. Every single time. It got to the point where I was absolutely obsessed with finding the right answer.

"So I'd come up with exactly what I thought she'd want to hear. 'To grow up and have a nice big family. To get all A's and go to Harvard. To break records in cross country'— See, I was a bit of a runner—but nothing I came up with ever received a new response. It was always just 'That's nice, dear' and she'd write it down in her journal. Every time," said Liz, growing a little teary eyed as she walked down memory lane.

"Did you ever get her to say something else?" Chase asked, needing to know more.

"You know I wish I did. Marion and I have talked about it out here before. She seems to have an idea what her answer is. But that's just Marion. She may not have everything figured out but she definitely knows what she wants out of life."

"I take it you don't?" said Chase and Liz huffed in response.

"Not in the slightest. Maybe one day I'll have it figured out. But the more I grow up and see the adults around me, the more I think that not everyone does figure it out."

"So you asked me what I wanted in life but you don't even have your own answer to it? Filthy pool, missy." Chase further dodged the question.

"Because maybe when I hear yours, I'll have a better idea of what my own is."

"Oh so you just plan on copying me? I see how it is," joked Chase.

"Inspiration and thievery are two entirely different entities, my dear Watson." A grin spread across Liz's face.

". . . you've been dying to say that haven't you?" asked Chase, already knowing the answer.

"Oh you have no idea. Sherlock is my hero."

"Yeah, I like the BBC show." Although it had been years since Chase had binged the series online.

"Wait, there's something other than the TV show?" she said, straight-faced. Chase took a moment, not really knowing how to react. Was she being serious? Did she really not know about the Sir Arthur Conan Doyle stories? Hell, it even said so in the credits to the show.

Chase's trepidation was met with a huge laugh from Liz. "Oh my god, I'm obviously kidding. I totally had you going. Come on now. Me read good. I've gone through *Adventures of Sherlock* like twenty times. That is my shit. Although I won't lie, I do enjoy me some Cumberbatch as well," she said, successfully lightening the mood.

"That was slightly terrifying for a second," said Chase, relieved. It would have been just his luck to find a cool girl who ended up being culturally ignorant.

"Gotta keep you on your toes," Liz said, bringing her knees up to her body and resting her arms around them.

"You've offended me and I now think I'd rather just go back to the mess hall," said Chase sarcastically.

"Oh. Well if cramped is your style then please take a look to your right." Liz motioned over to the bathrooms, resembling a tour guide in her tones and hand movements. The building couldn't have been more than fifteen feet by fifteen feet, housing showers and toilets and sinks for one of the camp's genders. A duplicate building stood next to it for the other. Chase had just thought it was an equipment building when he had seen it earlier.

"You've got to be kidding me."

"I told you, this place is practically a five-star resort. . . in North Korea."

Chased wanted to laugh at her joke but he couldn't. He had frozen. The silence of the night seemed to be broken by a repeated *"splat!"* that resounded in Chase's head. Sitting on the ground, nearly three feet from his outstretched leg, sat a bullfrog. Instead of a frog, all he could see was a red and green mush.

"Got a problem with frogs?" Liz inquired.

"You could say that." Chase still hadn't taken his eyes off the frog which finally did him a favor and jumped out towards the lake and out of sight.

"Okay, you have to explain this very moment." Liz's enthusiasm was worrisome as she leaned forward, wide-eyed and smiling.

"Hey, what're you two doing?" the authoritative voice struck through the darkness and startled Chase. A flashlight shined on them, making Chase immediately feel guilty. *Liz had said this was okay, why would she lie?*

"Chill out there, spaz. It's just Marion." And Liz was right. Marion lowered the flashlight and rolled her eyes. Bundled up in a dark hooded sweatshirt, she did not look pleased to have found them out there.

"Of course it's you. Always up to no good," Marion said, seemingly joking.

"You know me, always trying to start fights and murder fellow campers," exclaimed Liz.

"Well while you're busy stargazing, I'm busy trying to get all the girls rounded up like cattle so I can lead them to their sleeping quarters. So will you please join me, madam?" said Marion, putting a little English accent on the end and curtseying a little.

"Do I have to? Can't I just sleep out under the stars?"

"Done it before. Not all it's cracked up to be. Very wet. And not in the good way." With this, Marion finally turned towards Chase. "Mr. Watson right? Don't you think you should be heading to your bunk?"

Chase froze, not really sure what to say. Was he supposed to be back at his bunk? He must have been if Marion was out to get Liz. But then why would Liz not have said something earlier? He should have waited around for an official announcement, not just gone out because Liz said they had free-time.

"Chase, I told you, you should have—" said Liz, but was quickly cut off by Marion.

"I think that he can speak for himself, Ms. Thompson."

"I. . . umm," Chase mumbled. He was absolutely terrified. Wasn't Marion supposed to be Liz's buddy and confidant? Yet Liz looked like they were in huge trouble, staring at the ground and hardly saying a word now that Marion had changed her tone.

"Mr. Watson, please return to your cabin," Marion said with authority. "And make sure it doesn't happen again."

"Yes, ma'am. Will do." He tried to make eye contact with Liz but her eyes refused to raise. Chase walked away from the lake and as he did he could have sworn he heard giggling behind him. Then he heard howling laughter and had it confirmed: *Yup, they were fucking with me.*

Walking around the side of one of the cabins, he looked around, hardly believing how different he already viewed the camp. He was excited to try out the rock wall and lounge around on the beach. The canoes looked like they wouldn't even float, and he couldn't wait to test that theory out. The mess hall was definitely to be avoided, but outside of that, he was ready for whatever challenges Watanka brought his way. It was sure to be a good summer.

Chapter 7
Sally

GETTING CORRALLED INTO THE CABIN that Sally would spend the next month in wasn't exactly a pleasant experience but she made do. At least she was finally finding out where she would sleep. That didn't stop it from becoming a madhouse the moment all the girls walked in and realized the beds varied drastically in terms of quality. All at once they sprinted, trying to locate a bed that wouldn't squeak or leave lumps in their backs. Sally stood near the rear, not really caring much about which bed she was given. She just wanted her stuff. The counselors had taken it earlier and Sally didn't like the idea of it being handled without her permission. Her counselor, Marion, stood at the back, laughing at the sight of the girls going crazy over the beds.

"Hold up," said Marion, raising her hands to get everyone's attention. Surprisingly, it worked, with most of the girls turning towards her and listening intently. "Your stuff has been placed at the assigned bed. Which means that Nancy can get off Alice's bed any day now."

Sally looked over at the twins and the brunette dressed in pink jump off the bed, pouting as she did. She wasn't too happy about losing her prime spot. The other girls were just glad to have a place to lay down.

"Why the hell are we getting assigned beds? This is stupid," the pink-wearing Belar twin protested the rule.

"Alice is right, we've never been assigned beds before. This is dumb," the green-wearing Belar twin said, as if she *had* to affirm her sister's statement.

"Did you not see what *just* happened?" Marion responded sternly.

"You could have avoided that by telling us before we got into the cabin and just assumed," snapped Alice.

"And miss out on you pouting like someone half your age? Never. It's too adorable," Marion said, smiling wide. "Makes me want to pinch those pouty cheeks of yours."

"You suck." Nancy rolled her eyes. This seemed more like usual procedure between them rather than any animosity, or at least from what Sally could tell.

"No, I just really like seeing your sister pout since it's just so gosh darn cute. But since she's not a big baby, I just have to settle for you," Marion said, acting like she was going to pinch Nancy's cheeks.

"I really hate you sometimes," Nancy mumbled through gritted teeth.

"Oh I know you do. And again, it's adorable," Marion remarked, hugging Nancy. *What an odd relationship,* Sally thought as she found the bed that housed her luggage.

Sally had packed light for the month, with simple short and shirt combos for every day. The website said they had free laundry so she was going to be sure to take advantage of that.

Liz's bed was next to her own, a fact Sally was happy about. Liz seemed like a cool girl from what she had seen. Plus, she was friendly with that cute boy Chase. Sally had been waiting for a moment to spark up conversation with her but Liz hadn't really left Marion's side during the group stuff. The time was perfect.

"So I take it you've been coming here a while?" Sally inquired. "You seem like quite the vet."

"Oh yeah. Years and years. Camp veteran and all that jazz. No worries, not a suck-up though. Marion is just really cool. Total hippie. But yeah, I'm not like weird or anything by being friends with the counselors right? I mean, they're totally normal people. And now I sound super defensive, don't I? Well, hell. I think that hits all the points at least. Totally normal person here," Liz said as if she was in severe need of some Ritalin.

Sally looked over at Marion who helped one of the girls flip her mattress, revealing a nasty stain on the other side and ultimately leaving it as it was. While she looked like she was fun to hang out with, she was still the head counselor so Sally had her doubts. Just as she had doubts about the laundry after seeing just how much of it Liz had packed.

"How's the laundry here?" Sally asked.

"You're kidding right?" said Liz, laughing as she did.

"That's not a good sign." Sally already regretted not packing more. She could practically hear her mother saying 'I told you so.'

"Unless you enjoy having your clothes come out dirtier than when they went in. Because then you'll be in heaven," Liz joked.

"Great. . ." Sally wasn't sure what she was going to do once she ran out of clothes, but she quickly decided that would be a problem for future Sally to sort out.

"Okay ladies, I'm leaving you to it. My cabin is right next door so if you need anything go there. If I'm not there, Carol will be and she will be more than happy to answer every question you may have. . . and probably some that you didn't even ask. All the lights go off at 11pm. No exceptions. Except if there's a cute boy just dying to get in your pants, obviously." Some of the girls erupted into a fit of giggling. "Kidding. The entire camp is on a timer and *errrthang* shuts off at eleven outside of the main office. Besides, you're gonna need all the beauty sleep you can get. Depending on who your counselor is, you may be in for a super fun day or a super. . . day. But just make the most of it. The camp experience is what you make it. Good night my sweet princesses," Marion finished, closing the door behind her. Sally could see what Liz was talking about; Marion was pretty great.

The twins had begun arguing at the other side of the cabin, still annoyed that they didn't have the beds that they wanted. Sally was quickly reminded of why she always got along more with boys than with girls. The shrill voices and pompous demeanor made her crave something a little less hectic. These girls were absolutely crazy. And they made themselves hard to be ignored, with their voices piercing through any nearby conversation.

"Fine, you basic bitch. Maybe you'll be the next one to end up splattered up against the side of some toolshed," Nancy threatened.

"Oh please, like I'd miss out on camping to get deflowered by one of the boys from this camp? Yeah, right. One of those lucky boys over there might get a finger somewhere south at Final Bash, but deflower? No, no, no." Alice shot back. *What on earth was she talking about?* Sally thought, looking over at the other girls, trying to gauge if she was the only one left in the dark. Maybe she should have been paying a little closer attention.

"What are you going on about?" said Samantha, as if she were reading Sally's mind.

"Final Bash?" Nancy started. "It's not the wittiest name but it's pretty much the end of the summer bash that the counselor's let us throw that—"

"No, the whole murder thing." Sally interrupted, not needing to hearing Nancy talk anymore about partying.

"Oooh! I want to tell it!" Alice shouted.

"You? You can't tell a story to save your life. Liz is so much better." Nancy leaned in towards her sister. "Don't you remember that girl? God, she was so basic. What was her name? Sandy? Betty?—I don't know, doesn't matter—she was so scared she got her parents to come pick her up the next day. All because of Liz and her *fantastic* storytelling. Fucking genius."

"Poor girl." Sally made the mistake of saying.

"Eh. She was a bitch anyway."

Liz continued to put her stuff away, seemingly annoyed at the inclusion of her name to begin with. Finally, she broke the silence, "I don't think that story is a good idea."

"Oh come on, Liz!" Nancy exclaimed. "You are so fucking money. They can't just expect us not to talk about it."

"Bullshit," said Brenda, a stout Mexican girl with an attitude. She'd been glaring daggers though Nancy from the corner, but had finally had enough of Nancy going on and on.

"What's that?" Liz peeked her head around Alice at Brenda, perturbed by her intense tone.

"This is so much bullshit. This is all a bit. Nancy there is a shit actress. And Liz, you're not much better."

Liz cracked her fingers, drawing all of the attention in the room towards her.

"'A bit' eh? Didn't you notice how. . . off Al seemed once the year 1991 was mentioned? Wasn't exactly the most normal of reactions, was it? See, '91 was a special year for Al and one that he never forgot, no matter how much he tried to. It's not something that we just tease to try and scare you off. This is something that Al has to live with for every day of the rest of his life. And if you're not careful, you will too. See, this happened long before Al was even running the place. Long before the bald head and the beer belly. He was just another counselor. His dad, Abe, was still holding onto the family business and grooming his dear boy to be the heir apparent. Didn't think that Al was mature enough to run it quite yet but he was well on his way."

"How could you possibly know that?" asked Brenda, her arms crossed in defiance.

"Are you going to let her tell the fucking story?" the Belar twins sounded off in unison. Brenda sat back, rolling her eyes yet still silent, part of her wanting to hear more of the story, the rest just wanting to prove Liz wrong.

"As I was saying, Abe was still holding firmly onto the family business and Al was a counselor—not even head counselor, mind you—and that didn't sit well with Al. Not one bit. It got so bad that he just couldn't take it anymore. He was going to do something about it. Something. . . radical. So on the last day of camp in 1991, he goes to the main office, reaches under the front desk, and pulls out the magnum his father kept for trespassers. He was gonna end it all. Shoot his brains out all over the precious grounds of the camp with his dad's .357. He had the suicide note written and everything. Stole the gun out of his father's desk; even cleaned it to make sure it wouldn't jam. He did everything he needed to prepare, and didn't have a second thought once. He was dead set on it, with only one final step remaining.

"But all of that changed with a single blood curdling scream. He was mere seconds away from pulling the trigger when it started. His first reaction was to protect the campers; he had the gun so he had a responsibility. He ran to the cabins, stumbling and falling as he did. Al was never the most agile. He kept following the screams, through the woods. Once he came to them, he couldn't figure out what was wrong. It looked as quiet as ever. Everyone was out camping for Final Bash and the cabins were empty. Or so he thought. Were the screams coming from elsewhere?

"A shadow moved across one of the cabins and he went to investigate. He wasn't prepared for what he'd see upon opening that cabin's door. No one could have been prepared for what was in there. There had been a massacre, the entirety of the room covered in blood. Two campers were dead on the floor, bits and pieces of them scattered about. The sight was too much for Al to handle and he fainted, right there in the doorway. They say that fainting is the only thing that saved his life. Because he wasn't alone in that cabin. The one that killed the two campers still remained. When Al awoke, all he saw were police sirens and some disembodied voice telling him his father was dead."

"Wait, are you trying to say that Abe fucked one of the campers?" interrupted Mary-Ann, a girl with far too much cleavage.

"What? No! What the hell is the matter with you? Let me finish the story. You see, the killer passed up on killing Al because it wasn't necessary—"

"Wait, who's the killer, did we already get to that part of the story?" Samantha blurted out.

"Okay, maybe I need to describe how storytelling works to you folks but sometimes leaving out certain details and then revealing them at another time is to greaten the effect," Liz tried to calmly explain.

"I just thought you forgot. . ." Samantha said with an edge.

"Holy fuck," Liz said to herself, then turned to Alice. "Go right ahead."

Before Alice can even get a word out, her sister's hand was to Alice's lips, keeping her quiet, and urging Liz to finish the story. Sally agreed, along with most of the other girls. Liz was much more of a natural storyteller than the girl who just earlier told of the awkward time she got fingered in the back of her grand-parents' car. It was anti-climactic.

"Okay, are we done? Can I do this," said Liz, looking at the others for any objections. "Okay then, where was I? Oh yeah, so this had just been a fit of—god dammit. You know what?" Liz had enough of the whispering and eye rolling from Samantha and Mary-Ann. "Fuck it, the killer was a camper who caught his girlfriend having sex with another one of the other campers. Boom!" Liz was annoyed at having to rush through her story but satisfied by the widespread disappointment.

"Awww," the Belar twins echoed each other's sentiments.

"Shut up, you two have heard this story a million times," Brenda spat back.

So much for her not caring about the story.

"Doesn't mean we can't appreciate it," the girls said together. It was odd just how in sync those two were. Sally had never been around twins and, while these girls certainly were an odd example, they seemed to fit every stereotype she knew growing up.

"Wait, so how did Al's dad die?" asked Brenda, on the absolute edge of her bed.

"He left his place to investigate a strange noise." Liz commanded the room with every word she spoke. "Ended up getting an axe in the face for his efforts."

"You'd think running a summer camp, he'd be a little more up on his horror movie clichés," Nancy added.

"You'd think so but how many times have you investigated an odd noise, just to find nothing there? Well what if something was there? Hell even if you were smart enough to bring a bat, would it really make that much of a difference? An axe wielding psychopath is still an axe wielding psychopath."

It scared Sally just how right Liz was. In that situation there wasn't much anyone could do. Would a gun have helped? What about the gun Al had taken from his father? Would Abe have had that had it not been for his son? Sally could vividly remember the times she heard a strange noise while babysitting and immediately took care of it. How vulnerable was she being without even realizing it? She suddenly felt a little more sympathy for the idiots in all those Jamie Lee Curtis movies.

"Was it in the main office? Is that why that big window is broken?" asked Samantha.

"No, you can thank 'Wild Thing' over there for that," Alice said, pointing at her sister.

"You should have caught that ball," Nancy replied.

"You should have thrown it better."

"Okay wonder twins, deactivate." Liz settled them down. "Like Alice said, the window wasn't from that. You wanna know more? Visit the house."

"The house? What house?" Sally asked. She hadn't really thought about other houses being around the lake, she had just assumed the camp owned the entire area. She couldn't see any other lights on across the lake in any direction. It was nothing but forest. This was the first she had heard of any house.

"Just because we're told not to venture off into the woods, doesn't mean that area magically doesn't exist, dumbass," Alice said and Sally's eyes went to the floor.

"The house is where the Shepard's used to live. Al grew up there actually. But he hasn't stepped foot in it since. He absolutely refuses to. That's why there's all those 'Trespassers will be shot' signs on the west side of camp."

"Not like it works though. You remember that sick party the boys threw in there last summer?" said Nancy.

"Yeah, and I remember you getting boned in the upstairs bathroom by Darren Matthews. Uck," Alice gagged.

"Whatever. He was sweet."

"He was five foot nothing with a speech impediment. You have a disgusting weakness for losers."

"So is that it?" Brenda butted in, not wanting to deal with the Alice and Nancy show. "Is that all the resolution we're getting?"

"They cleaned everything up. Al took over the camp. We're here now. End of story. It's not a real complex one. Would have been a bit better had I not been repeatedly interrupted," Liz said and glanced down at her watch.

"Thanks for the wisdom," said Mary-Ann, rolling her eyes.

"You want real wisdom?" Liz tucked her bottom half into the covers. "Just try not to bring any boys back here. Best wisdom I can give you."

"Thanks for the parental advice, mom," said Mary-Ann, clearly not taking to the advice as it seemed to interfere with her plans to hook up with every cute boy in the camp. At least that's what Sally assumed based on how much she put her boobs on display.

"Hey I'm just looking out for you. No one wants to lose their V card in the cabin where a double homicide happened. Okay. G'night!" Liz said abruptly.

What was she talking about? The campers were. . . murdered here? In this cabin?

Before Sally even had time to ask, the lights turned off, leaving the room in pitch black. When Marion said lights off at eleven, she meant lights completely off at eleven. Her gaze went to the window, where she could have sworn she saw someone, buzzcut and all. But with a blink, they were gone. She quickly deduced it as paranoia and moved on. She had more important things to worry about than the darkness playing tricks on her. How could someone just go crazy and kill a bunch of people? Was sex really enough to incite such an action? Was Al still traumatized from it? But one prevailing thought, lingered in her mind: When could she go and investigate that house?

Chapter 8

Louie

"THANK FUCK THAT'S OVER," Louie groaned, pouring half of a beer down his throat. He was just glad to be done with the campers until morning as Marion had taken the first night of rounds. The first day of camp was always so hectic that, by the end, he had to resist every urge in his body to leave and never look back. He knew that things would eventually settle down but that didn't make his body ache any less.

Louie threw his empty beer can into the roaring campfire, much to the chagrin of Marion, a quasi-environmentalist. All of the counselors—Diane, Keith, and Barry— were gathered around the fire, beers in hand. Carol was noticeably absent, as she rarely joined them at night, despite it being a near every night occurrence down at the fire pits on the beach. She greatly disapproved of their alcohol consumption and refused to ever take part when it was present. Her loss. Besides Louie didn't have time for that now anyway, it was a cause for celebration. Their first day of dealing with campers was over. Somehow the beer tasted even better than it had the previous two weeks at the fire. Maybe because now it had a purpose: stress relief from the insanity of the campers. Louie wasn't sure if it was a good idea but he popped open another beer anyway. "If I have to deal with one more immature little shithead, I may just lose it."

"Oh, they're not that bad this year!" exclaimed Marion. She was probably right, but Louie couldn't resist the urge to argue.

"Yeah, easy for you to say miss 'I pick the best campers for my group.'" Louie knew the accusation had little merit but, given how much Marion did around there, it was unwise for him to poke the beast.

"You realize I have absolutely zero background on eighty percent of these kids right? And the court-assigned ones I give to our perfect citizen molder, Carol. So if you get stuck with shit then I'm sorry Louie but that's just the world collectively trying to make you eat a shit sandwich. No collusion necessary on my part," Marion stated matter-of-factly. Louie could sense how annoyed she was by the accusation. He was never quite good at sarcasm.

"Yeah, I know you don't. Just. . . yeah, ignore me," Louie said, defeated.

"Done and done." Barry had just returned from a pee and was already unbearable. *Fuckin Barry.* Louie didn't like Barry. Not even a little bit. Barry reminded him of every bully he had ever encountered in high school. The way he talked, the specific words he used, his mannerisms. There was no one that left a worse first impression on him. And he ended up being as big of a douchebag as his appearance let on. The years had just soured their relationship further with Barry constantly berating him in front of everyone else. This time though, Barry followed it with an "Only messing with you, Louie."

Louie? What the hell is he playing at? Louie thought. Barry wasn't one to say he was joking. Because he rarely was. Let alone the fact that he wasn't calling him 'Louise', a nickname that only Barry prescribed to. This was odd on Barry's part and Louie didn't know what he was playing at, but what he did know was that he didn't like it. Before Louie could overthink the situation, Diane was quick to send the conversation in a different direction.

"Why did the last two weeks have to end?" Diane shook her fists at the sky. Louie always thought Diane was pretty cool but she was also a little too girly for Louie's liking. She would often get too drunk and become the "we need to be friends forever" kind of person. Not that it wasn't cute, but her lack of contact during the off-season made Louie question her honesty in it. And not to mention that he found it difficult being friends with those that couldn't hold their own. The multiple nights of getting carried back to her cabin the previous two weeks made it clear which category she fell into. Still, she was a lot of fun, and Louie still held out hope she'd drunkenly stumble into his cabin one night. A guy could dream.

"Best part of camp for sure. Makes me feel like a little kid in a candy shop. The whole camp to ourselves and no kids around," said Barry.

"Minus one Carol and you really have yourself a party." Louie couldn't help himself while Diane and Barry nodded in agreement.

"Oh she's not that bad," Keith proclaimed. Keith was Louie's cabin-mate, so they knew each other pretty well but never quite understood his friendship with Carol. At least the rest of him was pretty decent. Outside of the occasional beer by the fire, Keith was the definition of health and fitness. He ran five miles and did yoga every day, keeping a strict diet in the process. How someone could be that handsome and not bang every hot girl he came in contact with, Louie would never know or care to understand. Still, it was a nice change of pace having someone around that seemed like a genuinely good person.

"Not that bad? Excuse me?!" Marion could hardly control herself, readying up all of her ammunition. "She wakes up at 5:00 a.m. every day. And her being the loudest person ever when she's getting ready means that *I* get up at 5:00 a.m. every day. *Then* I get to wake up, terrified, as she's staring directly at me, just waiting for me to open my eyes. Every time. No matter what minute it happens to be. Is she there the entire time? If so, for how long? Why is she staring at me? Why can't she just wake up and not stare directly at me, like any normal person would? There's a million and a half questions I have for Carol and why she does the things she does yet my questions will never be answered because she'd just come up with something else that was even more annoying and intrusive. So yes, she really is *that* bad."

"At least you don't have to deal with 'Mr. Pushups' over there," Louie said, signaling to Keith. "The man does like a thousand a day—"

"Five hundred." Keith corrected him.

"Oh, I'm sorry, don't mean to be hyperbolic, Mr. Pushups," Louie snorted. "Regardless, that man sounds like Hulk Hogan in *No Holds Barred* when he does his pushups, and he wakes his ass up at 6:00 a.m. to do them so yeah, he may not be eye-fucking me awake every morning—which by the way, Keith, you should totally start doing, really increase the serial killer vibe in the cabin—the push-ups are still enough to make any normal person go insane. So I think I feel you."

"Hear that, Keith? You're getting compared to little ol' Carol. How you feeling about that, chief?" Diane asked, running her hand along Keith's forearm.

"I'm perfectly fine with it. Carol is a pleasant person. She's just really passionate about her job," said Keith.

"Thas putting it-t lightly," Diane slurred her words, taking another swig of her beer. She was well past the point of hammered. *Maybe tonight.*

"Who needs one?" Barry said as he stood up, walking to the beer filled cooler. "Diane? Louie? Keith, I know you're done. Marion?"

Diane and Louie motioned for one while Marion just shook her head. She never was much of a drinker.

"Oh come on, one and done?" Barry questioned her.

"I have rounds in. . ." Marion checked her watch. "Forty-five minutes. So I'm thinking that doing it drunk isn't an option."

"Psh. I do my rounds drunk," Louie blurted.

"You do everything drunk," Marion said before turning to Diane. "And how are my little munchkins doing? I love the toddlers. . . as long as they're not my problem."

"Well, they're h-hardly toddlers," scoffed Diane. "I think the youngest is nine. Al is going to have such an easy time with them at night. Though there's this little girl Holly and she is absolutely adorable. Little chubby and always has a big smile on her face. Oh my god and that giggle. Slay me now. I want to adopt her. You know, as long as I only have to deal with her for part of the day."

"I wish I could be guaranteed a fat daughter," said Louie, trying to outdo Diane.

"Wait, you want a fat daughter? What on earth would make you specifically want a fat daughter?" asked Diane, hardly able to control her laughter and failing as she spat out a little bit of beer in the process. "And I mean that in the health way, not in the superficial way you're all thinking."

"Are you kidding me? I'd much rather have to take her for some dialysis appointment than have her getting railed by every guy from here to California," said Louie.

"People have sex. Deal with it dude," Diane said as casually as possible. *Was that a hint?*

"While that may be true, when it comes to 'Daddy's little princess', sex is not to be had. Ever. In the eyes of her father, she will die a virgin."

"Oh yeah, then how would you explain all the pregnancies in the world?" asked Marion sarcastically.

"Mary."

"Wait you mean of—"

"Of Mary and Joseph. No sex had, yet babies were made. It's every father's dream scenario. I'll just make sure she takes that route," Louie said.

"Oh yeah, is this what your dad taught you?" asked Diane, shaking her head.

"I have three sisters. Where do you think I got this from? I learn by example, darling." Louie's dad certainly gave him more than enough reason to actually think this, but it was less an ideal and more a general thought on the subject. Louie just found it funny.

"I think you're taking more of the 'learn through fear' route," said Keith. "Always fearing that your hypothetical daughter is gonna do what's only human nature."

"No, taking the fear route is the Al Shepherd way of living, am I right?" Louie said, trying to make a joke but without any proceeding laughter. *Shit, these guys can't really be that tense about this. People even joke about 9/11 now. I probably shouldn't say that.*

"Hey, I mean nine—" Louie started, but was thankfully interrupted.

"Louie, you certainly do love sticking your foot in your mouth don't ya, buddy?" Keith was charming, even when Louie didn't want him to be.

"So what are the chances the Belar's are gonna spill the beans tonight?" asked Barry.

"Oh god, I hope not. The last time that happened night one, we had that girl's parents threatening to sue us for 'allowing such a thing to happen.' Like it was our fucking fault. I wasn't even born then," Marion said it with a mocking tone. "What a fucking joke."

Louie remembered that. He thought it actually was a joke when it was first mentioned but before he knew it a lawyer turned up at the camp, delivering papers that nearly caused Al to have a heart attack. The family didn't have much to go on but they were clearly out for money and willing to do anything to get it. (Un?)Fortunately for Al, he didn't have any money for them to take so the lawsuit died, but as did Al's passion for the camp. Louie was glad though, the less Al cared, the more fun could be had.

"Wait, I thought it happened in the house?" asked Keith.

"It did. That cabin wasn't even built in '91," Marion explained. "Liz just likes to say it happened in that cabin and make my life a living hell. It's this special testing of patience where she does this thing, and I see how long it is until I have to kill her. And the Belar's just love stirring the pot."

"As long as that story stays far away from my campers' ears, Liz may continue living," Diane stated. Louie imagined Liz telling Diane's group of younger campers the story and the mayhem that it would cause. He couldn't help but smile thinking about it.

"Oh please, in this day and age, I bet that's not anything big. The Internet has scarier stories than that. Honestly I've never seen the big deal," Louie reasoned. It was honestly what he believed too. The way he saw it, murders were such rare occurrences that a repeat was much less likely given that one had already happened at Watanka. Marion once told him that was just his way of trying to reason with his fear. He wasn't sure which he believed. "I feel like that's life though. A series of lessons and interactions that ultimately lead to an untimely demise."

"Okay, Psych 101. I'd just like to think that not everyone just up and dies," said Diane.

"Oh so you're one of those immortal sympathizers?" Marion joked.

"No, I'd just like to think that there's something more at the end of the tunnel than just suffering. Like, I wanna go out quietly, in my own bed, in my sleep, at the ripe old age of two hundred—shut up, we'll be advanced enough by then—not to mention with a dozen grandchildren filling my house."

"Wait, so in this scenario do the grandchildren all live with you or are they there for like a party?" Marion asked

"Yeah, like, celebrating your death?" said Louie.

"I think it's usually called celebrating life." Keith clarified.

"I know what I said."

"They can't really be that great of grandchildren if they're celebrating your death like that. Who's going to watch them now? Is this a *Lord of the Flies* scenario?" Marion continued.

"You guys suck. They would be there because they'd would want to be around their sweet grandmother while she's dying," Diane reasoned but the others refused to let up.

"You know, I've heard no mention of their parents. So are they dead in this scenario? Is that why you only have grandchildren at your house?" Marion crossed her legs and assumed an investigative stance.

"Are you trying to be a makeshift foster care?" Louie asked.

"Wait, did you kill your children and take *their* children because you secretly hate adults and only want to be around children?" Marion wouldn't let up.

"So she's just going to kill her grandchildren and take their children when they have them?"

"Don't be silly. . . she'll be long dead by then."

"I hate you all." Diane pouted.

"Did you at least leave a manifesto?" asked Louie.

"A what?" Barry countered. "What are you even talking about?"

"Come on, a manifesto! If you're gonna do something that makes you into a monster, wouldn't you want people to know why?"

"In this case, it'd be the murder of her kids, so I don't think people really care about 'the why?' Prolly caring more about when her appointment with the needle would be," countered Marion.

"Oh come on! That's total horseshit! Because of DNA evidence, we almost always end up finding what happened, how it happened, where it happened, and who it happened to. 'The why' likes to elude to us. Because there's not always physical evidence for that. Sometimes it's all right up here." Louie moved his finger to his temple. "And it's some of the most pivotal information of all."

"Why should I care about some sicko's reasoning? They're evil. End of story," Barry protested before looking over at Diane, who shot him a glare. "Shit, sorry. Obviously not in Louie's stupid scenario. You would never do that."

"You're not getting the point. The why *is* the most important aspect. The dead aren't coming back to life and the place where it happened isn't suddenly *not* a murder zone. But the exact reason for the murder? That's where you separate the truly evil from the impulsive. Did Diane know what she was doing and did it anyway? Or did she have some backwards reasoning for why it happened?

"What can of backward reasoning could she have that could possibly be anything but evil?" Keith quizzed him.

"Peace and quiet."

"Jesus Christ, Louie!" the group resounded.

"I'm kidding! Lower the pitch forks. All I'm saying is that most people don't inherently do bad things and think they're bad while doing it. There's got to be some method to the madness. I just like to know what it is so that I can read the warning signs."

"So I take it you're a big fan of Doctor Doom," mocked Marion.

"You can diss supervillains as much you want but they have the right idea. Why try and take over the world and go through all of this work, if you're not even going to have your reasoning heard about by the people that are trying so hard to stop you? Otherwise you'll just be marginalized with all the people that came before you. No, if you really want to stand out, you have a manifesto."

"Sometimes I really don't understand your logic, Louie. Still, I think the most important thing to take out of this is that we all believe Diane would kill her children," said Marion, trying to get back on topic.

"Seriously I hate all of you." Diane groaned.

"Hey, I'm sure you'd be super nice about it though," Louie remarked. "You'd probably just poison their nighttime snack. Let em die peacefully. No one wants to go out in some horrific, painful way. That sounds terrible. Hell, if I could pick my way of death, I'd definitely go with dying in my sleep. So it's really a compliment, Diane."

"Hell, if you're just wanting to die in your sleep, I've got a pretty stiff pillow and I've seen enough

Cuckoo's Nest to know the technique," Marion joked. She proceeded to put her hands up, holding an imaginary pillow and pushing it towards Louie, who acted like he was suffocating. He stopped suddenly and cocked his head to one side.

"Wait, does that make me Jack Nicholson?" Louie asked. "Because I can totally deal with that."

"It also makes you brain dead," stated Keith.

"Worth it. I'm now a badass."

"Oh Louie. . ." Diane chuckled.

Louie could have sworn Diane shot him a seductive look after she spoke, but he wasn't sure. The lack of blood rushing to his head and heading elsewhere was at a peak. Or maybe that was for a different reason.

"I've got to go drain the main vein."

The moon was out in full force, illuminating most of the walk away from the fire towards the woods. Trying to get far enough away that the others couldn't hear his stream, he stopped at the tree-line, satisfied with the distance. It was hard to see too far into the woods but still, he took a quick peek to make sure no one was there. Last thing he needed was a camper saying he had exposed himself to them. He unzipped his pants and relief washed over him. Considering he had drained a six pack without breaking the pee seal, it was long overdue.

He could hear the others back at the fire laughing and hollering something. *It must have been Barry being an idiot. Only he would make such a mongoloid noise.* Otherwise the night was oddly quiet and Louie couldn't believe how much he enjoyed the serenity. He had been so exhausted and angry because of the kids but the beer was doing a good job of suppressing it. Besides, from this point on it was all second nature. He knew that some of the people at the camp didn't want to be there but getting the opportunity to be out at a lake for a month during the summer? It didn't get much better than that. Maybe that was it, maybe he was just being more positive about it this year. Maybe that positivity would bring him the best summer yet.

He leaned his head back, took a deep breath of fresh air and looked up at the stars. They were so bright. So beautiful.

A twig snapped from what sounded like just feet away and Louie was quickly drawn out of his daze. He swiftly finished up peeing and zipped his pants back up. His eyes scanned the forest, trying to see if there was a deer or other animal nearby. No matter how much he squinted, it was nearly impossible to see more than fifteen feet in front of him, given the thick coverage of the trees. Why did he have to walk all the way over to the woods to go to the bathroom? He should have just gone by the pits. Now he was just hearing weird creepy noises and scaring himself for no reason. He leaned against the tree he had been peeing next to and peered deep into the forest.

"Hello?" Louie gulped and immediately regretted saying anything.

Great, now you're going to get murdered by a psycho axe-man.

He quickly retreated away from the tree-line, the hairs on the back of his neck standing up. He didn't like this. He had seen far too many horror movies and drank far too much beer to not be paranoid. And he knew he shouldn't have smoked that joint earlier. It didn't matter how much he reasoned with himself, a thousand scenarios went through his head and all of them ended with his own violent death. Diane had told him that the strain would bring on paranoia but Louie wasn't sure if Diane realized how much his brother had tortured him with scary movies and how unlikely he was to snap out of it. He just didn't trust the dark.

Deciding that he'd had enough of the woods scaring him, he retreated back towards the fire, glancing over his shoulder as he did. *What the hell?* Louie thought as he saw something move behind the tree where he was standing. Did he just see that? Did that really happen? *Not again, Louie. You just went through this.* No, it must have just been his eyes playing tricks on him. He really needed to just stick with beer. He returned to the fire, still unsure of the movement in the woods.

****

Louie sat back down with the others at the fire and a figure in the darkness continued to watch him. To watch all of them.

Time to get started.

PART TWO

Chapter 9
Ralph

RALPH WAS THE FURTHEST THING from a morning person. Usually his nights would be spent watching Adult Swim and playing guitar, with mornings being less the start of his day and more the end of it. So it was surprising to him that when the giant bell at the front of the cabin started ringing, and found himself being awoken with ease. The crisp morning air, the streaks of sunlight entering through the thin cloth window liner. Maybe he could get used to the whole camping experience.

At the very least he was getting away from his hometown, which couldn't have come at a better time. Breaking up with his girlfriend of eight months, Ashley, wasn't easy. But they were going to be away from each other anyway, and High School was just around the corner. It wasn't worth being tied down during the summer. Especially when she was going to spend her break at her grandma's place in Florida. It was only a matter of time before one of them was tongue deep in someone else and breaking a heart in the process. He decided to be responsible. Plus, camp looked like it was going to be fun.

Maybe it was because he was sick of *hearing* about the camp and introducing himself to others that he just wanted to start the actual summer camp experience. Find out what it was like for himself. He wanted to get past the awkward stages of learning the routine and the people around him. It was his first time at anything like it and he just wanted to feel comfortable again.

It helped that Ralph was placed in, from what he could tell, the best group in the camp. His counselor, Louie, appeared pretty laid back and fun, reminding Ralph of this senior who got kicked out of school for bringing in special brownies for all the teachers. The previous day when they had to introduce themselves, Louie just said to talk amongst themselves.

"You're gonna be here for a month. Forcing you to learn each other's name at this very moment doesn't do any of us any good and just forces you to hate me," he had said. Judging by the crazy outburst in one of the other groups, Ralph decided he was onto something.

The days at Watanka couldn't have been any worse than the boredom that would come with summer vacation. At least at school he was forced to be social but over break he'd just spend time in his room, playing old video games. Getting him away got him out of any kind of relationship mourning process.

It was also one of the reasons he looked forward to camp so much: forced interaction. Even Louie's "Hey dudes, time to get your shower on so we can all get some grub" was a welcome change. Louie was either really good at his job or really bad, but either way the camaraderie was nice to Ralph.

Finally deciding it was time to start the process of getting up, Ralph stood, reaching under his bunk to grab his toiletries. Pulling the bag onto his bed, he was completely unaware of the open zipper and everything proceeded to fall to the floor. It seemed to fall in slow motion as the embarrassment of the situation felt like it washed over him for days. He looked up, ready to be made fun of by one of the other boys. It was prime joke material and he wouldn't blame them for it. He awaited their harsh words, laughter and finger pointing. Only that didn't happen. Those actually awake just looked over, sometimes saying to themselves, "that sucks" but otherwise just going about their own business. The guy next to him, completely covered in tattoos and therefore in Ralph's estimation, a little scary, quickly knelt down to help.

"Shit man, talk about bad luck," he said, putting Ralph's toothpaste and deodorant back into the bag.

"Yeah, that would be my middle name," Ralph said, a little intimidated by the large tattooed man who he questioned was even young enough to be at Watanka.

"Tell me about it, man. I've just been waiting for something like that to happen to me. Let me tell you, you think you have bad luck? I may as well have bad luck as my first, middle, and last name. Speaking of which, the name's Santa." He extended his hand out.

Ralph immediately shook it but he couldn't help but chuckle as he did. It wasn't just that he said his name was the alter ego of old Saint Nick, it more had to do with the fact that he was also a large Mexican man covered in tattoos. An odd nickname for anyone with that appearance but even more so given his age of what sure wasn't more than seventeen. Ralph felt like he was in a movie and half-expected a musical number to break out at any moment.

"Before you even ask, my Christian name is Santiago and my first tattoo. . ." he pulled up his sleeve. "Was this bad boy!"

He revealed a tattoo of Santa Claus, a very colorful and extravagant image featuring a stereotypical Saint Nick. It fit in nicely with the other tattoos, some featuring tribal symbols but most just old cartoons characters.

"Okay, good to know. Was a little thrown off at first." Ralph really wanted to address how odd the moment was, but decided to ignore it instead, too worried of what Santa might do. Santa just chuckled.

"Yeah, most are. Grams always used to call me it so that means my sisters would, which then meant my schoolmates would so it just kinda ended up stickin'. Trust me, a bunch of gangbangers shouting for Santa is a pretty entertaining sight to behold."

Ralph wondered if the name had any gang affiliation after he used the term "Gangbangers" but he was too scared to ask. For one, he didn't want to offend him but more importantly, he didn't want to be the type of person that would ask that question. Why should it matter what his past held? They were at the camp now and all equals so why would it matter if he had some trouble hundreds of miles away? After sitting in silence for a few moments, Ralph soon realized how rude he was being by not offering up his own name, so he rectified it.

"Well it's nice to meet you, Ralph. Honestly, after yesterday I wasn't sure how this camp was gonna go," Santa continued. "Been feelin' like a fucking fish out water. Had one of the counselors say some nice things to me 'cause she liked my Foghorn Leghorn tat, but outside of that it's been nothing but terrified looks and whispering."

"Ever think about just wearing some sleeves to cover them up?" Ralph said, trying to offer up any kind of helpful advice but quickly deciding he should have just stayed quiet.

"Ha! As much as I'm sure others would appreciate it, I doubt that'd really solve the problem. Still got that very visible aspect of the whole being a large Mexican man. And the thought of wearing long sleeves all summer long has me sweatin' already. Santa don't do too good in the heat, brother."

Ralph showed sympathy but understood where the others were coming from. Santiago was large, tattooed, and held himself like he had just come out of gangland. It wasn't exactly the most approachable appearance, especially given most of the campers' trepidation towards socialization in general.

It wasn't like he fell into that category as well. Ralph certainly had a little concern the night before when he realized his bunk was directly next to said scary-looking person. Those fears were quickly absolved after talking to him for a few moments. In fact, Ralph wasn't sure if there was a nicer person in the camp—besides that one wacky counselor.

"Well I need to get to that shower before these other guys actually manage to get out of bed. Santa don't do cold water."

Unfortunately for Santa, as he would find out shortly, there was no such thing as "hot" water at Camp Watanka. No, at best one could sometimes achieve air temperature water, which still felt absurdly cold. Ralph found this out when he stepped into the shower and it felt like a bucket of ice was dropped over his head. As mad as he was at first, he saw the silver-lining, telling himself, *Hey at least you're awake now.* Too many mornings of this though and Ralph was sure he would fall ill.

When he exited the shower, cold and shivering, Ralph went to the sink to brush his teeth. It was cramped and he could only get access to the sink to moisten the bristles of his toothbrush before being pushed back into the crowd. He opted to go outside and just spit out the Winterfresh/saliva concoction that had brewed in his mouth. In front of "The Bathhouse"—as the sign on it read—Ralph looked around hoping to find a water spigot.

His eyes wandered freely, finally landing on the toweled up midriff of a perky girl at the girls' bathhouse. Realizing exactly what he was doing, he looked up, staring directly into the eyes of the midriff's owner. Busted. Trying to counteract the perception, he quickly looked away, helping to avoid the look of disgust that was sure to adorn her face. He could hear giggling behind him but he kept his eyes forward. He felt like such an idiot.

Off in the distance, he spotted a water spigot next to the lake; only problem being its current occupation by a cute girl washing her hair. Ralph wasn't sure he wanted to risk it, with the other girls and their giggling still freshly resounding in his head. But anything would have been better than just standing there. He started debating whether he should go over or just wait but before he could even make up his mind, his feet had carried him to the water spigot, making the decision for him. The girl was leaned over the flowing water, washing the soap from her hair.

"I just need one more minute. Having a little difficulty getting this shampoo out. Dang water pressure," the girl said, not even looking up at Ralph. "Be happy you're not a girl and don't have an entire mane of hair to deal with."

"You know you might have better luck in the showers," Ralph reasoned, his voice cracking a little.

"Nuh-uh. Nooo thank you. That place is an absolute madhouse. Have you ever had to be around a bunch of girls, some having to shave their legs, others just trying to wash out the half a can of hairspray from their hair? It's not exactly a pleasant experience. At least this water doesn't turn me into a human popsicle."

"You've got me there. I didn't realize water could be that cold without freezing." He looked back at the showers, not-so-fondly reliving the ice shower he'd just had.

She laughed at his dumb joke, a heavy tomboyish laugh. He wasn't sure if it was pity or genuine but he took it either way. She finally looked up, getting the final suds out of her hair. She grabbed the towel that lay in the grass and started drying her hair vigorously. Ralph took notice of the Superman shirt she sported. He hadn't met many girls that liked to wear superhero shirts. None of the girls back home would do that. Especially not Ashley.

"So either you like Superman or you're looking at my boobs. Considering these are solid A's, I doubt it's the latter. So I take it you like Kal-El?" she said, throwing Ralph off completely. He could hardly make a sentence in his own head, much less with his mouth. The longer he stayed silent, the more suspicious he looked in his motives. Ralph knew this yet he still couldn't manage a word.

"Okay, maybe *you were* looking at my boobs. . . or lack thereof."

"No, no, no! Sorry, my brain just kinda locked up," Ralph finally blurted out, figuring honesty was likely the best option. At least, that's what his mom would always say.

"So your answer is. . ." she was still playing with him, wanting to see how he got out of this situation.

"Oh yeah, I'm big into Superman. Christopher Reeves though, not that Henry Cavill stuff," he added, wondering if he'd just made his second friend this morning.

Maybe this camp thing wouldn't be all too bad.

"Oh god!" she exclaimed. "Do not even get me started. *Man of Steel* has got to be one of the worst superhero movies I have ever seen. That was like *Daredevil* bad. It's like the director of some cheesy action movies with a fetish for slow-mo decided to never read an Action Comic or look at the previous movies."

This comforted Ralph, immediately responding with a passionate "Yeah, what a mess. Literally. How many buildings did they have to destroy in that end fight? Hell, Smallville pretty much just isn't even a town anymore. It's just rubble. So now we're supposed to cheer for a guy that lets his home town get completely destroyed—massively aiding in its destruction, actually."

"I'm pretty sure the Superman we all know and love would be smart enough to not take down skyscrapers full of people," she affirmed, finally done drying and deciding to wrap the towel around her head.

"'But he's young and brash. He has to *become* the Superman we all know and love.' Psh, bullshit. Sounds like someone is just trying to make up for their own terrible writing."

"Yeah, you know, because you have to *learn* how to not kill thousands of people. Otherwise, that's just like a basic function."

"At least half a million people died during that fight. At least," he said, gurgling at the end as he rinsed his mouth of toothpaste.

"And then he's so fucking upset that he has to kill Zod, the guy who just tried to destroy the world, right after not being upset at all over the hundreds of thousands of human beings that were crushed to death due to that little scrap. How heroic." The sarcasm rolled off her tongue with ease.

"And don't even get me started on Lois Lane in that movie. She makes some of the stupidest decisions ever, yet we're supposed to commend her for being so brave. For what, wandering off in the middle of the Arctic and being lucky enough to stumble upon an alien spacecraft, where she moves through the world like an idiot in a horror movie? 'That's a big alien spacecraft. Better go explore it!'"

"Margot Kidder was so much better. My boyfriend is insane and swears that Kate Bosworth was the best Lois Lane. He said 'She resembled the comics Lois the most' or some crap. She's a go-getter willing to take calculated risks; not scaling a glacier at 2 a.m. so that's an improvement. But I still I drug tested him shortly after. The results came back negative." She laughed it off. Ralph was still recovering from the use of the word "boyfriend." Sure, he didn't even know this girl's name but she was actually into Superman. And good Superman too! It was hard to not be at least a little disappointed. Still, at least he met someone he could talk to. And a girl at that. Plus, who knows, maybe it could turn into something down the road.

"Do they have tests for insanity? Because you might need to do that. As much as I hate *Man of Steel*, I may hate the Superhero Soap Opera known as *Superman Returns* even more." Ralph continued the conversation, trying to steer away from the boyfriend.

"Tell me about it. I about ended things the moment I found out about it but he likes *Doctor Who* so he's not all that bad." She looked over at her cabin where the over-enthused counselor was corralling the girls into lines, trying to get them all ready to go to breakfast. "Well, well, well. Looks like it's my cue to leave. It was nice meeting you. . ."

"Ralph. . . Lieber. And you—"

"Sally. O'Neill. If you can remember that then I'll love you forever. Everyone always seems to remember it as Sandy or Sarah. Even got a Sal once, which I guess is right, but I think Grandpa thought I was a boy the last couple years of his life so I'd still count it as a miss."

"Wouldn't dream of forgetting," he gushed, but she didn't give him a response. Was that too much? Was she weirded out by it? He didn't have time to ask, not that he would have, because before he knew it she was sprinting off to her line at the flagpole. He watched her closely as one thought repeated in his head, "Why the hell did I get back together with Ashley before I left?"

"Ralph!" someone yelled from off in the distance. Ralph looked towards the cabins and spotted Santa, who waved his hands, trying to get his attention. "We gotta go to breakfast, dude. You missed Louie's roll call."

Ralph made it back in just enough time to grab his glasses off his bunk. He proceeded to join up with his group, headed by Louie, and then marched over to the flag pole to begin the day's activities. First, there were a couple of morning rituals to be had, something that caught him off-guard, but it made sense quickly, given where they were lined up at.

The pledge of allegiance was harder for Ralph to remember than he thought. It was even harder for him to recall when the last time was that he even had to recite it. *Probably elementary school.* It just wasn't something that ever entered his life. Maybe if he was more into sports then he'd have been exposed to it more. Instead a slight chuckle came to his body, drawing an intense stare of disapproval from the loud blonde counselor. He couldn't help it, the whole thing seemed silly. He started to wonder if they were going to start coloring or craft something out of construction paper.

Ralph was half-expecting a prayer or moment of silence but instead Al stepped out from the main office and moved to the head of the lines. He had a huge smile on his face, calling some of the guys 'sport' as he passed by. Ralph noticed the huge name tag that read "Big Al" firmly attached to the breast of his shirt. Finally settling in, and receiving a happy greeting from his counselors, Al looked out at the campers with a massive grin, soaking in the surroundings.

"The first official day." Al exuded an intense happiness. "It's exciting isn't it? Couldn't have asked for a better morning, could we?"

"Absolutely not, beautiful morning," the chipper woman behind him said.

"Yes, Carol, the best." Al seemed to think the question was rhetorical given his annoyed look when Carol spoke up.

They were right though; it certainly was a beautiful morning. The fog was starting to fade and streaks of light shown down on the lake, giving it an ethereal glow. The sun was rising over the tree-line and gold streaks moved through the morning dew.

Any place that can look like this can't be that bad.

"And while I wish that every day would be as beautiful as this one, I know that's just not likely. Now I'm not trying to be a gloomy Gus. Some days are going to be brighter and warmer than others but I promise you, the good days will outweigh the bad ones. Just like your experience here at Watanka. Don't let a few things get to you and ruin your time because there's always sunshine right around the corner!"

"Beautifully said," Carol chimed in again. Ralph noticed Louie at the back, barely able to contain his laughter, causing some of the other counselors to smile and chuckle to themselves. Ralph looked down at his feet and smiled, knowing his days with Louie's group were sure to be fun.

"Now, there's a couple things that I need to go over. Yes, the rumors are true and given the massive heatwave hitting us this summer, we'll be providing extra swimming time," Al paused, waiting for applause but only receiving it from the counselors, mostly the blonde, who seemed to clap for anything Al said. "And I also wanted to announce the addition of a new activity! Thanks to our friend Keith over there, we're going to be able to reopen an old classic: the archery range!"

This actually drew some excitement from the camp. Ralph had overheard the previous night that the Archery range had been closed because someone was murdered there. He didn't believe it, especially given that it came from the Belar twins, and needed clarification. So he went to Louie about it and his laughter was all Ralph needed to know that he had been ribbed. *Stupid twins.* He should have known better than to trust them. And even though he'd never used a bow a day in his life, he still had a certain interest in learning it. After all, Katniss and Legolas looked pretty damn cool using one.

"Yes, yes it's very exciting. As some of you know, I've been wanting to bring that range back for years but lack of equipment just wouldn't allow it. Step in, Mr. Tucker over there who has graciously donated several bows and hundreds of arrows. Yes, he's been a swell addition to the crew. I think he might have something to say," Al said and motioned Keith over to join him.

"Now I understand that some of you may have a misconception of what archery may be. We're not going to be jumping off horses and shooting flaming arrows. We will be taking our time and learning all of the basics. I've been bow hunting since I was nine-years-old so I know my way around a bow and arrow," Keith continued. "You will too if you take it seriously and listen to what I have to tell you. Al has been gracious enough to provide me with the opportunity to pass on this fun past time to you. I mean, who doesn't want to say that they learned how to shoot an apple off their friend's head?"

Al's eyes grew wide and Ralph could practically see the number of lawsuits going through Al's head after that comment.

"I'm kidding," Keith interjected. "That's not really what we're going for. I welcome anyone that wants to come join. I promise it'll be a blast."

Keith looked at Al, clearly no longer wanting to talk, which Al happily obliged him, sending him back to his group. Suddenly archery didn't sound like quite what Ralph was expecting. It looked like Sally was into it though, so he was looking forward to signing up.

"So y'all have that to look forward to. We've also obviously got rock climbing, kayaking, and, *ahem*, pottery, amongst other things. So you can. . ."

The sirens started subtly but then their presence was felt more and more as the source drew closer and closer. At first Ralph just assumed it would start to fade, an ambulance passing through to a nearby town or something. Instead the siren just grew louder and louder until finally a pair of headlights emerged through the morning dew, a pair of flashing red and blue lights up top. The police vehicle sped up the dirt road with some urgency, drawing a look of concern from Al.

In fact, all the counselors looked a little worried. Marion was whispering something to Al. It looked like Louie tossed a baggie of something into the bushes, but of what, Ralph couldn't be sure. Carol just stood, hands behind her back, rocking backwards and forwards, heels to toes. She seemed amused by all of the excitement more than anything.

"Maybe we should get these hungry campers to breakfast," Al suggested, his voice booming but also cracking with concern. "I'm sure all of this excitement has just stirred up those appetites even more. So let's get some eggs and. . . cereal into these bright young minds."

Carol agreed, starting to usher the campers towards the dining hall. The other counselors followed suit except for Marion who followed Al to the cop, who had just exited his vehicle. His partner stayed inside, doing something on his laptop, typing away furiously. The cops seemed suspicious of the camp, but Ralph wasn't sure if he was just reading into things. Cops always intimidated him and seemed like they were sniffing out trouble. Even though Ralph was far from a troublemaker, his fear of the law was very real.

While Al and Marion sorted out the situation with the cops, Ralph was ushered into the dining hall with the rest of the campers. No one knew what was going on but that didn't stop the rumor mill from churning up ridiculous theories.

"Alice told Tommy that Nancy said they found a bunch of marijuana plants out in the woods and that they belong to Al. Said that's how he's been making his money all these years and that the camp is just a front. He must be loaded and he's just stuffing it all away, waiting to run off to Aruba or something."

"I heard that they found a bunch of kiddie porn on Al's computer so they're here to take him away. Probably why he runs this camp. Gets pictures of us boys for his collection. God, I can't even imagine how many cameras are around here."

"No, no, no. You're wrong. They came because Al murdered his wife. See, he decided he finally had enough and took her out back and wam. That's why he's been so happy."

"Al doesn't have a wife."

"Exactly."

Ralph found it amusing that no matter who was telling the story, the reason the cops for the cops arrival was always to get Al for something. It wasn't like Al was a bad guy, but no one liked to see authority crumble more than a bunch of pre and pubescent kids. Whatever it was, it couldn't have been too serious because the policemen left without taking Al in their squad car. Or doing anything really. In fact, Al seemed to be in an even better mood after the police had left. It was anyone's guess as to what they wanted. The conspiracy theories were sure to run rampant but Ralph knew better than to believe any of it.

Getting his breakfast—two waffles doused in syrup and three sausages—Ralph made his way over to Santa, who was saving him a spot.

"I don't know, man. You really think it's not at least a little real?" Santa was engaged in conversation with the boy to his right. Ralph thought his name was Chase.

"No it is absolutely fake. It's more like a simplistic ballet routine sometimes featuring tables. . . or ladders. . . or chairs," Chase said.

"Those hits are real as hell though man. They be like *bam, bam!*" Santiago mimed chair shots, even giving his own reaction to receiving a chair shot, something that required flailing arms that ended up hitting the poor girl next to him. Santa profusely apologized.

"If you keep doing stuff like that, I'll argue wrestling with you any day," Chase laughed. The girl Ralph had seen by Chase's side the night before joined them out of nowhere and took Chase away, whispering something into his ear. Whatever it was, they left in a rush. Those two were thick as thieves.

"Probably going for a bit of the ole in out," said Santa, right when the two were out of earshot.

At first Ralph didn't get the joke, shooting Santa a look of confusion. By the time he got it, Santa had already moved on, mentioning something about basketball. Eventually, the conversation ended up exactly where Ralph had expected it to: the police visit that morning.

"I don't know, it all seems pretty normal to me," Santa shrugged it off. "If there was actually a problem then someone would have been arrested. That's how it works." He chomped down on some burnt toast and scrambled eggs.

"Still it could've been something serious," stated Ralph.

"And you're worrying about it, why?" Santa asked. And he was right. Why was Ralph worrying about why they were there? It didn't matter so long as everything was okay. And the police left didn't they?

They wouldn't have just up and left if things weren't okay. So everything had to be fine.

"You're right, it's stupid. I just. . . I saw that Donny kid leave in the middle of the night and he wasn't back for a while. Something just didn't seem right about it."

It wasn't something that really bothered him when it first happened. He saw the kid leaving, figured he was using the bathroom and didn't think anything of it. But with the police that morning, it all seemed more suspicious. He looked over at where Donny sat and saw him talking with some cute girl. He didn't look harmless per se, but something also seemed. . . off about him. His leg shook and his eyes darted around. He was nervous. But what did Ralph know by a look? It's not like Donny's buzzcut was going to tell him anything.

"He probably just pissed the bed and didn't want anyone to know so he did some stealth cleaning," Santa reasoned.

"Then what do you think the police were here for?" Ralph queried.

"Chances are they just found weed on one of the counselors. Hell, did you see how much Louie was sweating during all that? I think that one brunette girl snagged the bag that he ditched. Guess we figured out why he's always so mellow."

But there Louie was, standing over with Keith, and he looked as calm as could be. In fact, it was Keith that seemed to be nervous and freaking out. They were speaking in hushed tones but Ralph could see it on their faces that something had happened. His curiosity got the best of him and he started over towards them, wanting to find out for himself. Upon reaching them, Keith was ready to leave, brushing past him and saying to himself under his breath "I am so fucking dead."

"What was that about?" Ralph asked.

"Don't worry about it. He's just havin' a rough day." Louie took a huge swig of coffee.

"What's there to worry about? Is that why the cops were here today?" Ralph asked these questions at lightning speed, drawing a look of ire from Louie.

"Woah there. Ease up, detective. Nah, man. Don't worry about it. What can I do for you. . . Ralph?" Louie said this last part as if he was just drawing a name out of an invisible hat and just lucky to guess the correct one.

"I was. . . uh," he stumbled over his words, trying to think of something. "I was just wondering if there'd be time to go back to the cabin, I forgot some sunscreen."

"Sunscreen?" Louie asked, befuddled and looking back at Ralph's table. "You realize Santiago has some, right? You know, in that place you were just sitting?"

Sure enough, there sat a big bottle of sunscreen right where Santa was sitting.

Congrats Ralph, you are the world's worst liar. Also, unimaginative.

His terrible detective work would have to wait.

The rest of the morning went fairly seamless, with the excitement from the police slowly fading with the rising sun. Ralph went with his group to the kayaks, the first activity of the day. He was excited for it at first until Louie explained that since it involved being in the water, they'd have to go over safety protocols. It's not like it mattered though; his parents already signed his life away, giving up any right to sue outside of negligence. This was all just window dressing.

By the time Louie was finally done going over safety, the sun was boiling down on them. So hot that Ralph could feel every piece of clothing he had on, sticking to his body. *Did I remember to put on deodorant?* Ralph thought to himself, trying to subtly check and make sure he had no pit stains. He was relieved when he saw that he didn't but quickly suspicious when an odor hit his nostrils. Was that him? Or was it one of the other campers? Ralph squeezed his arms to his body, trying to avoid letting the smell escape.

So Ralph's mind had been a little preoccupied when Keith brought his group over to join Louie's shortly before lunch. He said he needed to make a phone call and that it was really important. Ralph would have asked Louie but he knew he'd have received the same derision as before. Whatever it was, Ralph still didn't know enough to put anything together. Outside of Keith's short outburst, it was all a mystery.

So while Ralph had listened in, making sure not to miss out on any vital information, one phrase kept entering his head:

You are so fucking dead.

Chapter 10

Keith

"JUST ANOTHER BEAUTIFUL DAY IN PARADISE." Keith stared out at the Lake and the sun began to set just beyond the tree-line at the water's edge. Some of the other counselors may have contained a note of sarcasm there, but not Keith. He absolutely loved the fresh air and constant physical activity. Being there was a nice reset from the constant struggles of the real world, where he constantly had to be at his best and train without reserve. This place was supposed to serve as his very own pause button. Not like that mattered anymore though.

The letter had come during that day's afternoon activities and Keith knew he made a mistake the moment he decided to open it. The anxiety had gotten to him and he couldn't stand to wait. Instead, he asked Louie to watch his group so that he could open the letter and the celebration could start early.

Celebration. . . riiiight.

At least he had a beautiful view to come to during hard times. He was able to stare at the lake, watch the sun's rays bounce off, and try to forget all of his worries. It always worked before. Now he couldn't keep his mind off anything that didn't involve that letter in some fashion. No, this was the last thing that Keith needed to be thinking about and he knew it. He needed to just take his mind off of it, however impossible that may have seemed.

Most of the clothes he brought to camp could be considered "workout gear", so he didn't even need to head back to his cabin after making the decision to go for a run; he was already dressed for it. Going for a jog was always his way of sorting out his thoughts and put things in a better perspective. Back when he needed to decide between which scholarship he was going to take, he went on a 14 mile run to clear his head. From the beginning of the run to the end, his mind ended up changing completely and he was grateful for the journey. Otherwise who knows what school he would have ended up at? Moments like those were essential.

Keith darted into the forest, jumping onto the path that had become his usual route. It was hardly wide enough for one person to carefully walk on, let alone run, but he had taken this path for the past two weeks and had it mapped out carefully in his head. He weaved in and out the trees with ease. The entire route was four miles, and the various elevation changes provided for quite the workout, so Keith found himself taking it anytime he needed to cool down and get the endorphins going.

As he continued down the path, his blood pumped and sweat collected on his brow as his thoughts wandered. What was he even going to do next? This was supposed to be his chance to get to the next level. To make his passion into a career. The tears formed and started dripping down his face almost as much as the sweat beads that continued to pour out of him with each step. The salt in them burned a little but he powered through, using the pain as a motivator.

Keith must have taken his eyes off the ground in front of him for a split second because before he knew it he was tumbling forward, slamming into the trunk of a giant tree just off the path. The force of hitting it almost took his consciousness but instead just left him dizzy and lightheaded. He remembered in all the movies what it was like to be knocked out, waking up hours later with a lump on the head and no memory.

Instead everything just felt foggy and he couldn't figure out what was happening at first. But then he looked around and saw he was at the edge of the forest, within eyesight of the camp. *Why did this have to happen right at the end?* He couldn't have been out for more than a millisecond and rapidly recalled the fall. *It wasn't that bad. So much for the movies. . .*

Keith's fall must have made quite the noise because before he knew it, Diane was running down the path, a look of concern on her face.

"Hey are you—" Diane started to ask but stopped herself as soon as his saw his face full of tears. "Oh my god, what's wrong?"

"I fell. It's not a big deal," reassured Keith, trying to pick himself up but being stopped by Diane.

"Looks like a hell of a lot more than that." Diane knelt down and Keith quickly became very aware of the tears that covered his beet red face.

"I just. . ." Keith started but everything came rushing to him. The disappointment his parents would feel. The lack of respect he'd get from everyone that once respected him. Everything he'd lose because of one stupid decision.

The tears started up hard and he couldn't have stopped them if he wanted to. Everything about his life was now up to question, all because he didn't put his best foot down. He didn't try with all that he could. He couldn't have. Otherwise things would have worked out just how they had in high school and then college. Things always worked out. Always.

"I just. . . I don't even know what I'm doing. All this training, all this love for the game, what does it amount to? So I can just be head basketball coach at a high school that sees me as a disappointment?" Keith could barely get the words out through all the tears.

"What happened, Keith?" Diane sat down next to him, putting a consoling arm on his shoulder.

"They turned me down. Didn't even give me a shot before they took every dream that I've ever had away from me. How can they even do that? I had tryouts scheduled and they just told me not to come. Didn't even want to bother. God dammit!" He punched the ground next to him in frustration. How could this be happening to him? He may have been a complete mess but how could he be wrong? Those bastards screwed up, not him.

"What? The pros?" Diane asked, still confused as to why exactly he was so upset. Keith wasn't surprised, it was an odd situation to have stumbled upon: a man who could barely get words out through the blubbering mess he'd become.

Dad would be so ashamed of me right now.

"I'm sorry, this is embarrassing." He tried getting up, but again, she put a hand on his shoulder and motioned him back to the ground.

"There's nothing to be embarrassed about, Keith. You need to talk to someone. And what better person than the one right in front of you." Diane smiled warmly but Keith could hardly even acknowledge it with his own.

"I don't even know what free time is. Everything has been spent preparing for this. Every waking moment. Watanka? I wish I could have gone to a camp like this when I was younger. Getting to just do fun activities or hang out on the beach. Make friends. It was always basketball camp or football camp or baseball camp. Any camp that was filled with people who just saw competition, not friends. Any camp that made me better. Better at a fucking sport that doesn't even matter anymore. All for some non-existent 'next-level.' I *needed* them to succeed. It was one after the other. I always had another thing to go to. I didn't have summers off. I didn't sit around playing video games with my friends late until the sun went down then rose again. I wasn't that kid. I didn't get to be. I was an athlete. That was my identity. And now what am I?" Keith finally caught his breath and looked at Diane who just looked at him with sad puppy dog eyes.

Is she even listening to me?

"Wow. Just when I thought you were Superman and didn't have any weaknesses" she swooned but he hardly cared. His entire life was falling apart.

"How am I even supposed to succeed? My entire life I just assumed I'd be playing a sport professionally. Coasted my way through school because of it." Keith sniffled, trying to hold back more tears. At this rate, he'd be out soon. "I'm not even sure I could do basic algebra now. Heck, most of the time I didn't even do my homework, it was just from online answer books. Now what? I'm just a dumb jock who's gonna wind up working in a factory. I should have just listened to my dad. I should have tried harder."

The words just bounced around in his head over and over. Did he really believe all of that? It was hard to see past the intense feeling of hopelessness. Every person that had ever doubted him were all proven correct in one fell swoop. He'd be lucky to make it out of this at all.

"Keith, I could be totally out of line with this but it seems like you're looking at this all wrong. You don't need to be anything you don't want to be. You think there are only two options for you: playing professional basketball or going to a factory. Why do those have to be the only things? Why can't you just find another approach? Why does having this one thing not work out mean the end of the world to you?"

"You just don't get it."

"What's there to get? Go somewhere else. Go to Europe and play. A lot of people do that. Hell my friend Nitsy's brother has been playing in Europe for two years and he played for a division III school that never even made the playoffs. There are options.

Sometimes you just have to open your eyes a little wider to see them."

Diane was right, that much was obvious, but it was still hard for Keith to actually admit to. It didn't matter anyway because there was no way his dad would let him do that. As soon as word got to him— hopefully not until Keith had some time to digest the information himself—he was sure to be driving up, wanting to come up with a game plan. Find other farm teams to try out for. Everything that *he* knew about getting to get to the next level. Keith had had enough of it. Enough of everything.

"What's the point in playing if it's not what I set out to do?" he asked, immediately thinking that it sounded better in his head than out loud.

"Honestly, I can't believe you even think like that. So what that one thing got in your way. So you're just going to quit? Sounds pretty childish to me." Diane's words cut deep. She was completely right and Keith knew it. He was acting extremely childish. Why would one obstacle mean everything was over? Granted it was a big obstacle but still. It just reminded him of how many things had been given to him throughout his life. Was he even worthy of the life that he yearned for?

He was naturally gifted so he had a litany of options in school. No matter what sport he did, he excelled at it. In basketball, he was the point guard. In football, he was the quarterback. In baseball, he was the short-stop and clean-up batter. He was always in the spotlight and he always thrived in it. But it had all come so naturally that it didn't even require much thinking on his part. Did he even deserve it?

By the time schools were seriously looking at him for college athletics, he just took the best scholarship on the table. It was a choice that was in front of him, no reaching out necessary. They came to him. The scouts courted him at his games, chatted up his dad, and usually offered to pay for some kind of meal at a get-together. This trend seemed like it would continue forever but suddenly the phone calls stopped coming. Now he was two years removed from school, with several failed walk-on attempts under his belt, barely able to stay afloat while he chased his dream of becoming a professional athlete.

"Thanks." Keith finally let out, truly meaning it.

"Oh yeah, sure. Little miss Diane and her infinite wisdom. We all know how much everyone appreciates it." She laid the sarcasm on thick.

"Yeah, well I do. So thank you." They both smiled at each other, looking anywhere but at each other's eyes. Keith wasn't sure if it was because she liked him or if she was embarrassed by the way his face looked covered in tears.

"I'm going into the city in a couple hours. Would you like to come with?" Diane asked. *That was out of nowhere.* A trip to the city was all that Keith needed at that moment, especially with Diane. Maybe a little excitement was what he needed and who knew when the next time for that would be? Was there even an implication there? Maybe it had just been too long since he'd had sex and was going through a traumatic experience so the body was overcompensating. *But then she did just bite her lip.* It seemed like these were all the signs. Should he be nonchalant about it? Should he be more straight-forward? *Fuck it.*

"Okay, but only if it's a date," he urged, catching Diane off guard after his prolonged silence.

"I. . . well yeah," she was barely able to get it out through her nervous laughter. He had read the situation correctly.

"Then I'll meet you at your cabin at seven," he said, finally having a smile come to his face.

"You better clean yourself up," she said and he finally noticed just how dirty he was from the fall. His knee was pretty banged up as well, with blood forming in little beads. It looked worse than it felt though, with Keith able to ignore it for the most part.

"You sure you don't want me to look like this? I figured I'd be going for the deep woods survivalist look." She provided him a polite chuckle.

"Just let me go jump around in the mud a bit so I can get on your level and we should be good to go." Diane smiled uncontrollably. "I need to get back to the kids though. One of the boys thought he lost his grandfather's watch during our scavenger hunt today so I had to go look for it. Thankfully it was just on top of one of the stumps next to the fire pits. Didn't prevent me from getting eaten alive on my way out here though. Little bastard better be appreciative."

"Here let me. . ." he said, holding out his hand to help her up. "You know, those kids don't realize how good they have it. I don't think anyone else would have gotten that for him."

"Oh, so you're saying you wouldn't have?"

"Me? Of course not. It'd be lost for the ages." He grinned wide, his eyes darting back and forth between her eyes and her lips.

"I'll see you in a bit, hard ass. Keep your head up." And with that she was gone, leaving Keith to stand there, grinning like an idiot. It may have been small, but it was finally a win. And God knows he needed it. He noticed Carol, peeking out from behind one of the cabins, but she disappeared when he looked directly towards her. She was likely just trying to keep an eye on the camp, but her ways were a little intrusive. Keith didn't sit on it for long as one unfortunate fact remained: he still needed to deal with his father.

Deciding he could probably use the extra pump before his date, he started back down the trail, this time paying a little closer attention to the path at his feet. His knee throbbed throughout the run but he powered through it, finally returning to his cabin after a four-mile trek. He returned to an empty cabin and was able to quickly make it to the showers, unoccupied thankfully. For some reason the kids were all in the dining hall. *A little early isn't it?* Looking forward to a little privacy, he found himself annoyed somewhat to find Louie inhabiting the cabin when he returned from the showers. The six pack at his feet— half empty—didn't help matters. He quickly decided not to let Louie in on any of his basketball problems. Louie was unlikely to be supportive in his current state.

"Dude you were supposed to watch my group for me," said Keith.

"Calm down. Al and Marion are doing some safety lesson. All the kids are with them. The counselors have officially been dismissed for the night. Looks like I really interrupted a difficult time in your life. Enjoy your spa day?" Louie had a slight edge to him. The kids must have gotten to him.

"Huh. . . wonder why she didn't tell me that?" muttered Keith.

"What? Who?" Louie asked abrasively.

"Diane. I just saw her. She didn't mention anything about it. Guess that makes sense why she was able to leave her group. . ." Keith trailed off towards the end, almost just saying it to himself.

"Diane? That girl'll take any excuse she can to go smoke a cig in the woods. She thinks no one's wise to it but I can smell that shit on her from across the lake. Wait, why were you in the woods with her anyway?" he questioned suspiciously.

"Running. You know me. You won't believe this though, I've got a date." Keith was excited to be able to tell someone of his success but he was still confused by Louie. Had Keith mentioned that he had seen her in the woods? How could he have known she was there?

"You know, somehow I do believe it," said Louie, rolling his eyes. "Diane, I take it?"

"Hey, you know you could be a little happier when good things happen to your friends. It's not always a slight on you. Life is rough for all of us. Trust me."

"Yeah, that perfect six-pack and those All-American good looks must make your life pretty tough. I bet you only have like. . . three girls that think about fucking you in a given day. What a rough fucking life," said Louie, his tone somewhere between annoyed and complimentary. "You don't even realize how much that is not a normal thing, right? Like at all. I wish I had that many girls even thinking about me. Doesn't even have to be sexual. Could just be 'Hey, that guy sure is pleasant.'"

"And how exactly do you know they're not? Are you a mind reader? If anything I'd say you're the master of *anti*-social situations," Keith huffed.

"Because I don't look like you and that makes me qualified," Louie reasoned. "I'm the guy that girls think to themselves—or even out loud—'he was funny.' And that is it. Positively the only thing. My face comes up and that is literally the only thought that comes to their head. Their brains won't compute anything differently."

"Your self-confidence is just oh-so appealing, Louie. I'm surprised you don't have the girls lining up for you when you've got such blaring machismo."

"I'm very confident in myself." Louie brushed it aside. "I'm just not delusional. I'm not one of those funny guys who beats himself up because he can't get the hot girl. I get it. I'm the guy who gets the girl who wants to sleep with the funny guy. Can't say they're the most mature but hey, I'll take what I can get."

Poor Louie, Keith thought to himself. *Just doesn't seem to get it. Maybe he'll figure it out one day.*

"You know, someday you're gonna meet a nice girl that is your perfect fit and all your resentment towards women will just disappear." Keith tried to give him some advice, make him see that being so negative all the time wouldn't help him in the long run, but he knew where it would likely lead.

"I think I'll just follow the normal path," said Louie, cracking open a beer he'd retrieved from his mini-fridge. Apparently the six pack at his feet was empty.

"Which is?" Keith asked, genuinely curious of what Louie's idea of "normal" could be. He'd started the process of getting around for his date, trying to pick out a nice shirt and tie combo, without looking forty.

"Just marry someone I can barely tolerate and grow stagnant with till eventually death takes us both." He sipped on his beer as if to reward himself for a job well done.

"God, you're a negative person, Louie."

"Which is it?"

"Which is what?" Keith asked, clueless.

"Are you calling me God or Louie? Because I usually prefer one name per sentence when possible."

"See, you're a funny guy. Use that charm on a girl." Keith tried putting his tie into a neat Windsor knot, but failed miserably.

"Yeah right," Louie chuckled. "Hasn't been working out for me so far."

"Oh come on, what about that girl you thought you might get with? You seemed pretty confident about that girl from last week." On the third try, Keith got the tie the perfect length.

"Well, some guy with a six pack decided to come along and swoop her up instead. So it looks like I'm shit out of luck." Louie raised his beer in a fake salute.

Oh crap. The thought had never even entered Keith's mind that Louie could be interested in Diane. He had mentioned having a crush on some girl but Keith always assumed that it was Marion. And being the ignorant fool he was, he'd just been talking about his date for the last five minutes. He couldn't help but feel like a complete idiot, cringing at his own stupidity. But that didn't help settle the giant monkey in the room. He was parading it in front of Louie without even realizing.

"I'm sorry, Louie, I didn't even. . . Honestly, I thought—"

"It's fine," Louie interrupted. "It was just a little crush anyway. Not like I had a shot. Would be kind of stupid to call dibs on something that wouldn't happen anyway. No hard feelings. Really."

Louie patted him on the shoulder and plopped down on his own bed, grabbing a book and immediately diving into its pages. They sat there in silence for a while, with Louie reading his fantasy book and Keith throwing a baseball up into the air as he lay on his back, essentially playing catch with himself. Every now and then Louie would shoot Keith a glare, as if asking him to leave the cabin. Keith didn't want Louie mad at him just because of a date.

"Look if you don't want me to go on the date—" he started but Louie was quick.

"Okay then I don't want you to go on a date with her!"

"—then I'm sorry and hope you realize what you're asking is extremely immature," Keith finished.

"I don't know why you said anything then if you weren't going to change your mind." Louie greatly resembled a child having a temper tantrum, straight down to his crossed arms and pouty look.

"Because I thought you were going to be a mature adult and say 'No, don't worry, it's fine. It's not like I had a thing with her anyway. Go for it.'"

"Go for it? You think I'm gonna tell you to go on a date with the girl I'm into? Are you out of your mind? You really are s-some piece of w. . . work." Louie grew sloppier with every word, adding a violent stomp at the end of his sentence. He threw the book in his hand off to the side. "Not like I'm readin' this anyway. . ."

"That's what an adult would do! An adult would get over it. It's not like I'd be mad if you got a date with her. It'd mean she was into you and I'd be happy for you. That's how adults handle situations. This isn't high school, Louie."

"Oh it's just so easy to be happy for someone in hypotheticals isn't it? Bet you've gotten your way your entire l-life. You know, it's not. . . not so easy for the rest of-uss," Louie threw barbs at Keith but he refused to bite. He wasn't going to be dragged down into a stupid argument. He was finally in a good mood and Louie's pettiness wouldn't change that.

"Your negativity is really affecting me right now, so I'm gonna take the mature route and leave the situation." Keith tried being as calm as possible. He just needed to leave and get some fresh air before either one of them said something they regretted. Unfortunately, his date wasn't for another hour.

Not wanting to come back to the cabin again that night, Keith patted his pockets and searched for his wallet. He grew a little more worried, with each pat that yielding no results. It wasn't in any of them. What could he have done with it?

"Crap. Have you seen my wallet?" Keith said, looking in his previous day's clothes. *It has to be in here somewhere.*

"Wallet? Nah, man. I don't think so. Can't say I really check for it when I'm in here though, I'm usually too busy being negative."

"It's got to be in here somewhere." Keith ignored Louie's comment. He didn't have time to deal with his childish games so he continued his search in silence.

"When's the last time you had it?" Louie asked, finally being useful.

It was then that Keith realized exactly where it had to be. He had his wallet at breakfast and he hadn't been back to the cabin, so it had to be with him on the run.

It must have fallen out when I whiffed it.

It made sense that it would be there but it was the last thing he wanted to deal with. He was already dealing with enough bad energy right before his date. But he couldn't exactly take Diane out without money. It happened to be a vital component of the whole date experience and the last thing he needed for his ego was for Diane to pay for the date. He was too "old school" for that.

Keith left without saying a word to Louie, unwilling to take whatever insult he had stored up. Now that Louie was out of beer there was no telling where he'd go with his jabs and Keith had more pressing matters to tend to.

Once he reached the forest's edge he looked down at his sports watch: 6:40 p.m., he still had plenty of time. Darting off down the path, he made sure to keep his eye on the forest bed, wanting to avoid a repeat stumble, not to mention having to shower again on top of that. Soon he came upon the area where he had fallen—obvious due to the disturbed foliage and snapped sticks from his fall. Then there was the giant tree that he had run into. How could he forget that? Some of the bark was peeling off from where his knee had scraped up against it. He leaned down, scoping the area for any signs of the wallet.

Off in the distance he could hear kids playing and someone yelling about staying off the rock wall. *They must be out of that safety meeting*, Keith thought, smiling at the thought of what it'd be like to be a kid at the camp. To get to enjoy all the activities without any worries or fears of what the next day would bring. *God damn I wish I was a kid again.*

He spotted the black leather of his wallet peeking out of a mound of leaves and a smile spread across his face. It would have completely blended in if not for the giant maize and blue M that adorned it. He leaned over, picking it up and wiping the dirt and soot from it.

That could have ended very badly.

Keith hadn't even noticed the hooded figure that rose from the darkness behind him.

****

This exact thought had entered their mind over and over but never in their wildest dreams could they have imagined the rush that would follow. The cold steel of their blade cut at Keith's Achilles tendon, slicing it in half and sending him flying to the dirt and foliage like a ragdoll. He grabbed at his leg, looking around like a lost puppy dog. He had no idea what was coming. He half-shouted but a swift kick to his throat stopped that with a *crunch!* The blood splatter was more intense than expected, nicking what must have been an artery. Keith tried to stop it with his hands but instead gave himself crimson gloves, the blood flow just too much to stop. His eyes moved from his wound, up to his would-be killer, his face unable to hide the absolute terror he felt inside. Their appearance sent shivers down his spine with the black hood leaving just enough light, to view the dark mask underneath, covered in green moss. Expressionless. Fearless. Remorseless. Their blank stare, piercing through the dark abyss of the eye holes, where their true emotions hid.

"Please, I don't know why you're doing this but just. . . please stop," Keith pleaded in a gravely tone, finally able to get some words out that were more than just whimpers. The blood continued to rush from his heel, a pool forming at his feet. His face grew paler with each passing second. The wound gushed and gushed—more than they had ever dreamed. Keith was quickly losing his strength. It wouldn't be long, with his face nearly ghost white. No, it wouldn't be long at all.

Now you'll be the first of many.

They plunged the long blade down again, finishing what they started. Keith no longer struggled. He no longer whimpered. He just laid there. That's all he'd ever do. Just lay.

Chapter 11
Marion

"I AM SUCH AN ASSHOLE." Louie buried his face into a crumpled up sweatshirt. He had been like that ever since Keith up and vanished: a self-blaming mess. He had been crying into his pancakes throughout most of the morning. Marion was past the point of annoyed, nearly wanting to strangle him. The remaining counselors agreed, trying to get as much distance between themselves and Louie as possible.

"Not this again," groaned Barry who shook his head disapprovingly, echoing the sentiments of those around him. He was seated next to Diane, who twiddled her thumbs, sipping on a cup of coffee. Her emotions had ranged from sad to angry and the randomness and veracity of it wasn't the prettiest sight to behold. At least she was subdued at the moment though. Carol just sat there, reading her newspaper and trying not to scoff every time that Louie said "asshole."

"You guys just don't get it," Louie reasoned. "Keith would still be around here and we wouldn't be having to bust our asses picking up the slack. It's all my fault."

At least that much is true, thought Marion, who certainly was feeling the brunt of having one of her counselors up and leave on her. It wasn't the first time this had happened, and likely not the last, but she was surprised at who the perpetrator ended up being. She figured if anyone were to leave without warning it would have been Louie.

"He had an opportunity and he took it. It's really not a big deal. If you were offered a, I don't know . . . professional. . . Halo contract." Barry grasped at straws, trying to come up with anything that Louie could possibly be professional at. "I'm sure you'd be out of this place in a heartbeat. Especially if you'd been working so hard for it. Easy choice. Have a little perspective, Louie."

"One, you've now proven that you have absolutely no idea how the video game industry works and sound like a complete tool. If I wanted to be in a Halo league, I would be in a Halo league. But do you even know the rigorous drug testing that goes through that type of sport? Of course you don't. I'd be disqualified for my Adderall prescription alone. Two— and this is really the most important one—it is not up to you to decide whether this is a big deal or not. I was the last person to talk to him, he and I were roommates, and I'm the one that knows what was going on," Louie stated, trying to sound as authoritative as possible but coming across more childish than anything.

"Uh technically the last person to talk to him was—" Barry started but was quickly stopped.

"Okay fine, the last person that *saw* him before he left. The conversation did not go well and I know that if I hadn't been such a dick then he wouldn't have left. It's all I'm saying," said Louie for the umpteenth time, before burying his face back into the sweatshirt.

"You sound ridiculous right now. You just need to drop it and let it go. You sound like a scorned lover," Marion groaned, not wanting to deal with him at all.

"She's right, there's no reason to do that to yourself," Barry added.

"You guys can think whatever you want but I know the truth," concluded Louie, trying to put a nail in it.

"You are such an asshole," exclaimed Diane, standing up and getting in Louie's face.

"Can you please just cool it with the—" Carol tried to say but was cut off by Louie who either didn't realize she was talking or didn't care.

"Thank you! At least someone can see what I'm talking about," Louie complained. Marion choked a little on her sandwich, laughing at the fact that Louie was thankful for the insult.

"No, you are a self-centered piece of shit," Diane started, her face growing more and more red. "Why the fuck would you ever think that this was about you? People have lives that are bigger than some alcoholic talking shit to them while they're hammered. You know, one of these days you'll realize that you're not right about everything. In fact, I'd say you're wrong a helluva lot more than you're right."

"And on that note, I really must be going," Marion announced, ready to make her exit.

Not that she had much of an issue with leaving such an awkward lunch, but Marion also wasn't wanting to return to the office either.

Lesser of two evils I suppose.

She quickly left the mess hall, glad that she had at least a little time to make progress with office work while the kids were busy at lunch. It had grown so hectic that, especially with recent events, they were quickly getting behind on bills and payments.

When she arrived at the office, Al was halfway through a coke—not a week after swearing off all caffeine—and appeared a little more jittery than usual. Marion figured he'd have been on edge about Keith, but it appeared he'd also succumbed to one of his vices. She took off her sweatshirt and plopped down in the seat across from him, ready to move on and go over camp business.

"I fucking hate that jock," Al blurted, completely drained.

"Oh you do not. He was a hard worker," Marion reasoned. "The campers loved him, he was a friend with all the counselors—even Carol. I'd say that makes him a catch. He just had an opportunity and took it. So don't be like that."

"The headache that motherfucker has caused me is enough for me to want to contact him and tell him that he needs to refund any money that I paid him during his first three weeks. Because he did not fulfill his contract and I refuse to be taken advantage of. No, ma'am. I refuse. God, and to even think about the work I put into getting that archery range back up and running. I even changed the brochures to put that bit about archery being a quiver full of fun back in," Al fumed.

"Al, do you have any idea how ridiculous you sound right now? Hell, Keith did most of the work clearing out all the weeds and brush anyway. And he provided the bow and arrows. And the hay bales for the targets. That's like a quarter of our budget! He helped us out a ton and it wouldn't even be possible in the first place without him so what are you even talking about? Have you been drinking?" she asked, wondering if it was more than just an emotional outburst.

"Ridiculous? I don't think so." Al ignored the question. "You should be right on board with me right now. You know our finances. This fucks us. This totally fucks us. I can't even believe he'd do something like this. He knew what hot water we were in and he specifically told me he wouldn't let me down. He promised me. Job interviews mean nothing nowadays; they'll just say anything to get themselves hired. Millennials just don't give a fuck about obligations, they're all about what will help them out the most. Selfish pricks, all of them. Society is just a fucking mess these days. And this is all just the beginning. Now people are gonna be dropping like flies."

"What do you mean?" Marion was amused at first but a little concerned at that last part.

"We were barely able to keep control of everything going on with six counselors, now we have five. They're gonna start complaining about not having enough to do. Then they'll just go spend the rest of their summer playing video games and texting each other. I know what we need to do! We need to make sure that they can't call home. That's it! No one leaving and asking their parents to come pick them up. Phone privileges revoked."

Al was growing ravenous in his tone and Marion did not like it. He hadn't touched a drop of alcohol in years. Why now? And taking away the kids' phone calls? That was just begging for angry parents to be calling all the time. It was like Al was just wanting to create more work for himself. And for her.

"Do you hear yourself right now? Is everyone going fucking crazy? This doesn't change anything. We already have the kids from Keith's group divided up into mine, Louie's and Carol's. It's been a week and everything has been totally fine. You're freaking out over nothing." she tried to be the calmer of the two. "You still didn't answer my question. Have you been drinking?"

Suddenly the office door was thrust open, banging up against the outer wall of the cabin, with the perpetrator really wanting their entrance noted. It startled Marion at first but then she saw it was just Carol—not Louie as she originally feared—and she felt relieved. She was tired of Louie trying to get Keith's contact information just so he could pester the poor kid about why he left. They already had enough difficulty getting ahold of him themselves, it wasn't going to do any good for Louie to try. No, Marion was quite grateful it was Carol who stepped in through the door. But that quickly dissipated.

Carol plopped down in the chair next to Marion and noisily started tapping her foot on the wooden floor. She was obviously mad but Al refused to make eye contact with her, clearly not wanting to deal with another problem. Carol took the tension in the room as her own doing and as such tried to command the room with loud sighs and incessant tapping. Finally, Marion took the reins and decided to ask her what she needed.

"We lose one counselor and suddenly I'm expected to change my entire schedule around? Do you have any idea how long I've worked on perfecting it? This is, and I'm sorry for saying it, but this is complete and utter horse doo-doo," Carol snorted, annoyed she even had to resort to such language.

"Look, I know that you have a very meticulous schedule planned out and I know you've worked very hard on it," Marion began but not before Carol had to start back in.

"A schedule that has already been rough enough to keep up to date with all these willy nilly meetings and happenings that are going on."

"Carol, we were forced to have that safety meeting. It's the one thing the cops asked us to do. I'm sorry that it interrupted whatever activity you had planned—"

"It wasn't just any activity it was my pottery. The most underappreciated art form and practical application that our camp offers," Carol interrupted.

"I can't go back in time, Carol. So I'm not really sure what you want me to do about that." Marion continued. "You're just going to have to deal with minor tweaks. We all have a lot on our plate and I already have enough of a headache without adding your bullshit to the pile."

"Well you wouldn't have that much of a headache if I could just take over a duty here or there," said Carol, just trying to weasel her way into

Marion's job. "With Keith being gone, surely you could use the help. I mean, I already offered to take more of his group since I wouldn't want to over-burden you, Marion."

"How about you just do what we ask of you?" Al finally chimed in. "It's what employees do so it'd be lovely if you just did that."

"You're asking me to give up my pottery class and go do archery. I should not be punished just because you had some irresponsible boy that Marion hired decide to up and leave. If anything *she* should be punished for having such terrible judgment in character," Carol looked down her nose at Marion, who debated whether every outburst Carol had would just be a play at her head counselor position.

"That's not the point, Carol. The point is that you're the only person here with any real kind of experience with archery and you have the opening in your schedule," Al stressed, trying to be as nice as possible.

"I told you that I don't have an opening. That's when I teach pottery!" said Carol, putting her foot down figuratively and literally.

"You have two signups!" Al stated bluntly. "And that's just because the Belar's know that they can just sit there and gossip in private since no one else is around. Have you seen them produce one pot? Because I sure haven't. I'm not going to have any more of this camp's resources wasted. And in this day and age, pottery is a waste. So you're going to do what I'm asking you to because I'm asking it and I'm the boss. That's all there is to it."

Carol couldn't even look him in the eyes. Tears formed under her own but before she would let them fall she dismissed herself and was gone from the cabin in a flash. Marion would have been a little thankful she left, except that she knew what she'd be dealing with back at their cabin.

"That may have been a little harsh," Marion said after several minutes of silence.

"I don't have time to babysit these counselors. I have enough trouble babysitting all these campers. Did you get things settled with that Lieber kid?" Al questioned.

"Yes, he said he was with Sally, it's all been sorted out. Carol just needs to calm down—in more ways than one."

"You can say that again," he said, taking another swig of the coke. If it even was coke.

The rest of Marion's day consisted of Arts and Crafts, a thrilling game of capture the flag which her team won, and a pizza dinner—something the campers were ecstatic about after the previous two nights of some kind of weird pasta made with a mystery meat. Reality kicked back in as the two showers in the boy's bathhouse went out completely, followed by the girls' toilets.

When the day was finally over and the campers were back in their beds, Marion couldn't help but crave a real cigarette. Something to just allow the tension in her shoulders to release and let her go to sleep. She hadn't had one in months and while she still puffed on her e-cig daily, avoiding real cigarettes made her feel some form of health awareness.

Not that it mattered anyway, her stress was sure to be back the moment Carol walked through the door with another problem. While it didn't affect

Carol's job performance, it certainly didn't make her any more pleasant to be around. She received three complaints from campers in her group that she was being particularly mean and snappy. Marion understood that pottery was important to her but it was still just another aspect to the job like any other. *She'd complain less if I had her scrub the toilets with a toothbrush. . . maybe.*

This probably attributed to her bad judgment when Diane said she wanted to have a party and agreed it was a great idea when it clearly wasn't. Even though she wouldn't admit to it out loud, Keith's sudden departure definitely affected Diane, so mixing in alcohol and a bunch of horny guys couldn't have sounded like a worse idea. Unfortunately, Marion's usual judgment was stressed out beyond belief, and didn't care to tell her no. So she agreed to go over to Diane's cabin, even though every part of her body was telling her just to stay in her own cabin. Then she remembered Carol would be there.

"So what's on the menu tonight?" Marion asked before she was even fully through the cabin's door. She regretted saying it the moment she saw the state Diane was in.

"Well, I still have plenty of vodka left and w-whatever's in that fridge is faaaair game," slurred Diane. She had decided to start early based on the red cup in her hand which she proceeded to take a big chug of its contents.

"You're really going hard tonight, eh Di?" asked a concerned Marion, kneeling next to her bed.

"Why not? Not like there's anything else to do in this place." Diane sighed, taking another swig from her cup. Diane was often one to get sloppy drunk but there was a violent temper to everything she said like never before. It worried Marion. It didn't help that Diane could hardly prop herself up on her own bed.

Breaking the tension without even realizing it, Louie and Barry walked in, arguing over something involving video games. Barry looked disinterested.

"So glad you guys could come," Diane said playfully, raising her red Dixie cup high and almost falling over in the process.

"Yeah, it was a really long walk," Barry joked, drawing a sideways look of annoyance from Louie. It never seemed to matter what Barry did, but it always drew Louie's ire.

Those two just can never get along.

"So why exactly do we have to be inside this cramped cabin drinking when we could be outside at the fire like we do pretty much every night?" Louie wondered aloud. And he wasn't wrong. The same thought had definitely occurred to Marion but she just assumed Diane wanted to switch things up. She was wrong. Sort of.

"The fire is fun and all but how are we going to get any privacy out at the fires?" Diane uncomfortably teased.

"Why would we need privacy?" Louie bit like a rabid dog.

"Al wouldn't appreciate us playing strip poker out there in view of all the kiddies, now would he?"

Diane took everyone off guard with that comment. It wasn't like Marion was opposed to the idea since she was really good at poker and found the thought of Louie having to finish the night in his boxers hilarious. Still, it was becoming more and more evident that Diane wasn't fit to be drinking. As much as she trusted Barry, she couldn't say the same for Louie, who was just looking for an excuse.

"I think you've had enough," Marion suggested, trying to take her drink away from her. She refused though, pulling away and spilling some of her drink all over of the floor.

"Excuse me! I believe I'm a grown woman and can do whatever I damn well please," exclaimed Diane.

"Yeah, well I believe you're acting like a child. So I guess we'll split the difference and call you a teenager," Marion said matter-of-factly.

Diane didn't like that. Not one bit. She charged at Marion, knocking her own cup onto the floor and causing Marion to hit up against Barry, who quickly stepped between the two. The cabin was far too small for so much drama, they were all practically on top of each other as it was. Diane's sloppy and broad movements weren't helping matters.

"Enough! Diane, you've clearly had enough to drink. Marion, stop provoking her." Barry stepped in, trying to be the voice of reason but only angering both girls.

"Stop provoking? Are you fucking kidding me?" Marion fumed.

"Too much to drink? Do you know who you're talking to?"

The fight lasted all of 60 seconds but it had felt like much longer. Between the insults that Diane threw and the nonsense Louie spouted, Marion had, had enough. She was sick of dealing with everyone else's issues. No matter what, they just kept coming to her with their problems and she went from head counselor to head babysitter. No one could deal with anything themselves and the camp couldn't hold itself together. She was done.

Forgoing the usual nightly tradition of the fire felt weird, especially after walking by the pits in order to go back to the main office, but given how mad Marion was at the others, its absence couldn't have come at a better time. She grabbed her sweatshirt from the office cabin and started her way back towards her own. As she turned she saw something move in the woods, not ten feet away from where she stood.

"Oh my god," she mumbled under her breath.

A person. *Wait, was that a person?* She closed her eyes, trying to adjust them more to the dark but when she opened them, she saw nothing. No one was around. She was completely alone. She peered into the forest but it remained void of any movement whatsoever. Was anyone ever there? Was she just seeing things?

"Hello? Is someone there? Look, I'm not having the best of days so I swear I'm not going to write you up if you just come out now so that I can send you back to your cabin," she shouted into the woods, but received no response. If it were a camper, they weren't going to just come out and give themselves up. She needed to do something to draw them out but what could she do?

So she just stood there, waiting for something to emerge from the woods. Something had to; she knew she wasn't just seeing things. She didn't imagine that dark black hood and that black mask. It couldn't have been a trick on her eyes. Even while she waited, part of her knew that she had to have just seen things in the dark. It may have been her eyes playing tricks but that didn't stop her from sprinting full-speed back to her cabin. Just in case.

Marion returned to her cabin as quietly as possible, not that it mattered given Carol's deep sleep patterns, but still Marion was raised to be courteous. Even if it was to someone like Carol who was raised to be the opposite. At least that's how it felt for her.

The worry was for naught as she looked over and saw Carol sleeping perfectly still in her bed, under the covers, a big creepy smile adoring her face just like usual. She wouldn't be moving an inch until the morning when her internal alarm clock went off and she made her presence known. Marion really hated mornings.

I'm done with this place, Marion thought. *This is the last summer I'll ever have to spend in this shit hole.* With that she took a drag on her electronic cigarette and dozed off to sleep repeating two words to herself:

"Final summer. . ."

Chapter 12

Liz

LIZ NEVER BELIEVED IN BAD LUCK but that was soon to change. It began with one of the snaps on her favorite bra breaking off, starting the day off on a sour note. It continued when Liz was told they were out of vegetarian options at breakfast after most of the girls at the camp had decided they were no longer eating meat (or whatever meat-blend Marge put together). *I shouldn't have told any of those bitches about doing that.* So she settled for a chocolate milk and strawberry pop tart. *Breakfast of Champions.* To make matters worse, she was then forced to help serve brunch because Carol needed time to prep the archery range, a new morning ritual for her. Al treated it as an opportunity for Liz despite her protests.

On top of it all, Chase was acting weird. She couldn't quite put her finger on it but it was clear something was on his mind and that something had to do with Liz. It was understandable given how quickly their—whatever it was they were in—had progressed. If *she* was scared, he must have been terrified. While she wasn't calling him her boyfriend, it certainly felt like it was there. They had been spending a lot of time with each other over the previous two weeks and things had moved forward but it certainly wasn't a talk she wanted to have with him at that very moment.

After the day she was having, it was a relief when Marion asked Liz at dinner if she wanted to smoke afterwards. Liz hadn't smoked in several weeks so she was happy to indulge. Plus, she had yet to catch up with Marion all summer given her hectic schedule in recent days. Everything was getting more and more complicated as the summer wore on. She needed advice. So she met up with Marion just after lights out, over near the woods next to the lake.

"You know, I wasn't even sure if this was where we were meeting or not," Liz whispered into the night, the moment she saw her.

"Oh come on, gotta stick with the classics. This spot is great." Marion was right, this was definitely Liz's favorite smoke spot. They walked a few yards into the tree line, coming across a massive oak tree, right near the water's edge. The brush and foliage around the tree was undisturbed—it had been too long since they'd met out there.

"So how much has Al been freaking out about Keith running off?" asked Liz.

"You know, I'll answer this one question but as soon as this torch is lit, the work talk stops." Marion raised the pipe to her mouth, lighter right next to it, just itching to ignite. "He's pissed. Pretty much wants to denounce all males named Keith and put a ban on any would-be professional athletes getting hired. So, you know, totally normal reaction. But hey, I get where he's coming from, as crazy as he may be. But Keith got an opportunity and he had to take it. I'm not going to be enough of an ass to hold that against him. When you got a chance at the pros, you've got to."

"So he *is* going pro?"

"That's what I heard. You'd think he'd be a little more courteous to give a heads up, but I don't come to expect much from our well-respected staff."

"Well then, I wish him the best in all of his future endeavors." Liz raised an invisible glass as a salute.

"And on that note. . ." Marion sparked the lighter and lit the pipe. It was time.

They smoked, doing little tricks back and forth like the "French inhale"—a trick Liz had perfected with a boy sophomore year—giggling to themselves as they kept one upping each other. Her mind wandered, drifting back to Chase. He was certainly the closest friend she had made at the camp—outside of Marion, of course. They formed a bond rather quickly and it was weird to Liz just how comfortable she felt with him already. Like they had been friends for years. But she couldn't deny that she was well past the point of having developed feelings for him.

Liz wasn't sure if the feelings were mutual but she felt like they were. She still enjoyed his company regardless. Not that she didn't get a little jealous when

Sally asked her if she was dating Chase and if it'd be okay if she were to talk to him. They weren't anything official but it certainly didn't mean that Liz was okay with another girl making advances towards him. Not like it mattered though, they only had a few more weeks together. Then they'd go their separate ways. *Dammit, why are things so complicated?*

Liz noticed Marion looking over at her but before she could say a word, Marion was already talking, as if reading her mind.

"So what's the deal with you and Chase?"

"Honestly?" Liz sat on the question for a moment. "I have no idea. I mean, he's totally someone I would date but. . . he also lives hundreds of miles away. Not like this is really going to be anything more than a summer fling. Not like a summer camp hookup is the most viable long term option. I'm not some delusional girl."

"Since when is a summer fling so bad? Not everything has to be a 'happily ever after' courting. I can't count the number of times that a simple fling has helped me out during a shitty time. Sometimes we just need a boy."

"Your feminist colleagues would be appalled."

"Oh shut up, you know what I mean." Marion groaned. "I can be completely happy by myself but that doesn't mean I don't like male company. Doesn't make me any less feminist. If I were a lesbian, I'd be all about the female company. I'm just more simpatico with the idea of someone completing me, driving me. Plus, there's the sex. Doesn't make me a terrible person, just means I like to cater to my base instincts."

"Yeah but how can you tell your brain that a relationship is just gonna be casual? It doesn't work like that. And I really don't think the heartache is worth it."

"So you're avoiding it because you don't want to get too attached? Sounds pretty weak in the reasoning department to me, missy." Marion leaned up against a tree, throwing a few choice pebbles out into the lake, hopping across before dying out in the darkness. Her eyes followed them as they pitter-pattered into the abyss.

"Look, I just don't really feel like falling for some guy when I know he's just going to be gone in a couple weeks. It's stupid."

"It happens. You're into him and you keep spending time with him, what're you expecting out of this?" Marion reasoned.

"Do I really have to even think about that right now? Can't I just enjoy this bowl?" Liz inhaled, taking a hit off the pipe.

"Do what you will, girl. I'm just telling you that just because it won't last forever doesn't mean you shouldn't enjoy it while it's around, or in this particular case—*he*. I mean, think of how many times you would have missed out on friendships if you had known they weren't going to last forever," said Marion, eyes half opened. Liz wasn't sure if she had been trying to be as philosophical as she sounded, but she made a good point. Or maybe she was just high.

"What about you?"

"What do you mean 'what about me?' You think that this is just going to turn around on me now?" Marion retorted. "No, no, no. We're still firmly planted in the 'Liz's problems' territory."

"And we took a detour. I'm in need of your sisterly perspective, that's how this works," Liz said nonchalantly. "Any cute prospects around the camp? Back home?"

Marion looked at her a moment, like she was debating answering her question at all. With a raise of her brow Liz made it clear any excuse would not be welcome. Eventually Marion succumbed with a sigh.

"Oh god. Well you've seen the counselors and, outside of newbie Keith who was super cute but now obviously gone, it's the same crew as every year. They're more family than anything. And there's no way I'd let Louie touch me. He's a bit too much of a pervert for my liking," Marion pondered as if checking off a list in her head.

"Oh come on, Louie is the best." As soon as Liz said it, Marion was staring down her nose at her.

"Oh please. I'm sure you can get away with god-knows-what as a camper around him but for me it's a living hell. He'll be so inappropriate that I sometimes have to take a moment just to reassure myself that he did in fact just say that. He once asked me if I would ever give a guy his 'red wings.' He completely loses track of his group, sometimes all because he doesn't want to take them anywhere normal in the woods, it always has to be some random spot, two miles in. The motherfucker still can't find his way out."

"Sounds about why I like him." It was true, Liz didn't see any problem with Louie. He was laid back and didn't seem to care what his campers were doing as long as it didn't get him in trouble. It made him pretty easy to deal with from Liz's side. Though he always seemed to have a hidden flask.

"Yeah well try being his boss, and then tell me all those things are great qualities."

"Yet another reason why I'm glad I'm not a boss."

"Oh I'm sorry, can I help you with your breakfast duties, Madame?" Marion said daintily.

"Oh fuck you." Liz playfully punched Marion on the arm. "You need to get me out of that."

"Yeah, I'll do that the moment you tell me that Louie is indeed as bad as I say he is."

"That's blackmail!"

"That's the way of the world, darlin'" Marion said with a southern drawl. "I don't know why you care so much anyway. I will shatter your illusion of him no problem."

"Oh yeah, how you managin' that?"

"Imagine dealing with a guy who you can tell is trying to picture you naked, like, any time you talk to him."

"What are you talking about? I'm in high school. All anyone thinks about is sex in high school. I'm around that constantly. If I were to start judging guys based on that, I would hate every human in proximity."

"God, I sometimes forget what little perverts we can be during puberty." Marion took a hit and blew a giant smoke bubble into the air. Liz leaned in, sucked in the bubble and started coughing uncontrollably. They had perfected that technique the previous summer. It was their unofficial way of changing the subject. Liz couldn't drop it though.

"That still leaves Barry."

"Barry?" Marion seemed offended at the suggestion. "Are we still on this? No thanks. Former jock just finally being hit with the realization that high school was the best time of his life? Yeah, not for me."

"Okay calm down. I was just making small talk. He was the only guy left. I guess I could have said Diane," Liz joked.

"I'd pick Diane over any one of 'em. I'd be in a lesbian partnership if it meant those guys were my only male choices," Marion chided. "I'm not sure it'd take that much to switch Diane though. She always gets a little too handsy when we drink."

"Diane is so sweet. She's destined to get knocked up by some idiot."

"Oh, absolutely. She has the worst taste in men. She fucked Barry two summers ago. She said she regretted it but still, it happened. But to be fair, Barry did have a six pack then."

"Wait, Diane fucked Barry and you never told me?" Liz was completely flummoxed. She figured Marion had told her all about the juicy sex gossip in the camp. It was usually a funny source of entertainment while they smoked.

Marion stopped what she was doing and looked to be in deep thought. *She definitely didn't realize she never told me,* Liz thought, a little annoyed.

"Oh hey, dick move on my part. Look, so Diane told me not to say anything but then I had high brain and just kind of assumed I had told you since that's pretty much the only thing I've purposely kept from you."

"Well that and Jake Tramer."

"Wait. . . How do you know about Jake?" Marion asked, shocked that Liz would even know the name.

"D to the I to the A - N - E. Duh."

"That little bitch—" Marion started but was swiftly interrupted.

"Hey, what're you doing over there?"

The voice shot out of the darkness in an instant. It took a moment to register just who it was but it clicked with Liz the second his voice echoed over again in her brain. Only one person could sound so clueless and from a different time period: Al.

Oh no, Liz thought, going into panic mode. How did they not notice someone walking up to them? Usually the noise would carry across the lake and give them more than fair warning. Yet somehow Al had managed to sneak up completely, the darkness almost entirely cloaking him. She felt like a deer in headlights. Running was futile, and would only result in more punishment. Liz felt as though all hope was lost.

But Marion was quick, rising to her feet and taking control of the situation. She dusted herself off and put the pipe in a notch in the tree next to Liz. She swiftly motioned for Liz to be cool, quickly letting her know she'd handle it. Liz wasn't sure though. She didn't want Marion to lose her job or something worse. The flashlight was almost on them, all their movement would be tracked from that point on. No time to hide.

"No worries, Al. I've got this all under control," said Marion.

"Shut up, Marion. You're not my mom," Liz spat out. Marion looked at her, confused and alarmed but Liz just decided to run with it. She slyly grabbed the pipe from the tree and palmed it.

"What's going on here? Is that marijuana I smell?" Al asked, reaching them and shooting them a stern look of disapproval.

"This bitch won't let me just do what I need to, to fucking survive this place," Liz said, hoping her attitude would cloak her terrible acting.

"Marion, what exactly happened?" Al asked but Liz was quick to retort, not wanting Marion to screw it up. Her spontaneous plan was already coming together sloppily enough.

"She caught me smoking and was in the middle of a bullshit speech when you showed up." It wasn't her finest hour but Liz hoped that at the very least if the lie didn't take, at least she'd earn some major friendship points with Marion for at least attempting to take the bullet. She even raised her pipe, giving it over to really drive the lie home.

Al looked between both Liz and Marion, not sure what to believe but just waiting to hear Marion's side.

"Like Liz said, I caught her smoking," affirmed Marion and put her head down in shame.

"I just. . . I never. Just when you were really starting to show some real promise you go and do something like this. I would say I'm disappointed Ms. Thompson but you already know that. I guess those extra duties were for nothing since you just want to spend the rest of your life in prison."

Al brought on the parental talk in a way that Liz hadn't felt in a very long time. He dismissed Marion fairly early on, saying that he didn't want her to hear the things he had to say to Liz. But ultimately, they stung all the same. Al wouldn't stop telling her how disappointed he was and how much she was throwing her future down the drain. She could have sworn she saw a tear in his eye at some point but Liz hoped she'd just imagined it. He said the repercussions for her actions would come immediately and he wasn't lying.

It had turned into a very difficult summer.

As if it weren't bad enough that Liz was taking the fall for the situation, something she still did gladly given its impact on Marion's career, her night time privileges had been revoked. Al made it clear she was to stay in the dining hall until bed, at which time she'd be escorted to her bunk by Carol. She would also be spending her days with Carol; easily the worst of her punishment.

Liz had been in Marion's group every summer and was the main appeal of the camp. She didn't know what it was like to experience Watanka without Marion leading the activities she took part in. Marion was always her counselor and never imagined that changing. Maybe had a different thought entered her head she would have been more hesitant to return to the camp.

The next morning the Belar twins made it clear they knew exactly what was going on with both of the girls mimicking the act of smoking a joint the minute they saw Liz. She just rolled her eyes at them.

Of course they know. They always know everything.

What made it worse was they've always known she'd smoked but now that she got in trouble for it, they bit on it like rabid dogs.

Liz went to the showers, taking part in a surprisingly lukewarm rinse, and returned to find the girls complaining about some kind of awards show they were apparently missing out on. Nancy was pissed that Al wouldn't get cable for the mess hall.

Alice made it sound like they were close to convincing him (with a nice donation, of course) but Carol put a kibosh on that plan and then told them to "fuck off." Liz doubted that last part. By the time she got all dressed and returned to the front of the cabin, the Belar twins were busy complaining about some girl from another cabin.

"What the hell is she even doing?" Alice asked, staring out at the girl spinning poi balls around her body to imaginary music.

"I've seen that at Lolla before and it's fucking stupid. Just for a bunch of molly-loving hippies," quipped Nancy, who seemed to be barely paying attention, just wanting to talk down about the subject. She could always find a way.

"I know the general thing that she's doing, I just don't understand why," Alice said, totally perplexed.

"Come on, can't be the first hippie spiritual person for you to encounter. At least I hope not. You've been missing out on a lot of good stuff if you haven't," Liz insisted.

"Yeah, well not all of us are giant potheads so it doesn't always appeal," Nancy spat out. The word was getting around camp fairly quickly, even before Liz had made the official move to the other group. By lunch everyone in the camp would know.

"Oh shut up, I smoke a handful of times and suddenly I'm a drug addict. Whatever." Liz rolled her eyes and pushed forward.

"Woah, putting words in my mouth, miss guilty conscience," said Nancy with a little too much innocence.

"Don't act like you haven't taken part in some green with me."

"I just don't understand what goes on in someone's head that makes them go 'I want to spin balls around my body while looking like a complete idiot," Alice reiterated, moving away from the accusation.

"I'm sure she doesn't think she looks stupid at all," Liz interjected.

"Yeah well maybe that's the problem. Not like everyone else cares about others opinions as much as you do," remarked Nancy, taking another shot at Liz.

"Oh so now I care *too much* about other opinions, is that it, Miss Freud? If your measuring stick is the dancing diva over there, then yeah maybe I care too much."

Liz spotted Marion walking across the grass to the main office. She hadn't noticed Liz at first but when she did, she gave her a half-smile and a nod of the head, mouthing "thank you." Liz just smiled back, glad that she was able to help her out. It certainly had come with a price.

"Liz, we gotta go," interrupted Samantha, a girl from Carol's group.

"You sure the pothead is gonna be able to join along?" Nancy hissed.

"Yeah, I thought you weren't allowed to have any fun anymore?" finished Alice.

"Umm. . . yeah, of course," Liz replied.

She wasn't entirely sure if she was still allowed to participate in rock climbing given that Marion was the instructor, but Al hadn't strictly prohibited it so she assumed it was fine. Plus, the last thing she wanted was to give them the satisfaction of her absence.

Ah the rock wall. While there were many things around the camp that felt unsafe, the rock wall was not one of them. According to Marion, Al had spent most of his last bank loan to get it, hoping for a surge of campers. While there was a slight surge, that died down fairly quickly. Liz still enjoyed it a great deal though, making improvements of her own every year. In fact, she held the record for female campers. Marion had the fastest overall but, given the time she got with the wall to practice, Liz didn't see it as exactly fair. Still, when Diane called for everyone to gather up at the rock wall, she couldn't help but feel a little excited. Physical activities weren't exactly her forte but something with climbing just clicked with her. And it didn't hurt to try and get back some brownie points with the girls.

It was easy enough getting everyone into one area but settling them down was another story. Marion hadn't arrived yet and Carol was feeling under the weather, so Louie and Diane were left to deal with the campers, who were restless. So everyone just stood and talked, the gossip of choice being a certain smoking incident. Liz couldn't believe her luck.

It took another five minutes until Marion finally arrived, hurried and out of breath. She apologized for being late but gave no reason as to why she was. She looked pale and sick. Liz questioned whether or not she would even be able to climb but instead Marion carefully put all the equipment on, strapping everything in and tightening it all up with ease. She looked a little ridiculous given that the wall reached 50 feet at his highest but it was a necessary precaution.

"Now I don't want anyone trying to get fancy and act like Spider-man when you're up there. I get it, it's fun to climb walls. But it's also not fun to break bones. So let's try and avoid that as much as possible so that then I can continue harassing you little terrors," Marion's voice provided some laughs. She seemed to be powering through whatever was drawing the color from her face.

"So is it cool if I did it?" Louie jested.

"No, Louie, you're allowed. In fact, do some crazy stuff. . . by yourself. I'll turn a blind eye. But as for the rest of you, watch and learn, and you'll be on your way in no time."

And with that Marion turned around and started to ascend up the wall. Louie made an inappropriate comment but Marion shook it off and continued to climb. Step by step, hold by hold, she made her way up the well. Ten feet. Twenty feet. She was up it so fast, Liz couldn't believe it. She was so quick and sure-footed with every movement.

Someone's been practicing.

"Just remember, you want to use all the mechanics we've been going over the last few weeks. Just because you're up in the air doesn't mean—" Marion started but cut herself off with a horrific scream.

In one sudden motion, the rope line holding her up snapped like a twig. Her hands reached out, trying to grab onto one of the holds, the rope next to her, anything. Her fingers grazed along the rock but failed to connect to anything secure. She couldn't do anything to stop her momentum. She just shrieked as gravity took her.

Marion came crashing thirty feet onto the dirt below and all Liz could do was scream.

Chapter 13

Chase

CHASE COULDN'T BELIEVE WHAT HE WAS SEEING when it first happened. Unlike what many others would later claim, the moment didn't fly by. It lingered on, almost as if in slow motion. He could see the terror in Marion's eyes as she fell toward the ground, trying to grasp at anything in order to catch her fall but grabbing only air. Every passing second felt like hours, watching and expecting the worse when the impact finally took place.

And it really could have been worse, Chase supposed. Had her weight been distributed differently she could have landed on her head and killed herself in a most heinous fashion. Instead she landed feet-first, her left femur snapping with bone protruding out of the flesh. The white of it just barely peeked through the mushy mess, and caused several of the kids to faint. Sure, she screamed bloody murder and it looked like one of the most painful experiences a human being could go through. But still. It could have always been worse. *I really have to stop thinking like that. This is pretty fucking bad,* Chase resided, the loud snap of the bone reverberating over and over in his head.

The camp was a complete mess for the next few hours with police cars and ambulances coming and going. *The cops around here must have absolutely nothing to do,* Chase thought. Which made sense given the camp's remote location. The deputies currently at the camp probably watched over the surrounding area for tens of miles. This made their response time all the sadder, taking nearly an hour to finally arrive at the scene. By that point Marion was passed out from the pain and Carol was off trying to cover all the blood with more dirt to prevent any more kids from seeing it and being traumatized.

Barry did his best to round up the kids and take them over to the lake for some early swim time but most were too interested in the events at the rock wall. Too much had happened for them to leave. It took Al threatening all of them, telling them to go or it'd be the last time they swam all summer, to finally get them to disperse.

After nearly twenty minutes, Marion was finally loaded up in the ambulance to head to the hospital. A few other campers suffering from shock also joined, but they rode in the cop cars. In total four people left the camp that afternoon. *What a fucking day,* Chase thought as the final car pulled away.

Over at the lake, Chase was finally able to talk to Liz who had just come back from arguing with Al, her face red with anger.

"Are you okay?" Chase asked already knowing the answer. Her face was pale and tears streamed down her cheeks. *She just watched her good friend break her leg in half, of course she's not okay you idiot!* "Sorry, that was stupid."

"He won't even let me go with her. Fucking Diane is. This is ridiculous!" Liz shouted.

"I'm sure they didn't know," Chase reasoned, trying to comfort her but she was having none of it.

"If it was Marion's choice I'd be on that ambulance with her right now. She's practically my sister for Christ's sake!" said Liz, glaring daggers at Al from across the camp. "All because he's a fucking jackass who hasn't gotten with the times. He has to treat me like I'm a fucking child. God, I've never needed a bowl more."

Chase knew he needed to do something, *anything* to help keep her mind off Marion so that she'd stop worrying. The idea came to him easily enough, but in hindsight he kind of wish it hadn't. There were a million different things he could have done in order to gain favor with her. And most of them weren't illegal.

"Just wait. I'm gonna have an awesome surprise for you," Chase assured her.

With Marion's fall behind them, the excitement for most of the campers dwindled down as the day went on, while Chase's grew as his anticipation for what he'd do that night came to a head. When the sun finally set, he knew it was time for his adventure to begin.

Chase certainly had worse ideas throughout his childhood but he couldn't remember any being as stupid as the one he was currently entrenched in. Sure, he'd snuck into his parents' room and tried to find his Christmas presents. He'd also been able to retrieve a plagiarized paper from one of his English teacher's before she could show it to his mother at parent-teacher conferences. But it was harmless kid's stuff. This was more serious.

Sneaking into the main office appeared easy enough in theory but Chase quickly discovered the level of skill it required may have exceeded his own. And he was going to need a whole lot of luck. With one of the windows boarded up and the others seemingly unable to open, there was only one way in or out of there: the front door. While he was certainly no professional, he knew an exit strategy was usually the staple of any good heist and just having the door made him nervous. There was nothing he could do but hope for the best.

Chase watched the counselor's fire from off in the distance, its flame still burning bright. He could even see their shadows being cast onto the forest behind them, like some kind of huge puppet show. They would be over there for a least a couple of hours, giving him the perfect opportunity to make his move. He'd told Santa to make an excuse if anyone asked where he was, which Santa happily obliged, always wanting to help out "young love." He wasn't delusional though, anything could happen at any time. A counselor could decide to go to the office to get something just because it randomly came to their head. The spontaneity of the world aside, Chase thought he was as ready as he'd ever be. The only piece of the puzzle that Chase really had to worry about was the most unpredictable of them all: Al.

Most nights Al was on Toddler duty, sleeping in the big bed in C4 and helping them with anything they needed in the night. Sometimes though, Diane would take those duties and Al would end up falling asleep on the floor of his office. If that were the case this night, Chase was going to have to scrap the entire thing. It wasn't going to be worth it if he was busted within the first thirty seconds of the attempt. He banked on Al being gone but there was really no way for him to know until he was inside which caused the knot in his stomach to grow.

Getting into the office didn't end up being much of an issue. He assumed he'd have to jigger the lock open with a hairpin—a process he was not exactly professional at. If all else had failed, he planned to just try to use his library card to jigger the lock open. Thankfully, it all came much easier than expected as the door opened with just a turn of the knob. It was unlocked. By the time he worked up the courage— finally convincing himself that the coast was clear—it was mere seconds before he was actually inside the building.

The layout seemed simple enough: the main office was in a room near the back, with the first room serving more as an entry way. There was a bathroom off to the left, a sign on it reading "out of order", and a utility closet to the right.

Now where could you possibly be?

Spotting a huge trunk under one of the windows, he walked towards it, opening it up and pilfering through the goods. This was definitely where

Al was keeping all the things he had taken from the campers. There were various cell phones, laptops, video games, and even some bottles of liquor; so clearly it was both the stuff they handed over at the beginning of the summer, and the stuff that had been confiscated in the time since. Even then, Chase still couldn't find what he was looking for. With half the trunk's contents laid out across the office, he finally decided it had to be elsewhere.

He moved to the desk, starting to rifle through the drawers, hoping Al had quickly placed it there since the incident had occurred just the prior night. It took all of one minute to search the entire desk but still it yielded zero results. Annoyed, Chase wondered if Al had just thrown it away. Then footsteps shuffled across the wooden deck just outside the office. It wouldn't be long until they were inside the office. Chase was screwed. Looking around, he appeared to have two choices: the bathroom or the closet. Not wanting to deal with whatever putrid smell could be originating from the toilet, he decided on the closet.

As soon as he entered it and shut the door behind him, he took note of the obvious smell of marijuana. His eyes darted around, seeing a bunch of cleaning supplies and toiletries. Then he saw it; the thing that he was looking for, the item that would help turn Liz's day around: The blue pipe Al had taken from her. It sat on one of the shelves, a lighter laying right next to it.

Oh Al, you hypocritical bastard.

The front door opened up and multiple feet shuffled into the office. *Two people? Three?* Chase quickly looked around the closet, hoping for a way out. There was a window but it was near the back of the closet, behind a bunch of cleaning supplies; he would surely make noise trying to go out that way. He looked up at the ceiling, wondering if he could pop one of the tiles out and get out that way. *It's not the movies, I doubt they could even support you.*

It was hard to tell how many people were there, let alone who it was but he could have sworn he heard Al's voice at one point say "Keith?" They weren't really talking, it seemed to be just—were those. . . passionate moans of intimacy? Was that what that was? Chase couldn't tell but his desire to leave increased ten-fold with the weird moans that started permeating through the thin closet door. If he was going to leave, it had to be immediate.

He maneuvered his body past the mops and the brooms, almost knocking a dust pan onto its side. A storage shelf holding varying degrees of chemicals sat under the door. *The perfect ladder.* Chase moved his foot forward, testing to see if it would even hold his weight; it was only plastic after all. With a quick hop he rested his weight on the bottom shelf and prayed. Thankfully the shelf held up, bending a little in the middle but otherwise sustaining his full weight. Making his way up, shelf by shelf, he was careful not to knock over any of the cleaning supplies. Getting near the top he balanced on the shelf, trying to see if there'd be any possible way to open the window above without making a ruckus. Then the decision was made for him.

His foot crashed through the shelf, breaking it in half and sending half the cleaning supplies to the floor in a loud flurry. *Okay they definitely heard that.* He pushed at the window, shoving it open and pushing his body through the frame as quickly as possible. He heard the door of the closet open just as he plopped down to the ground outside.

As Chase ran for his life, hoping like hell that whoever was in the office didn't identify him, he could have sworn he heard someone scream after him. *You're not gonna get me.* He would just deny any accusations levied his way. It'd be easy enough. Hell, if it had been Al, Chase wasn't so sure he could even remember his name if he saw him let alone identify him in such little light. But as he ran, the wind hissing in his ear, he couldn't help but think he heard the word "help."

Chase was still coming down from the massive rush that sneaking into the office provided when he returned to his cabin. Half the campers were asleep while Ralph, Santa, and Donny were all up, and appeared to have been waiting for him.

"Ayyyy" the boys resounded as Chase walked in. Santa must have told them he was up to something. The bottle of rum at their feet spelled trouble for Chase's secrecy.

"I don't have any idea what you're talking about," Chase responded to a question they didn't ask but wanted to.

"I'm not sure what you mean. We clearly didn't say anything," said Santa, trying to act as clueless as possible.

"Whatever you're thinking and *had* been talking about, I don't know anything about it," Chase replied.

"Oh please. We're quiet enough. No one else knows outside of us. Everyone else has been sleeping," Donny explained. "So what'd you get? Santa said you were pulling some mission impossible shit."

He wasn't much of a bad boy back home so he relished in the moment. Getting Liz her glass back was sure to solve any lingering doubts he had with her. She'd be ecstatic about getting it back, he just knew it. However, he had no desire to let more people in on it than needed to know. He already had enough to worry about, not knowing whether or not he could be identified in the night.

"Look, I'm not telling you what it is but I will tell you that it was totally worth it," said Chase with a big smile on his face.

"Boo!" the boys all resounded in unison.

"Come on, you gotta give us more than that, bro," Santa nagged, trying to get some information out of him.

Chase debated just lying to them to appease their need for conclusion but instead he left them with, "If I told you, what do you think the chances of me actually keeping it would be?"

The next morning at breakfast, Chase half-expected everyone to be standing and huge round of applause to meet him upon his arrival. The epic adventure he just went on could only be celebrated with such. But instead he entered the dining hall without alerting a soul — outside of Marge who was motioning him over to get his food before she threw it out. *Ah, the unfortunate consequence of a secret.* It was okay though, there's only one person I need to know about it.

He obliged Marge's request and took the lukewarm plate of biscuits and gravy, before making his way over to the area he assumed that Liz was at. When he reached the tables, the Belar twins shot him a half-smile—Chase wasn't sure just how fake they were but assumed the worst—quickly starting to whisper to each other. Couldn't be about Chase. Could it?

Before he could think on it, he noticed Liz and sat down next to her, practically bouncing up and down with excitement. He couldn't wait to tell her the great news.

"I think I have something that may make you a little happier."

"Chase I'm really not in the mood," she sighed, dejected. She didn't look to be having the best morning but that's why Chase was there. To fix it.

"Don't speak so soon."

Chase made sure that no one else could see the bag, keeping it well below the table. He opened it up, just enough so she could see the blue of her pipe. Liz's eyes lit up and suddenly it was all worth it.

"You are a fucking knight." She grabbed him, hugging him tightly.

"It gets better." Chase reached into his bag and pulled out the small, blue pouch from his bedroom. Untying it, he opened it up, just enough for Liz to see and her smile widened.

Then the sirens started up again.

Chase's mind raced a mile a minute. Were they there for him? How could they have known that he broke into the main office? That person must have seen him when he ran away. It must not have been as dark as he thought. Would they arrest him or just leave him with a slap on the wrist since he was a minor? Regardless of outcome, Chase knew it couldn't be anything good.

"Why the hell are they back? Is this really happening again?" Liz asked, putting both bags in her purse and thanking Chase with a tug on his hand.

"It's probably just them bringing back Marion," Nancy deduced.

"They don't turn their sirens on if something's not going down, stupid," Alice yelled at her sister just wanting to start a spat.

"Maybe they're just wanting to make an entrance," offered Nancy, going for the bait. "You know Marion."

"No. Something is definitely wrong." Chase leaned closer to the window, looking out at what appeared to be a crime scene. The cops had sectioned off the area around the main office. Carol had been talking to one of the detectives for several minutes, tears streaming down her face. Whatever it was, it was clearly big.

Did something else get taken? Are they gonna find my finger prints and accuse me of whatever happened. The possibilities in Chase's head felt endless and none of them were good. The hole in his stomach was growing as he gritted his teeth and hoped for the best.

Shortly after the cop cars arrived a vehicle labeled "morgue" followed, and everyone's stomachs collectively dropped.

"This camp is so fucked up." Brenda had to sit, the situation being too much for her.

"Holy shit. Do you think it's Keith? Maybe Al killed him and stuffed him in the floorboards," Alice theorized.

"God you're like a vulture. Why on earth would that ever be it? This is real life not one of those stupid horror movies you watch at Dad's," her sister responded. They went at it for a little bit, calling each other insults ranging from 'Daddy's Little Girl' to 'super-bitch.'

"Will you two just stop? This isn't about you," said Sally, speaking up for everyone.

The Belar twins may have interjected had it not been for Santa, who was walking across the lawn returning from his cabin, casually walking by the scene of the crime like it was nothing.

"There's no way he can be that oblivious," said Samantha, pushing her way past some thirteen-year-old girls trying to get a view.

Santa was definitely overacting his part of the oblivious camper as he almost walked right into one of the police officers. They quickly turned him around and Carol stepped in, ushering him over to the dining hall.

That's when they saw it: the body bag. They had taken it out of the main office and were in the process of getting it in the back of the ambulance. *How could there be a body bag? That means there was someone dead in there.* Chase felt like an idiot having these thoughts but it was all his brain could process. How could someone have died in there? He was in there last night and everything was fine. Were those really sounds of passion?

"Oh my god," Ralph gasped, shaking his head and looking like he was about to vomit. Chase quickly looked around, doing a body check, trying to figure out who could be in the body bag. Before he could even think it himself, Santa entered the mess hall and put a stop to the speculation.

"It's Al. He's dead."

Chapter 14

Louie

THE NIGHT AIR WAS COOL and the fire was warm, but things weren't the same. No, not to Louie. Hanging around the campfire was always something to look forward to throughout the day. It would usually lead to some stress relief and genuine fun times with the other counselors. Yet there they were, sitting in silence not really sure what to talk about; their bodies completely exhausted. This was Diane's first night being able to get away from her night duties with the toddlers, and Barry and Louie were around each other more than enough recently.

It was still hard to believe what had even happened over the past few days. Louie certainly wouldn't have considered himself Al's favorite counselor but he had been involved in his life for several years so there was some kind of emotional attachment there. He just couldn't decide if it was enough for him to feel sad about it. He was certainly confused about the whole incident—Al seemed like he had more years left in him—but he couldn't really consider it enough for even the smallest of tears to form.

Heart attacks are unpredictable. That's just a part of life, I guess.

Al hadn't exactly hidden his dislike towards Louie. In fact, Diane had told him of the many times Marion had to vouch for him, with Al usually seeking to fire him. Louie couldn't blame him though. He had been drunk during most of his second year there and he wasn't exactly the best at hiding it. Water bottles full of vodka seemed genius to his drunk brain, but that didn't help the overwhelming smell that would ruminate from every part of him. Wasn't his best idea. But Marion was always out to try and help him.

He was honestly more upset about what had happened to Marion than anything else. No one deserved to go through that kind of pain. Falling nearly thirty feet just to have your leg snap in half? He had replayed the moment over and over in his head, trying to think of anything he could have done differently to get there in time. He could have broken her fall with minimal damage to both of them. He just needed to be quicker. It was pointless to even think about now. Marion was the best climber out of everyone and it still happened to her. All Louie could take from that was that anything could happen, out of nowhere. As was life.

One minute Louie was soaked in sweat, the next he was shivering, so the inconsistent wind was welcome by him. God knows it wasn't easy once he would try to sleep at night. That's when the heat and lack of moving air would really get to him. He could have sworn that the other summers weren't nearly as hot.

Diane and Barry sipped on their beers, staring at the fire but their minds clearly elsewhere. Louie sipped on his water, looking at the beers in their hands with a slight tinge of envy, but the feeling of disgust overwhelmed him more than anything. Alcohol was the last thing he needed. No, at that moment, all he really needed was some good old fashion conversation.

"I think I'm gonna head back to my cabin, guys." Diane yawned, removing the blanket from around her legs and readying herself to stand.

"Yeah, you're right, it's getting pretty late. I'll walk you—" Barry could hardly get a word out before Louie stood up and protested.

"What? No. Come on!" Louie pleaded. "It's been just me and Barry out here for what feels like forever. We need to take advantage of it. You never know when that stupid bitch is gonna take away our nights. Come on let's tell stories."

"I'm just exhausted. That's all there is to it. And that 'stupid bitch' has already taken away my nights."

"We're all exhausted. That doesn't matter. I just need some kind of fucking release. Anything. Can we just sit and talk?" Louie's voice reeked of desperation.

"Fine," Diane resided, firmly placing the blanket around her legs. "What do you want to talk about?"

Louie had to think about it for a moment. What did he want to talk about? He knew he wanted to converse, but hadn't looked much further than that.

Before Diane could start getting up, Louie was quick to blurt out the first thing that came to mind.

"If you could do anything in the world—and I mean absolutely anything—what would it be and why?"

"Easy," Barry chimed in. "I'd take Scarlett Johansson down to the fifty-yard line at 49er's field and give her the good, good."

"And I'm sure she'd really enjoy all fifteen seconds of it," said Louie, quickly turning to Diane before Barry could come up with a response. "What about you?"

Diane thought on it for a moment, a playful smile coming across her face as she cycled through the various choices in her mind. She giggled before finally deciding on one.

"I don't know, man. I have some pretty expensive tastes."

"Money isn't a factor. A billionaire has taken a shine to you and is willing to do absolutely anything for you."

"Eww, does that mean I have to have sex with an old man just to be able to get the money?" asked Diane, a look of disgust having spread across her face.

"What? No! That's not how this works. That's not how any of this works. Why would—just, no."

"Sorry," Diane resided, before finally coming up with her answer. "I'd probably just go to Cancun and hang out on the beach for a week straight with a margarita in hand."

"Of all the things you could do, you decide to do something that's totally possible for you right now? Mine was so much better," snorted Barry.

"He's not wrong. It certainly was. . . tame," said Louie before adding. "Not that there's anything wrong with that."

"Oh yeah, so what would be yours, Mr. Perfect? It's your game, let's see how to 'correctly' do this," proposed Diane, leaning forward with interest.

"Easy. I would have a candle-lit dinner with Jenny Powers on top of the Empire State Building."

"Who the fuck is Jenny Powers?"

"It's that YouTube chick, right?" asked Barry, completely oblivious and just grasping at straws.

"No," Louie laughed. "But good try. She was absolutely *the* most ridiculously hot girl at my high school. And she would have never even given me a second look during those years. It'd be like. . . The ultimate revenge for all those years of bad acne."

"Anything in the world, and you decide to fuck the popular girl from your high school? The girl who probably peaked as a senior? I take it back, Barry, this one is worse."

"It's not that bad," said Barry, drawing a glare from Diane. "I mean, depending on how high school went—"

"Like shit," Louie cut in.

"—Okay, well not everyone wants payback on someone from high school. I don't even think about those people anymore. People move on. You should too." Diane suggested.

"Come on, you're telling me that doesn't sound at least a little appealing to you? Going out with the hottest guy from your formative years. Come on, girls love dates."

"I wouldn't know, my last date—first one in six months mind you—decided to bail and go to Europe."

"Lucky bastard." Barry let it out before even realizing the implications. He quickly understood once Diane smacked him hard on the arm.

"Do you really think that's what happened?" asked Louie, somewhat shocked he asked it himself. It wasn't the first time he had the thought, but he hadn't heard anyone else share similar concern, so he buried it deep. He didn't even notice the silence, getting lost into a thought of if he really even questioned what happened. Maybe he just spoke nonsense. But for some reason, he couldn't shake the feeling deep down inside that something just wasn't right. It hadn't felt right all summer.

Of course it doesn't feel right, your brain isn't functioning, he thought, almost mocking himself.

"Obviously that's what happened. Why would we be lied to?" Barry shook his head, wanting to keep what little faith in authority he had left.

"I don't know. I guess there isn't any reason. It just. . . am I really the only one that thinks this doesn't feel right? I mean, look at Diane. Do you really think that Keith would just stand you up? Does that sound like the guy we know? No. Hell, he probably would have tried to take you with him."

This got a laugh out of Diane, who seemed to be thinking long and hard on what Louie had said.

"People change. Maybe he just figured it would be easier that way. Sometimes those are just the cards life deals you," Barry responded stoically. He threw his empty beer bottle onto the fire, smashing against the wood and tumbling it over a little bit. The ember burned brighter with each gust of wind, giving it new life with each breath.

"That about does it for me. Sorry, Louie. I'm exhausted." Diane stood up, with Barry closely following.

"Yeah, I think I'm gonna take off too. I'm tired." Barry yawned. He was so obvious that Louie could hardly even take it. They were both gone in an instant, seemingly going into their own cabins, but Louie wasn't sure. They could have easily slipped out when he wasn't paying attention. Either way, his nights of fun drinking by the fire had been reduced to so little.

"And then there was one." Louie sipped on his water.

He stayed at the fire for a moment but didn't want to be alone with his thoughts. Trying to get some rest was going to be time more well spent.

Louie awoke in a daze, hardly able to comprehend where he even was. Then he recognized the blaring noise from his alarm clock and the sound of camper's outside. Another day. He took a moment to get around but put his tattered shirt and gym shorts and stepped out into the morning sun. The campers were finishing up with their showers— apparently one of the other counselor's did him the favor of waking his group up. It couldn't have been Carol, since she was likely to be pounding on his door as an alarm clock had she noticed. He put his money on Diane. Sweet, sweet Diane.

"You look like hell, bro." Santa walked up alongside him, patting him on the back.

"I feel like hell so I guess it's an accurate representation," Louie yawned, his words trailing as his mind wandered.

"Don't let this place get you down. Life is what you make it. May as well make it a happy one."

Louie snorted. Was this guy really trying to tell him that he just needed to be happy? *If only it were as simple as that.* He dismissed it quickly.

"Easy to say when life isn't staring down the barrel at you," Louie sighed.

"Just because you're five years older than me, doesn't make your problems any bigger. You think that Al's problems were more important just because he was on this earth for longer?"

"No I think his problems outweighed mine because he was running a failing summer camp that many people relied on for their income."

"Fair point. But you know, I always used to say from the time I was five-years-old that when I grew up, I wanted to be an astronaut—"

"Is this gonna take a while?" Louie interrupted. He didn't mean to be rude, it was just hard not to be on edge at that point. "Because I'm not sure where Carol is but chances are she'll find some reason to yell at me for 'singling out one of the campers' or something."

"May learn ya something. Can you really put a time limit on that? Besides you're just out here till quarter-after anyway. May as well make the most of it." Before the words were even out of Santiago's mouth, Louie was shaking his head, but he continued. "I'll try not to bore you, *hefe*. Okay where was I— astronaut. Now, I lived with my grandma, uncle, mom, and two cousins from an aunt that I didn't see that much. Dad was a truck driver so he'd come and go. Wouldn't really see him much until finally just didn't see him at all. Mom provided everything for the family, even took care of my Uncle. See, my uncle Leon had special needs and would watch the original *Star Wars* trilogy on repeat. And when I say repeat, I mean 're-peat.' Some days he'd go one after another; *New Hope*, to *Empire* to *Jedi.* Other days I'd walk in and he'd just press play on *Return of the Jedi* over and over. So regardless of which it was, there was always a *Star Wars* film on in his room."

"I take it he loved the prequels then," jested Louie.

"Mom tried to show him one but he wouldn't stop crying, so we never went back to it. Loved that new one though. He just loved *Star Wars* with every part of his being. And so being around that love, I couldn't help but be addicted to it. It was the one thing that brought him joy in this world. So I took that with me and took it a step past where he could. I watched other space movies—*Alien, Last Starfighter*—and every time, I just became more and more obsessed. It was around the time I was able to study astronomy in a classroom that I got the news: Leon had passed away." Santiago sniffled, holding back tears but failing to muffle a lone sniffle.

"And so every time I took a class from that point on, I got more and more involved. I was doing things for Leon. Things that he always wanted to do but couldn't. But being in the place I was, it wasn't exactly easy going to school. If I could even make it the four-mile trek, I had to contend with more crack-heads and dealers than I was comfortable with. Sure, mom tried to take me as much as possible, and she sure did try. But sometimes she got called in for work and I just had to persevere. And I usually did. Even had a little pack of friends that I ended up going to and from school with. We made it without getting into a gang for so long.

"But joining a gang is just an eventuality in my neighborhood. So when one of us joined, we all did. The higher-ups are smart though, they start you on little stuff. Just some minor collections and break-ins. By the time they ask you to kill a man, you're already in so deep, your life is over anyway."

"Wait, you killed—" Louie couldn't believe he was being told all of this information.

"No, no, no," Santa interjected. "I was one of the lucky ones. I got booked after trying to steal this dude's 4K TV out of his garage. What the hell is a guy doing with a 4K TV in his garage anyhow? But that don't matter, he stupid as me for trying to steal it in the first place. They booked me and I was lucky enough to be sent here."

"Heh, lucky."

"Yeah, well those visits in juvie were an eye-opener. See how much it affected my mom. It was just another reminder of the fact that my life does matter, because it affects those closest to me."

"So is that how you ended up here?"

"Tracing it all back? I mean, I guess it could have been sooner, maybe even a little later, but my opinion of it all? Yeah, it started that day. Been trying to do everything I possibly could to get on the right path. To show that I'm capable of being of a productive member of society. I've learned a lot in the last few years. And the one thing I learned about being an astronaut: you can't have a record."

"Shit, man, you're more commendable than me."

"You keep the bar pretty low, Louie. Look, I know the likelihood of me even achieving that was so far away. Let's face it, it was a pipe dream. Astronauts don't come from the ghetto. But that didn't make me pushed towards it any less. It's what I wanted. It's what I needed. For him. At least, that's what I kept telling myself. And having it taken away from me over something so—well, juvenile—It just ate at me. For a long time."

"So what'd you realize?"

"That life isn't out to get me. Sometimes knowing everything is knowing absolutely nothing," Santa finished.

The statement stuck with Louie as he repeated over and over in his head. By the time the pledge of allegiance began, Louie felt a renewed sense of purpose.

Maybe it isn't too late.

Chapter 15

Carol

THE LAST FEW WEEKS HAD FELT LIKE A DREAM to Carol, who couldn't believe her own good fortune. Head counselor? It was everything that she'd ever dreamed of. And while it may have come at other's misfortune, she couldn't help but find solace in the old adage "everything happens for a reason." So while the surrounding events were clearly terrible, Carol truly felt it was for the best. Besides, the good that she'd do would well outweigh any of the bad that hovered over the camp's past.

Carol was finally seeing the camp with new eyes, as she took in every day with fresh breath. The birds practically sang to her as she made her way to the camper's bunks every morning. It felt like absolute heaven and it amazed Carol it took that long to get there. A part of her wished it had happened sooner. Watanka was already doing great under her new direction.

One of her first ideas to improve the camp was implemented with an hour of finding out the news. She had put up a new set of rules outside of the office that were going to shape the camp into the best place one earth (according to the flyer):

- Treat the camp, your counselors and your fellow campers with absolute respect.
- No profanity or disrespectful words will be used on camp property.
- Activities will be completed without complaining or certain privileges will be revoked
- Even if you do not agree with a counselor, you will follow their directions.
- If you are deemed a problem, you will be sent home without use of the previously employed "strike system."
- All campers must return to their cabin post-dinner.
- Above all, try and have the most fun possible while being the absolute best person you can be.

Carol didn't care what the others were probably saying while she hammered the laminated sheet of paper holding the rules, new regimes meant new sets of rules. Resistance was pointless. The sooner they got used to that, the better off they would be in the long run.

Sure, how she came by getting the head counselor position wasn't exactly what Carol always hoped for, but it still ended with the same result. She was now able to shape the camp into everything that she knew it could be. While she loved the camp before, she knew that it needed several improvements that Al just wasn't willing to commit to. And what better way to do that than to have the campers themselves join in on the fun?

She thought of the idea at breakfast and let out a "Eureka!" just as she served Samantha some scrambled eggs. She startled some of the campers with her enthusiasm but that didn't matter, sometimes brilliance just happened to strike at random times. How else could she have thought of having all the campers paint?

The entire exterior of the camp—outside of the archery range, which had already received a fresh coat of white paint—was in sore need of a touchup. The paint that remained was hanging on by a thread, merely flakes resting on wooden planks. A simple paint job would surely raise the value in the camp. *Why did Al never think of this before?*

By mid-afternoon Carol had split people into teams (why she refused to just put them back into the previously assigned groups was anyone's guess) and sent them off with a bucket. If they were as efficient as Carol figured, the entire camp would have a complete fresh coat of paint in just two days. Talk about a huge turnaround; the camp would be winning awards with Carol leading the charge. There's no way any of their improvements could have been done without her help. She was an innovator that was going to make summer camps bigger than they were even in the 50's.

But no matter how many positive changes she made, the other counselors seemed to get snappier and snappier. Some of them had even resorted to shooting her dirty looks from afar. They probably thought that she hadn't seen them, but she had. She knew what they were thinking. It didn't matter though. She was in charge and there was work to be done.

Sitting at the desk in the main office made Carol feel more power than she ever thought possible. This was several years ahead of her own vision board plan, but that hadn't mattered. Her plans were just moved up due to unfortunate circumstances. She paid tribute to Al by putting up several photos of him throughout the office. The one that sat on her desk was the biggest of the bunch, complete with Al's awkward smile and half-open eyes. She didn't care that the others gave her weird looks when they first noticed them. They just didn't understand her bond with Al. She'd do anything for him and paying tribute to his memory was the least she could do. In Carol's mind, he was so lucky to have passed at the happiest place on earth.

Carol would never admit it out loud but she was looking forward to having Marion back in the slight case that she needed guidance with the paperwork. While she was able to catch onto most of the main office stuff fairly quickly—despite how much Al and Marion had kept her out of it before—but there were still a few things she wasn't getting the hang of. Still, she hoped Marion wasn't expecting all of her duties back upon return. She had rightfully given them to her and made no mention of it being temporary. Carol wasn't wanting to have to get legal when it came to the verbal agreement but it hadn't slipped her mind.

As much as she loved the office work, it still ended up being a sacrifice. She had to give up her valuable time with the campers in order to properly get it done. She was the only person that she could trust with such important documents. It also meant more time that the counselors could avoid doing their assigned tasks.

It had become more of a problem the second day of her charge than the first. Maybe they just thought that the two page guidelines she'd given them were only suggestions. She quickly changed that after an intense yelling contest with Louie. They were going to do what she said and treat her with respect. Just like Al.

She was nearly a third of the way through the books for July when Diane and Louie stepped into the office cabin with looks of annoyance.

"Hello fellow counselors. How are you on this fine Thursday?"

"Gotta be fucking kidding. . ." muttered Louie.

"Not so great, Carol, and you should know that." Diane moved quickly past pleasantries and Louie's comment. "I talked to Marion and she said we can't have the kids painting or building or doing any kind of improvements to the camp."

"What? Why not? That sounds absolutely preposterous." Carol couldn't fathom it. This had to be Marion just trying to make a power play. Try and take away anything that worked so that she could just get her spot back.

Not on my watch.

"Something about child labor laws . . ." Diane said this so casually that Louie started busting up laughing, drawing a glare from Carol, her face growing red with anger.

"You know it's good for them. They need to learn a good work ethic and what better way than to do some good ole fashion American labor. Has no one read *Tom Sawyer*?" Carol slammed the folder on her desk shut and made Diane nearly jump out of her seat.

"Yeah, well that doesn't exactly help us if the po-po come in and decide to shut us down," Louie interjected. "Though you're welcome to take the fall."

His joke was completely lost on Carol, who just stared forward in disbelief, muttering to herself. She debated the situation in her head but clearly wasn't liking the outcome. How could anyone possibly take the camp from her?

"This is just ludicrous. I'm going to make some phone calls and get this all sorted out," Carol said as if she was going to actually be able to do something about it.

"And in the meantime?" Diane asked.

"Just . . . " Carol waited a moment, not really wanting to say it but knowing she had to. "Have them stop until I get it figured out. It shouldn't be too long. We'll just add some music time instead."

"Music time? We don't have any instruments, Carol." Louie was apparently trying to be helpful but failing miserably in Carol's eyes.

"What do you mean? I've got my guitar!" she nearly belted out in song on the spot.

"So you just expect everyone to sit around and sing 'Kumbaya?'" pondered Louie, apparently meaning to insult.

"Optimistic much?" Diane cut in.

"Are you two here just to be pains in my keister or do you need something?" Carol had enough of their interruption, wanting to get back to her paperwork.

"Marion asked us to come figure out payroll. Tomorrow's Friday you know." Diane stated the obvious.

"Yes, I'm aware. But you're just wasting your time because I already have it all sorted out. I did it early. On top of it." Carol smiled wide.

"Well she did still ask us to check and since she's our boss, I'd rather just check so we know for sure."

"I'm your boss. I'm telling you it's done," Carol said through clenched teeth.

"Look, I'm not trying to step on your toes with this whole interim thing," Diane said, knowing exactly which words to use. "But we really need to get this done. It'll take all of two minutes."

"Fine," Carol muttered. "Just know that this will not look good on your performance review."

The two both scoffed at the notion, took out the big binder on desk labeled "Payroll" and thumbed through it. Taking an excessive amount of time to find what they needed, Carol sighed loudly to let them know of her annoyance. She just wanted to get back to her paperwork. How else would the camp run efficiently?

"Woah, what the hell?" Louie cursed, breaking her concentration further.

"Why are our paychecks fifty short?" finished Diane, turning to Carol.

"Yes well there were certain fees that were just not being taken into consideration with prior management so that had to be corrected."

"Fees?" Louie thumbed through the folder. "You're taking out twenty-five dollars for water usage? These are our paychecks, you can't just decide to pay us less without notice."

"You're not being paid less, you're being given the exact amount you were given before. Unfortunately, certain taxes and fees were not being assessed previously, so those will be incurred from this point forward." Carol reasoned.

"Fees according to who?" said Louie, barely able to contain himself. Carol tilted her head, a little amused at how worked up he was getting over the situation.

"I've been doing double the work since Al passed, and you're wanting to pay me even less for it? That's bullshit." Diane pouted.

"You can be spoil sports as much you want, but that won't change a thing. We've got a camp to run! Can't let Barry have all the fun." And with that Carol stood up and made her leave. She didn't want to waste all of her day dealing with the counselors and their non-existent problems. No, she had bigger things to worry about.

Extremely annoyed that Diane and Louie were going to be in the office without her there, Carol stormed out in a huff. She was going to have to stop the kids from improving the camp for the time being.

No wonder Al had such trouble getting this place built back up. Everyone fights against change.

Crossing near the lake, Carol came upon the campers enjoying the water and beach; Barry was stationed up at the lifeguard stand keeping an eye on things. At least she had one counselor that would just do his job.

"How long have they been out here?" Carol inquired.

"Only about twenty minutes. Most haven't been in the water so there hasn't been much of an issue. Everyone seems pretty exhausted from all the painting. It's gonna be a big issue getting them to do it tomorrow. I think one of the Belar's was complaining about getting headaches from the paint."

"Enough of that. We won't be doing that anymore. I decided that they've done enough and it'll just get finished up at a later date," said Carol, not wanting to acknowledge her previous conversation with Diane. "Marge and I will do it after-hours."

"Okay, so are we going to be ready to send these kids to dinner in twenty?"

Carol panicked. Oh no, I forgot to go help Marge. She'll never be able to get it all together without me.

"Only if I get there quick." Carol started off towards the mess hall, not even waiting for a reply from Barry. After only a few feet she stopped, realizing she'd forgotten her custom apron and gloves in the office. There was no way she'd use the ones that Marge had. Those fit awkwardly and left her fingers with a weird rash. Plus, the apron wasn't befitting a proper leader. Neither would do.

She had almost stepped back into the office when she heard chatting inside and decided to listen in, hoping to hear some praise of her methods.

"I'm just counting down the days until Marion's back," barked Diane.

"Yes, please. Just get everything back to normal. Not have this damn schedule. I could go for that." Louie joined in on the mean spiritedness.

"Who's to say it'll even happen like that?" Diane questioned. "You really think that Carol will just give up power? Yeah, right. Now that there's blood in the water, that bitch is gonna bite."

How dare she! Carol couldn't believe the pure disrespect that they were showing her. They did this before and she would just ignore it but that was when she was just one of their co-workers. Now she was their boss. It wasn't fair.

"Please don't even say that. I'm not sure I could even deal with another two weeks of her fucking activities," sighed Louie, adding more fuel to the fire. Carol couldn't believe her subordinates were talking about her like this. *Is this the kind of stuff they would do to Al too?*

"Maybe we'll get lucky and *she'll* fall off the rock wall."

Finally having enough of all the insults, Carol thrust the front door open, alerting the others as she stomped her way across to them in a frenzy.

"You all should be ashamed of yourselves," Carol started up like a disappointed parent. "I work my keister off for this camp and am just trying to make the necessary improvements and what do you do? You go off and undermine me and mock my methods."

"Listen Carol, we're not meaning to—" Diane tried to say but was quickly cut off by Carol.

"No, you listen. I am the boss. I've worked my butt off to get here and I won't suffer your insults. I'm your superior and you all need to treat me as such."

"Woah, Carol, calm down, you're just the replacement until Marion gets back." Carol shot Louie a look of disdain the moment the words finished coming from his lips.

"Is that what you think? Wrong. This place is under new management and that is something that you are going to have to learn to live with. No more complaining and no more trying to rebel by not following your job description. We are here for these kids and that is our main purpose. We are molding the future and if you continue to care only about your own selfish interests, we will never be able to make this place what it truly needs to be. Al was an amazing person and I know that we all loved him. And I know that you liked Marion and enjoyed her more relaxed approach. But that's the style that got us into our financial predicament. Now I am doing something to try and change that and that means having to do things a certain way. I have taken over Camp Watanka and you will do what you're told, when you are told to do it. If not, you will be let go with no further payment, regardless of prior work." Carol stomped her foot down.

"What? You can't do that!" Louie and Diane echoed the same sentiment, not liking these revelations at all. Carol had done plenty of digging and had the proper ammunition prepared. They weren't just going to whine their way out of this one.

"According to the contract that you all signed, it states 'the employee may be let go and all pay held if said employee is in breach of any of the camp's posted rules' and seeing as how these have been posted rules for the past seventy-two hours." Carol raised her laminated list and shook it. "I'm going to have to ask you to do as you're told or leave my camp."

Diane and Louie sat there, completely silent. Carol had proven her point and knew it, brandishing a huge smile. She stepped past them and grabbed her apron and gloves. It was time to get to work.

"Does this mean you're not letting us have the Final Bash?" They chimed in just before she was out the door.

"What? Oh *that* thing?" Carol paused, wanting to draw the moment out for the two that had just insulted her. "I suppose that after a summer of hard work, you should be rewarded. Besides, it's a staple of the camp and we won't be doing away with any moments these kids can take with them forever. You can have your stupid Final Bash."

She was destined to be the boss that finally turned the camp around. Even if it meant being called a bitch every once in a while. *I wonder what other great leaders were called a "bitch" during their tenure?* That was okay though, she knew there were worse names to have. Like, failure. And under Carol's watch, she was going to make sure Camp Watanka never failed again.

Chapter 16
Sally

SALLY'S EYES SCANNED THE CAFETERIA for what felt like hours but couldn't have been more than a few seconds. She knew this because by the time she found what she was looking for, the line she was waiting in for lunch finally started moving. But she had more important things to do. Well, maybe not important, but more exciting things to do. And she conveyed it as such the moment she walked over to Ralph, deciding to just forgo breakfast.

"I'm about to blow your mind," Sally began, shifting her weight on her feet from side to side, rocking with glee. "This is going to be so cool."

"I'm not sure I even want to know," said Ralph, finishing his last bit of salad.

"So are you finally ready?"

"Ready for what?"

Oh come on, he has to know this, she thought, rocking back and forth on her feet barely containing her excitement.

"No," he huffed.

"But you don't even know what I'm—"

"Yes I do and I'm saying no."

"Oh come on, you big baby. It's going to be awesome."

"Going into that creepy house is not my idea of a good time. And it shouldn't be yours either." Ralph stood up and took his tray to the trash, Sally following behind the whole way.

"Oh come on, where's your sense of adventure?" Sally had a certain whine to her voice that she knew struck a chord with Ralph. It was obvious he liked her.

"I just don't really feel like getting kicked out of camp just because you feel like trespassing. I've already made it this long." Ralph seemed much less playful than he usually was. *Wonder what's wrong,* Sally thought but dared not ask. She was already having enough of an uphill battle with him.

"I mean you know, I can always—" Ralph was quick to not even let her finish.

"You are not going to bribe me with alcohol, Sally," he shot back, taking her by surprise. She hadn't expected him to say that, even though she should have. He knew about everything else.

"How do you even know that was what I was going to say?" Sally tried to act as offended as possible but knew it was useless right when he looked down his glasses at her. "Oh come on. You totally said you would. Plus, you're not gonna make little ol' me go all alone will you?"

Bingo.

Ralph turned, and Sally already knew what he was going to say before it even left his lips.

"Fine. When do we leave?"

Planning the journey through the woods ended up being a lot more difficult than Sally originally thought. Sneaking off when she was just scouting it out wasn't a big deal, she'd usually slink off when she was supposed to be going to the bathroom. Closing one of the stalls and crawling out from under—while disgusting—made it easy to declare her whereabouts. The last thing Marion wanted to hear was how the food gave her bad diarrhea, but she was always prepared to say it, just in case she was asked. But that was also when she and Al were still around. Now they were having to deal with the Tyrant known as Carol, who took her duty a little too seriously. It was going to take a bit more finesse in order to not get caught. But this wasn't Sally's first rodeo.

It took a little more lying than she wanted but having the Belar's cover for her seemed to be the best option she had. They didn't care what anyone else did if it didn't affect them and all it took was a pint of Whiskey, a gift from Sally's brother, to help coax them. It didn't matter much to her though, she had several. It always amused Sally just how much she would get from other teenagers just by giving them alcohol. She was always the person in school that would procure it, what with her having an older brother that was more than willing to purchase for her. But not being much of a drinker herself, she knew bringing some along would end up being a good bartering tool. She just had to choose to trust the right people. The last thing she needed was for Carol to catch wind. She could very well call the cops, a drastic solution but one she could easily see Carol doing.

Sally tried having some kind of plan in place for Ralph to get out, but he assured her it wouldn't be an issue. It didn't leave her feeling the most confident, but she didn't want to press him further. If he didn't show up at the spot near the edge of the forest like they planned, she'd just go alone. While it wasn't ideal, she wasn't going to miss out on this opportunity.

Sally waited on the edge of her cot, a book in front of her but not having read a single word in nearly half an hour. She ignored the other girls who gossiped about which boys they thought were the cutest and which of them had hit on whom. If Mary Ann were to be believed, every guy in the camp had hit on her at one point. Sally would have doubted it if not for the massive cleavage she always had on display and her reputation for giving blowjobs off behind the volleyball courts.

When the lights in Carol's cabin finally went off, Sally knew it was time. She'd been sleeping with the covers over her head for the past few nights so that it wouldn't raise any suspicion when Carol did her nightly sweeps. The first night, she felt Carol pull the covers back and check, but she hadn't done it the other nights, so she was counting on that. If she was caught, she didn't know what Carol would do and that made her nervous. At least Al was predictably lazy with his patrolling.

After positioning her bag and pillows just right, she pulled the covers over, completing the illusion. While it wasn't a complete match, she knew that the darkness would do its job in concealing anything painfully obvious. At least she hoped it would.

Getting out of the cabin proved a little trickier. Carol had stopped letting them leave during sleeping hours to go to the bathroom. She insisted they all go before bed as to avoid "any shenanigans that you *prematurely* sexually active kids could be up to." The other counsellors tried to veto it but they changed their tune after a heated argument in the office. While Carol wasn't able to put locks on the doors as she originally wanted, she put an alarm on each of the cabins that would go off if opened while armed. She had purchased them at Walmart for a discount with her own money, but they proved to be shoddy. Still, they were noisy so getting out of the cabin itself was no longer simple. Thankfully, they were still allowed to have fans in their windows, so she at least had one conceivable route out. That's where the Belar's came into play. They had perfect placement next to the window without a screen. Didn't make the issue of noise any less of a problem though. She just had to hope for the best.

By the time all the girls were asleep, or at least appeared to be, Sally snuck her way over to Alice's bed and tapped her on the shoulder. Her eyes opened immediately, and she slid over, allowing Sally to prop herself up into the frame. Before she was out the window, Alice whispered something to her, but it was hard to hear over the fans. Sally thought she said "be back later" but she wasn't sure.

Sally landed on the ground with a thud, not realizing just how far up the window actually was. It always looked so much shorter when she went through the plan in her head. Throwing her body up against the cabin, she tried to get a gauge on her surroundings. The office light was off but Carol's cabin lights were still on, which was a little worrisome. Usually she left the lights on to make it seem like she was in there while she was off on her patrols. That was the last thing Sally needed to deal with, let alone Ralph, who Sally doubted was the expert sneak, given his good-guy demeanor.

Making her way across the camp proved difficult when she came to the basketball court. She figured she'd be able to cross it and make it over to the edge of the forest where she was to meet Ralph. So when she stepped onto the concrete and massive lights turned on, illuminating the entire area, she froze. She didn't know what to do. How did they find her?

Those stupid Belar's sold me out.

She looked around, trying to see where the light was coming from. It couldn't be a flashlight, it was too bright. Finally, she saw it: the flood light, complete with motion sensor. But no one was around. Carol had just installed a sensor light around the basketball court. But someone would be there soon. So Sally made a mad dash towards the forest, trying to get out of the light before anyone came to investigate. Reaching the edge of the tree line, she darted behind the largest oak she could find. Peeking out, her eyes scanned around, looking out for any shapes in the darkness beyond. The lights went out and for a moment, she thought it may have gone unnoticed. Then she saw her.

Carol came waltzing out, her nightgown tucked in and a disheveled look on her face. She did not look happy. Stomping her feet down with every movement forward, she was out for blood.

"Okay, who's the funny guy?" shouted Carol. "The lights didn't just come on by themselves."

She waited for a moment, trying to get the assailants to reveal themselves but to no avail. Sally wasn't that stupid.

"We have a strict code of conduct that every camper must abide by. If you come out now, I'll be lenient with you. But if you don't, the consequences will be severe."

Sally debated for a moment whether she should just step out and take her licks. As annoyed as the new rules were, she had gotten quite close with several other campers and didn't want to miss out on Final Bash.

Fuck that. She doesn't know I'm here.

As if reading Sally's thoughts, Carol turned towards the forest. She stared deeply into the darkness. Sally knew Carol couldn't see her but that didn't help her shake the feeling that she was being watched.

"This is your last chance," she growled, putting her hands on her hips and waiting a moment for a response. When none came, she looked down and sighed, muttering something to herself.

Carol neared the tree line and Sally retreated behind the trunk, hoping she wouldn't go any further. She could hear grass rustle and twigs snapped.

Just as she reached the other side of Sally's oak tree, a familiar voice became Sally's savior.

"Sorry Carol. Didn't mean to spook you," said a downtrodden Louie, appearing from the darkness.

"God dammit Louie what the hell are you doing out here?"

"Umm following your rules?"

"Following my—what on earth do you mean?"

"You said that we would have to leave official camp grounds in order to smoke so I went out to. . . smoke."

"I. . . well," Carol stumbled over her words, already prepared to tear him a new one. She eventually found a problem. "And yet you decided to leave your kids alone without supervision? I can't believe you would even. . ." Her voice trailed off and she led Louie off towards the office, likely reprimanding him for whatever she could come up with that he supposedly did wrong.

With all of the commotion, Sally had failed to notice the figure moving up behind her. It was already within feet of her by the time she turned around. It took everything in her not to gasp as a hand covered her mouth, trying to muffle any noise she may have made.

It took her eyes a moment to adjust before she recognized the brown hair and glasses that she had associated so closely with Ralph.

"Jesus fucking Christ, Ralph. What the hell is the matter with you?!" Her heart nearly jumped from her chest with every beat.

"Sorry. I thought you'd find it more funny than terrifying. Clearly I was wrong."

"Yeah clearly. I just—" she tried catching her breath but it kept eluding her until other thoughts clouded her mind and helped her ignore it. "How did you get out?"

"You seriously overestimate how much Louie cares about following Carol's rules."

"Good point. And I'm sure that's the last thing on his mind right now."

"He'll brush it off. I already overheard him telling Marion that this was going to be his last year. "

Sally wondered if there'd even be a camp the following year, what with the number of people she'd heard proclaim they weren't coming back. It was past the point of just campers, and now the counselors were tagging along as well. And just when she was actually beginning to enjoy the place.

"So what way is this place?" Louie peered into the surrounding darkness. "I don't think I can navigate through this. Do you have a flashlight?"

"No. But your eyes will adjust. Doubt it's a good idea to have flashlights with Carol around anyway. She's got eyes like a hawk."

"Couldn't be too good if she wasn't able to spot you." Ralph moved past her, brushing against her a little. His touch sent shivers down her spine.

"I. . . uh. . . shut up!"

After nearly twenty minutes, and many bug bites later, they finally reached the house. It was bigger than it seemed the last few times Sally had snuck off to see it. She had suddenly become very aware of its foreboding presence, making her uneasy. She figured the opposite would be true since she wasn't alone this time, but she also knew she'd finally be setting foot inside. She hadn't thought she'd be this scared once the moment actually came, but now it was taking everything in her being not to shake.

As if the massive spider webs that adorned most of the house weren't enough, the forest that surrounded the decaying structure had crept up enough that even a tree branch had grown in through one of the windows. It was everything Sally expected from a place with the kind of history it had. It was perfect. Before Sally could even think it, Ralph was reading her mind.

"That place looks straight out of a horror movie."

"Oh come on, it's kind of cute," Sally insisted, trying to hide her own fear and be brave for both of them. But the house was making it difficult to concentrate on anything but its foreboding nature.

"People were murdered in there. That's not just some creepy house on some street that kids are just scared of because it's abandoned or the owners don't take care of it properly. Fucked up shit happened in there." Ralph swearing caught Sally off guard.

Is that the first time he's ever sworn in front of me?

"If you want to turn back we can," Sally sighed, hoping it was enough to get him to change his mind.

"No, I can handle it. It's not like—you know what never mind."

"What? You can't start something like that and then just not finish it. 'It's not like' what?"

"It's not like that murderer is still around and the same thing is going to happen to us."

They both looked up at the house, more and more creeped out by it. Sally laughed, trying to break the tension.

"You know, the killer's son could always just be going on a spree to avenge his parent." Sally theorized.

"And now you totally just stirred him awake by saying that. And in front of his own domain no less!"

"How do you know it would be a guy?"

"Oh come on. You seriously think some girl would lose it and try to kill a bunch of people? Nuh-uh. That's all guy territory right there. Michael Myers. Has a penis. Jason Voorhees. Zombie penis. Freddy Krueger. Probably burnt to a crisp, but still, has a penis."

"Those are movie villains, Sally."

"Okay well I was just going to stick with the easy ones but Ted Bundy, Ed Gein, Charles Manson."

"Manson never technically killed anyone," Ralph interjected.

"Are we really arguing semantics right now? Point is, women don't usually go crazy and do these types of things. I mean, that's just history."

"There's always a first time for everything."

"You're right." She changed her tone. "I guess this is finally the time to tell you that the only reason I brought you here was to murder you and start a spree, the likes of which have never been before. Mwahahahaha!"

Ralph's lack of response made Sally go into full panic mode. Oh shit, my stupid sense of humor. I totally just weirded him out. Oh god, this is so not going well.

"Well damn," he finally responded. "I guess that means I have to abandon my own plan since both of us can't be doing it. Then we wouldn't be unique."

Awkward silence followed as they hoped the other one was joking, given the devious looks on both of their faces. Finally, they both broke out into fits of laughter.

"Aww come on, you totally broke first," giggled Sally.

"No way, that was all you," Ralph insisted. "I didn't even have the faintest hint of giving it away until you started smiling and laughing. Plus, you said 'Mwahahaha.' How can I ever take you seriously after that?"

"Whatever, I'm totally blaming it on you." Sally turned back to the house, wondering when her goosebumps would go away.

"So we should probably. . ."

"Yeah, let's do this." Sally tried injecting her voice with a hint of confidence. She failed.

Stepping onto the front porch, the rush was almost too much to handle—every terrible scenario she just imagined went through her head on loop. Ralph clutched onto her hand as they moved forward, inching across the creaking wood splints. Spotting a bunch of rusted tools strewn about the porch from some long abandoned construction project, Ralph made his way over to one. He raised the hatchet up, a smile spreading across his face.

"Oh yeah? You gonna protect us with that?"

"Trust me, anyone within a two-foot radius of me is gonna have another thing coming." He swung the hatchet and made an exaggerated ninja call. "Waaaaaahhh!!!"

"Yeah, you look real fucking scary," Nancy's annoyed voice spat through the darkness and Sally and Ralph nearly jumped out of their skins.

"Jesus Christ, Nancy. What the hell are you doing here?" Sally turned and saw it was not only Nancy, but also her sister Alice and two boys that had been in Marion's group.

"Oh come on, you really thought we were just gonna let you have all the fun? No way."

"You were supposed to be my look out. Remember that?" It was hard for Sally not to sound annoyed. She was. She had scoped this place out several times with the intention of taking Ralph here. The more people involved, the less scary the house seemed to her. Too much protection.

"Don't worry, I've got us covered. I gave Brenda some Twinkies and ho-ho's. She'll be in a sugary coma." It was hard not to be offended by Nancy's comment, as evidenced by the eye roll from Ralph.

"You know, not all fat people can just be bribed with sweets."

"Yeah, and not all pretty girls can be bribed with alcohol but look where we are," said Alice, raising the pint of Whiskey Sally had given her.

"You know, technically since you didn't do your job, I should probably take that back." Sally extended a hand to take the bottle back.

"Okay," Alice said, holding the bottle out. "I'll just go fetch Carol and see if she wants to play hide and seek."

Sally knew there was nothing she could do and lowered her hand. They were going to be tagging along regardless. So much for her plans.

"Fine. Who are your friends?" she asked, a little more fire to her voice than she intended.

"Steve." Alice pointed to the blonde one that stood next to her. His square jaw and varsity jacket told Sally all she needed about him. They had apparently been going steady for days, but this was the first Sally had seen them together.

"And I'm Lucas," he said, extending his out to her. Sally ignored it for a second before Ralph stepped in and took it for a firm handshake. Lucas seemed the rocker type, which Sally had long ago pegged as Nancy's type. She was glad to see she hit the nail on the head.

"Well Steve and Lucas, it was lovely meeting you but Ralph and I really must be heading inside." Sally pulled Ralph back towards the doorway.

"Oh come on, you don't get the whole house to yourself." Alice groaned. "There's gotta be plenty of rooms for the taking."

"The whole point is to explore not to hook up," she shot Steve and Lucas a nasty look during the last part but they brushed it off with a laugh.

"Well hey, we can all still enjoy the house. Just. . . for different reasons." Alice pushed her way through, dragging Steve by his collar. Nancy stood next to Lucas with a big smile plastered across her face. She was ready to get this party started, raising up a pint of whiskey and wooing loudly.

"Jesus Christ, Nancy! You have to be quiet," Sally pleaded. "Otherwise what's the point if Carol can just show up?"

"You heard the lady," Nancy pushed past, stepping foot into the big scary house. "Let's go exploring!"

This was now the second house Sally had been in that had a murder occur inside of—at least that she was aware of. It was an odd thing to keep track of but Sally did just that, always seeking a further thrill. She stared at a dark stain on one of the wood panels, assuming the worst but not letting the words leave her lips. Ralph was already uncomfortable enough. He was had been gripping that hatchet fairly tight. On edge seemed to be the bare minimum for everyone at that point. And with good reason, as the house was creepier and creepier the further in they went. Sally almost didn't want to follow Ralph up the stairs, but her adrenaline carried her. When they reached the first room, she wished she'd stayed down stairs.

"Definitely looks like a whole lotta murder right there." Ralph not-so-eloquently took the words right out of her mouth.

The dark stain certainly looked like it could have been from excessive blood loss. The splatter even seemed straight from a gunshot wound. This would have synced up with all the stories Sally had heard. But something still didn't seem right. It seemed too dark based on all of the shows she'd watched. She had devoured as many Nancy Drew books as her local library would carry. Her television at home would rarely leave the Crime network. She knew this type of thing better than anyone with basic cable. And something still just didn't seem right.

"Certainly fits the bill. I'm not sure though."

"Oh yeah?" pondered Ralph. "So I'm curious as to what your analysis is, detective?"

She giggled at the thought of even being called a detective. He seemed genuine but she expected the sarcasm to bite back shortly.

"Well, my dear Watson, it could be anything. Hell, it could just be a spot where the roof leaks, so it gets exposed to water a lot. Warps the wood and all that."

"Then I guess there'd be mold on the other side then, right?" asked Ralph, circling around the hole, looking between it and Sally.

"It could be someone knocked over some dark wood stain and. . ." Sally started, unconvincing with her own words. "Yeah, okay. What're you thinking?"

"I'm thinking we have to find out, don't we? So we better crack the case, Mr. Holmes."

Ralph raised the hatchet up and smashed down on the wooden plank. He swung again, sending splinters into the air.

"You better be quiet, you're gonna wake the love birds."

Alice and Steve had gone upstairs minutes prior. The moans of pleasure that emanated from one of the nearby rooms stopped, as annoyed footsteps exited into the hallway. Apparently they didn't like being disturbed, as they entered the room, shooting Ralph and Sally looks of confusion.

"And you were complaining to us about being loud? Why the fuck are you hammering?" Alice asked in a huff, putting her shirt back on.

"I'm not hammering," said Ralph, pulling the plank up, trying to snap it off. "We're doing some detective work."

"By breaking the house apart?"

"Your friends are weird," Steve whispered into Alice's ear and tried to pull her away, back to what they were doing but she wouldn't budge.

"Okay, so what's the big idea? Think you're gonna unlock some grand mystery from breaking the fucking floor?" her voiced reeked of sarcasm but Ralph still pulled at the floor with purpose. Finally, it snapped off, sending Ralph slamming into the wall behind him—not expecting the sudden break.

"Congratulations, you now can say you've pulled a floor apart. This is truly a momentous occasion." Alice added, a hurried clap at the end.

"God, shut up, Alice," Sally yelled out. "Just because you don't care about anything that doesn't involve boys or alcohol, doesn't mean it's not important to some of us. So either you can stop being sarcastic or you can fucking leave."

Alice stared silently at Sally for a moment, letting out exasperated sighs and throwing plenty of eye-rolls to both Ralph and Sally. Finally, she placed her hands on her hips, came to a decision.

"Fine. But you should probably patch up your little boyfriend first."

"He's not my—" Sally started but was quickly cut off by Ralph.

"Umm, I'm totally fine. Just a fall."

"I meant your hand." Alice, trying to be helpful but still coming off bitchy. "Or do you just randomly bleed every once in a while? You know, I probably have a tampon for you in my purse."

Sally looked over and there it was, his right hand, clutching onto the wooden plank, had blood covering his knuckles. Was it from the wood? Or had he done it with the hatchet before? Ralph looked just as confused, looking down at his hand and then quickly looking over the rest of his body, trying to see where he cut himself. Sally walked to him and gave him the handkerchief from her pocket.

"Thanks."

Ralph wiped away the blood from his hand, trying to see exactly where it had come from. Sally thought she could see the culprit—a small cut on his left index finger—but it disappeared. A simple trick of the light.

"I don't get it. I'm not cut anywhere."

"Then where did the blood come from?" Alice clutched onto Steve's shirt, suddenly terrified of everything around her.

Ralph and Sally's mind went to the same place as their eyes darted to the piece of floor that lay next to them. He reached his hand out as Sally kept repeating to herself, *There's a logical explanation for this. There's a logical explanation for this. There's a logical explanation for this.*

Ralph flipped the brown stained piece over and there it was, completely illogical and without obvious explanation: a big red spot of coagulated blood.

"What in the fucking fuck!" Alice eloquently spat out. "Is that fucking blood? How is that blood? How in the fucking fuck?! How is it still. . . like that?"

"Isn't that the question of the day?" The words came out of Sally's mouth more on instinct than actual forethought. Her mind went a mile a minute, wondering how twenty-year-old blood could have possibly been there still? How could it still be coagulating all these years? Were the conditions just perfect enough that something like that could happen? No, that's stupid, how would this house be so self-contained when the rest of the camp was constantly exposed to the elements in such a humid environment.

"Sally." Ralph came to the conclusion just as Sally came to hers. Their eyes met and they didn't even need to say anything. That didn't prevent Alice's date from dully chiming in, not helping with Alice's current state of shaking.

"Does that mean it's fresh?" blurted Steve.

"Alice!"

The shriek from downstairs startled all of them. Sally had almost forgotten about Nancy and Lucas. Unless Lucas had suddenly dropped his voice a few octaves, she was willing to bet it was Nancy that screamed. They had confirmation seconds later as Nancy came plodding up the stairs, tears on her cheeks and bottle of whiskey—mostly gone—in hand.

"I can't find Lucas. He's gone. Eww what the fuck is that!?" Nancy freaked the moment she saw Ralph holding the bloody piece of floor. He looked at it awkwardly for a moment, before dropping it and picking up the hatchet instead, further terrifying Nancy in the process.

"What do you mean you can't find Lucas?" questioned Sally.

"He was supposed to come up here to check on you guys and all the god damn noise. So I waited like five minutes and nothing. And I kept hearing you guys walking all over upstairs, so I just figured you guys were doing something stupid and weren't inviting me."

"This is so stupid," Alice announced. "We're in a scary house. You drank way too much of that whiskey. Problem solved. Now where's Lucas, Steve? Is he hiding in one of the rooms to try and scare us?" Alice asked Steve.

"Hey, don't look at me." Steve raised his hands, proclaiming his innocence. "If this is a prank, I'm being played just as much as the rest of you."

"Great," Alice sighed. "That does us a whole lotta good. Well we need to find your idiot friend so that I can tear into him. . . that sounded better in my head."

Nancy, Alice and Steve walked downstairs, shouting insults about Lucas, trying to coax him out. Anything ranging from "Don't be embarrassed, I'm sure it happens to a lot of guys" to "Lucas, you're grounded!" Nancy sounded like she fell down the last few steps, blaming it on the darkness rather than her own drunken stupor. The moonlight had disappeared behind some clouds, making the house nearly pitch black. They used small lighters to lead the way. Sally almost walked down when she looked back and noticed Ralph, completely still at the top of the stairs. He appeared deep in thought, gripping the hatchet firmly in his hand.

"Are you doing okay?"

"It's just. . . moving around? We didn't even leave the hallway." Ralph was right. The only noise she should have noticed were the hatchet on the floor and the two love birds joining them. Outside of that they had been still. Ralph's eyes followed around the room, trying to peer into the darkness. Trying to make sure it was just them up there.

Suddenly a voice broke through the night, leaving behind more of a shiver than the silence even managed. They were simply two screamed words:

"Alice, run!"

It took a moment for Sally and Ralph to gain their bearings and even understand what was being shouted at them. It took the scuttling of Nancy and Steve's feet below till it hit them that they needed to move. Fast. Whatever it was that got Nancy, it was bad. Sally could hear it in her voice. They darted down the stairs, running towards the porch but quickly halted as a scream rushed towards them. "Holy fuck, turn around! It's here!"

A shadow moved across one of the windows. Someone was making their way across the porch towards the front door. Ralph took action, grabbing onto Sally's arm and leading her deeper into the house. They ran through the hallway, darting between the pillars that made up the crumbling dining room area. Sally was practically blind but somehow Ralph made his way through the darkness. She started to venture off a little but as she did he grabbed her hand and pulled her toward him, shutting a door behind them.

In the darkness it took her a while but she finally noticed his fingers held up to his lips, motioning her to be quiet. Stuffed in a closet, they had little room to move even if they wanted to. They could remain perfectly still and the door would still squeak randomly. They just had to pray. As soon as the thought left her head, someone entered the room, signaled by the familiar squeak of the old house.

She tried limiting her breathing but it was hard. She'd been scared before, but never to such a degree. Every urge she thought she'd have in a situation like this was completely gone from her, leaving nothing but a scared shell. What were they to do if the closet door was suddenly pulled open? Charge the mystery man? What if the man had a gun and just shot through the closet door? Should she drop down to make sure the bullets were above her head?

I can't believe I'm even thinking this. I'm going to be fine.

As if tempting fate, the mystery figure stood at the other side of the door. Sally cursed herself silently. She heard the heavy breathing and knew it was past the point of her overactive imagination. This was real. She braced for whatever was to happen next, ready to attack in whatever way her body would let her. Then the feet just shuffled away, heading back towards the front of the house. It was a good thing that Ralph was able to find that closet.

Come to think of it, how was Ralph even able to make it through the house?

Suddenly the thought of Ralph holding that hatchet wasn't nearly as comforting to Sally. Was this his plan? Was he just trying to scare all of them? What help had he really been? Maybe the heavy breathing was just him? His firm grasp on her wrist didn't help settle her nerves as her paranoia set in. She needed to make a run for it and she needed to do it fast. She knew that the backdoor was just through the kitchen to the left of them. She had to move.

"Sally, don't run."

That was all Sally needed to hear. She rammed her knee into Ralph's side and followed it with a kick to his crotch, sending him tumbling to the ground. He let loose of his grip on her and she sprinted off towards the kitchen. As she reached the back door, she heard the footsteps behind her and then Ralph's voice picked up.

"Sally!"

She unhooked the latch and thrust the door open, running out of the back of the house and towards the forest. She glanced behind and Ralph was already practically on top of her. He grabbed her by the shoulders, wrestling her to a halt.

"Sally, please just stop." Ralph could barely breathe. "Jesus, Sally, I'm not gonna hurt you. I'd never do that. What's gotten into you?"

"How do I know you're not. . . not just doing this to fuck with me? You sure did know the layout of that house pretty damn well, Ralph."

"Do you hear yourself right now? I can't even. . . Oh my god."

Ralph stared past Sally, his mouth agape. Sally almost didn't want to turn around, not entirely trusting his reaction. But as soon as the tears started to form in his eyes, she couldn't help but turn, and then she understood.

Nancy sat, motionless, her body propped up against a large mossy tree. Sally couldn't tell from any obvious wounds as to what happened to her, but with all the color drained from her face, the outcome wasn't looking good.

Then her eyes opened, almost staring right through Sally. Her lips shook as the words that left them were barely audible.

"Run."

Nancy keeled over and vomited all over the moss covering the bottom half of the tree.

Terrified, unsure of what was happening, Sally and Ralph turned to run far from the house. Sally wanted nothing more than to leave this place behind them. Go back to camp. To find out what was happening. But all that came to a stop before it even began as they tumbled into a figure that had snuck up behind them in the dark. A flashlight shined brightly into their faces and Sally could no longer see, her entire vision entering weird spectrum of yellow and white. While her eyes adjusted, the flashlight lowered and they could see the person wielding it.

Carol's face lit up.

But the smile that usually filled out her face was replaced with an angry scowl. Sally looked past Carol's shoulder and breathed a little sigh of relief:

There stood Alice, Steve, and Lucas, like three kids in detention, all looking down at their feet.

"Guess we didn't do as good of a job as we thought." Alice's eyes wouldn't leave the ground.

"Guys, I don't feels so g-good." Nancy's drunken voice struggled with every word that she tried to create. Sally didn't realize just how much she had been taking down of that pint.

"I expected more out of all of you. Especially her," said Carol, motioning over to Nancy who laid her head on the ground, almost putting it in her own puke patch. "This is what happens to minors when they ingest alcohol at such a young age. Your body is just not ready for it. You'll be good to learn that."

"This is ridiculous," Alice muttered, rolling her eyes.

"Ridiculous, eh? How bout I start with phoning up your parents and telling them they need to pick up their kid by tomorrow afternoon? Think they'd like dropping everything in their lives so that they can come pick up their disrespectful kids? And you can forget about ever coming back here either. Think that'd just be ridiculous?"

The teens hurled insults at each other the whole way back. Carol just shook her head, disappointed in all of them. Sally lead up the rear and one thought echoed in her head, *Where the hell did that blood come from?*

PART THREE

Chapter 17

Chase

MOST OF THE CAMPERS seemed at least a little excited when Carol announced the re-instatement of a camp-wide softball tournament. Everyone but Chase. He just sat there, wondering to himself how *any* form of sport could be the level of fun that Crazy Carol made the tournament out to be. She spouted out more adjectives for the word "fun" in a twenty-second period than anyone Chase had ever witnessed. Just when he thought she couldn't be more ridiculous than she already was, something like this would happen and prove she could always take it a step further.

The other campers ate up her announcement. The older ones loved the competition and the younger ones figured that anything the older kids thought was cool was especially so. Adding the fact that they wouldn't have to take part in the mandatory pottery class was enough for most. Even Liz was excited that the old softball diamonds were finally getting used again.

"Al shut them down like five years ago because it took a lot to maintain and he didn't think that kids cared about baseball or softball anymore," Liz explained. "That's why we have the half-finished basketball court with no basket."

"I just thought it was a really lovely slab of concrete," Chase jested.

"No one could say Al never tried. He just wasn't much of a. . . completionist. At least he has Carol to annoyingly continue his work. Lucky him."

"Yeah. . . lucky Al. Sure worked out for Carol, didn't it?"

"Not this again, Chase." Liz had heard enough of his theories.

Chase was having a hard time of being convinced of anything. Things just felt strange. In his mind Carol was just batshit insane and trying to get her way, no matter how much she tried to make it seem otherwise. She was simply trying to add something in order to give the kids some sense of "fun", while she still prevented them from doing the other things they actually wanted to do. The rock wall had caution tape up over it ever since Marion fell. No matter how many campers lobbied for its return, Carol claimed it was too dangerous to try again this year. She said she "cared about all of us too much to see us hurt." Then the volleyball courts had been deemed "too sexual" for a short while, but Marion made a deal to get those back, thankfully.

Doing more good than Carol, even in a hospital bed.

And the kids were actually falling for her spiel. They just didn't understand how stupid it all was. This was just another way for Carol to try and flex her power muscle. This wasn't for the kids. But as the time finally drew closer, Chase found something very strange happening: he was looking forward to it. He saw past Carol and whatever reasons she may have had for reinstating the tournament and realized it was just an opportunity to let loose. And he really liked baseball. Softball was like a baseball, he supposed.

The morning air had hints of mildew and freshly cut grass as it filled Chase's nostrils. He stepped onto the wet grass of the softball field with renewed pride, forgetting his previous trepidation in one breath. He had forgotten just how much he enjoyed the sport. He played baseball as a younger boy, even making the All-League team in fifth grade, taking pride in some of his base-stealing skills. Softball was the same— outside of the underhand pitching, which Chase could get used to. Baseball was something that escaped him as his youth evolved into teens and he became more obsessed with video games. Didn't mean that he wasn't well versed in the world of MLB 2007-2012— not that, that was relevant now. Not unless his ability to hit home-runs in game somehow transferred to real life. As much as he wanted it to, he doubted it. Still, he figured that he was at least somewhat ahead of the curve, in that he knew the positions and what each of them had to do. He had a decent arm and knew how to track down fly balls. He didn't consider himself the most athletically gifted but he still got the job done when he needed to, especially after his growth spurt the previous summer that stretched any remaining baby fat off of him. It had been a long time since he'd swung a bat, but outside of the athletes, he wasn't sure who else actually had, outside of gym class.

After breakfast that morning they had been marched out to the old diamond, where Carol stood, baseball cap awkwardly atop her head, and a clipboard in hand. Her shorts were hiked up so high, Chase debated how she could even breathe. She stood on the pitcher's mound like it was some kind of podium. Puffing her chest out, she looked out at the kids, a prideful smile adorning her face, like she was about to accomplish something world-altering.

Picking teams ended up going exactly how he'd expected: Carol stood at the front of the group and decided who would be on each of the two teams— hence the clipboard. She said she was doing this in order to "be fair" but Chase suspected it was just another muscle of power that she wanted to flex. *God knows that things couldn't go a way that Carol hadn't deemed fit. She may have an aneurysm otherwise.* It was annoying, but coming to be expected from her. At least it was harmless.

After being placed on a team devoid of any of his friends, Chase quickly understood what she was going for: separating the ones closest to each other. Even Alice and Nancy were split up, resulting in quite an uproar from the twins. Carol proceeded to scold them till they finally settled down. She didn't even have to threaten them anymore, everyone knew what the punishment was: being sent home.

This would have been a godsend for most other years, but for some reason the campers had been banding together more so than usual. Liz had said it was the fact that Marion was in more control the first half than she ever was before which made it more fun. Then the campers banded together in their mutual hatred for Carol during the second half. Not exactly the way Al probably envisioned it, but it was the most tight-knit the camp had been in years.

At first it seemed like a decent idea; getting sent home early and getting to enjoy a little more of the summer. But that quickly disappeared as they saw the first person get sent home. He was a boy from Louie's group that had back talked Carol after she kept trying to get him on dishes duty. He refused. He was somewhat of a hero during the first few hours but then, when a speeding car drove up to the office and an angry older man stepped out, everyone knew it was big trouble. He didn't look like much of a tough guy with tears rolling down his face as the angry man dragged him off.

Carol implemented a policy of no refunds after a certain date, and it made the kid's father furious. He seemed like a tough enough kid but the cries that resonated from the office were hard not to hear even from the lake nearly 100 yards away. The kicking and screaming was just icing on the cake. The thought of being sent home early was no longer as tempting as the campers first thought. Otherwise, Chase figured more people would have tried to get kicked out. Dealing with their parents' wrath wasn't always the worst option.

As Chase expected, the less gifted kids were placed either at catcher or right field, with more of the star athletes going for pitcher, short-stop and second. Chase took up his spot at third base, a position he had grown quite fond of during his little league days. He had enough of an arm to get the ball to first, but his defensive area was much less than that of second and short—two positions he actively avoided. It was just enough for him to feel comfortable; a rarity with himself and sports.

The teams were allowed two hours of practice and then the "tournament" would begin. It was confusing as to why it was even called a tournament when only two teams were taking part, and therefore the only game played would be a championship, but Carol refused to listen to Louie, who just laughed it off and proceeded to overuse the word "tournament." Everything felt slapped together, but at least the competition was getting them away from the cleaning and policy. Although Chase wouldn't have put it past Carol to spring that on the losing team.

Each team was assigned a coach between the counselors. Given that Marion wasn't back yet, and Diane was lording over the little ones, the choices ended up being Barry and Louie. Barry had played baseball in high school so he was fist pumping at the announcement, while Louie just kind of yawned and walked over to his group. Chase was thankful to have Louie as his coach.

Unable to escape Carol and her rule, she had placed herself in the role of Umpire, even wearing a slapped together version of an ump's outfit.

When the teams finally separated, Louie led his over towards left field, where he sat down in the grass and stared up at the sun for a moment. It only took a few seconds for his eyes to start watering. For a moment, Chase thought he was seriously crying, but then he opened his mouth.

"I'm not going to lie to you guys," Louie began. "This is the single most important thing that has ever happened in any of yours or my stupid lives. We have been irrelevant to time until this very day, July somethingth, two thousand-whatever. This tournament will go down in the history of the United States as one of the greatest tournaments in the history of thrown together summer camp softball games. Get out of here *Sleepaway Camp* cause we're coming for you. *Meatballs*? Psh. They don't even know 'bout us! That top spot is ours! Because we're the. . ." Louie paused, thinking for a moment and 'magically' regaining his composure. "Wait, what's our name? Come on, let's get a team vote. Remember, it may be the most important decision you've made in any of your lives up to this point."

"The Dickbags," someone shouted.

"Sheep Orgasm," another followed.

"Bag of Oats!"

"Oh come on," Louie shook his head. "We're at a summer camp. At least stick with the theme, you heathens. And I don't want to hear that language out of your mouth, Randall."

"The paint cans," yelled Chase, looking over at Carol, who'd made no friends of the campers after the paint fiasco. Most of the kids, as well as Louie, smiled wide at the suggestion.

"Boom! We've got our name. Chase in the clutch." Louie stood, trying to take on whatever persona he happened to have in regards to a baseball coach. Chase figured it was a mixture of *Bad News Bears* and *A League of Their Own*. At least, those were the two movies that came to his head first.

Louie tried to get the team to do some basic drills but most of the time was just spent sitting around, talking about how important the tournament was. Louie had gotten most of the team joking about it. Chase was glad they were able to have some fun with it, but with Barry coaching on the other side, he wondered if this was going to be a lopsided display of athleticism.

Thankfully the team proved more adept at actually playing the sport than they were talking about it. As soon as everyone was placed in a position and Louie was hitting balls out to them, everything just seemed to click.

At one point Carol came over with a pile of old camp t-shirts that she said they could turn inside out and make into team uniforms. Louie took the opportunity to argue with her over getting proper time to make the best uniforms possible but Carol was having none of his procrastinating. They were to make their uniforms immediately so that the game could commence before the incoming storm made it impossible. It didn't matter to Carol that the storm was supposed to hit 30 miles west of them. She refused to sway from her schedule.

"You make sure that you get everyone lined up along the third base line right when you hear my whistle sound." Carol, thinking Louie needed an example, whistled sharply at him. "See, like that."

Once Carol went off to the harass the other team, Louie handed out a bunch of colored markers. With everyone having different ones, the shirts each ended up having unique color schemes. Given that it was just a paint can, Chase didn't think the task would be too much to manage but the results varied from person to person. Some looked like paint cans, others looked like big blobs of color. Chase laughed when he noticed that Louie's blob resembled that of a penis.

"So tell me, does anyone else feel like we should just be doing shirts versus skins?" suggested Lucas as he eyed the girls across the way.

"Yeah, that's definitely not happening." Alice was disgusted it was even being suggested.

"As much fun as that sounds, I'd rather not go to jail. But thank you so much for your suggestion, Lucas. You are just full of great ideas. But maybe next time try a little harder if you want to see me with my shirt off. So overt. Disgusting. Back in my day, guys had class." Louie was joking more than usual and it made Chase wonder if he'd been drinking again. It wouldn't have surprised him, with Carol's reign of terror still in full force.

As if on cue, Carol's whistle sounded.

Louie quickly got his team over to the diamond and lined up along the third base line. Apparently Carol had not given the same message to the other team, as the Water Rats were left waiting. In the meantime, Carol cleaned off all the bases with a small brush, originally intended for art, now something she could repurpose to make her feel like an official umpire.

After a few minutes passed, the other team finally walked over, each clad in white with some hand drawn insignia on it. Chase couldn't quite make it out and his mind quickly wandered away from it as he tugged at his own uncomfortable shirt. Why hadn't he tried grabbing one of the mediums? The larges were more like extra-larges and his shirt draped so loosely around his shoulders that he wondered if it'd fall off.

He could see Liz near the edge of the group, smiling wide and pointing down at her team shirt. The crude design was done with generic green and brown marker but it was easy enough to figure out. As Chase read the name, he could practically hear Liz suggesting it, and the glee in her voice when she did.

They were the Bullfrogs.

After a rather nasty rendition by Carol of the National Anthem, they were finally ready to play some softball. Carol made it clear that they were not allowed to lead off, but they were able to steal so long as they left the base after the pitcher started their motion to the plate. Otherwise, it had the same basic rules as baseball. Carol would be acting as umpire—an obvious fact given her ridiculous homemade umpire mask that hung at her side, but one she still wanted to officially announce to everyone.

The game itself was a healthy back and forth. Once it started, Chase remembered why he loved baseball in the first place. The thrill of competition. It was something that he enjoyed but often never pursued. But this was something he could do. And he did it well. Especially at third base.

He had one of the stronger arms on his team, making some of the better throws of the game from third. This led Louie to think it would be a good idea for Chase to take center, given that six runs had been given up by their then-center fielder, James. Chase hated the outfield and he made it known as he rolled his eyes at Louie. The infield was his comfort zone in something he already was out of his element in.

As his took his position in center field, Chase had the eerie feeling that he was being watched. He looked around, expecting to see someone—maybe a wandering local—peeking out from the woods. Instead his eyes went back to the field and the only person looking at him was Carol, waiting for him to get his head back in the game.

By the time the sixth and final inning came around, there were already two outs as Chase approached the plate. The game was up to him. His team down 14 - 16 with a man on second base, he spit whatever he could manage at the ground, regardless of his dry mouth. His nerves were starting to get to him as he hit the dirt off his shoes with the aluminum bat. He wasn't sure why he was doing it, but he always saw MLB players do it, so he figured it had to be useful in some way.

Even though it was an impossibility, he kept picturing himself hitting a homerun, sending it clear over the fence, and getting a victory lap around the bases. He could practically hear the crack of the bat and see its trajectory off into the woods beyond. It wouldn't have mattered what happened after because he would have tied it up and it would be out of his hands.

Instead the first pitch came in and Chase missed wildly. He couldn't decide if it was just a bad swing or if the ball was just out of the strike zone too much. Either way, it was his fault. And the laughter from the other team didn't help matters. He gripped the bat a little looser and stared ahead at Santa, who looked like a pitcher to be reckoned with up on that mound. It wasn't like they were professional, and it was still underhand as to avoid any injuries, but with Carol's strike-zone, it was hard not to want to swing at everything. The probability of being struck out by a bogus pitch was high.

"You ready for this curveball?" said Santa with a big smile on his face.

"Oh yeah? How exactly are you going to manage to throw a curveball?" Chase joked. "I'd really like to see this untapped softball skill that you suddenly have, Santa. And I'd also like to know why you waited till now to showcase it."

"Just you wait, it's my specialty," declared Santa.

"Last I knew your specialty was presents, not curveballs."

"Enough of the trash talk," Carol butted in, ruining all the fun. "We're not here for that."

When the next ball came careening toward him, Chase tensed up and swung with all his might. The crack of the bat was almost like he had envisioned, with the ball soaring off into the sky. It traveled and traveled, further and further, but there was one problem: the trajectory was not how he imagined. At all. The ball had floated off towards the side, deep into foul ball territory.

That meant he was at two strikes.

Waiting for the pitch, several scenarios entered his mind: he would either strike out in a blaze of glory, he'd get out on an easy grounder to one of the studs in the middle, or he'd pop up into right field where Jimmy, who hadn't caught a ball all day, would make a miraculous catch and save the day for the other team. The fact that no positive scenario entered his head was slightly troubling.

Staring at the ball as it left the pitcher's hand, he watched as it made its way toward him, as if in slow motion. By the time he swung, he thought he had for sure swung too late but instead, with a pop of his bat, he saw his ball soaring over Santa's head and towards the short-stop. Chase started running but felt it was pointless until he saw the ball lifted higher and over the shortstop's glove. It was a base hit.

He rounded first and started making his way towards second but quickly stopped as he noticed the center fielder already had the ball. Everyone from the bench yelled at him to stop which he ultimately did, not wanting to be the stupid hero. He'd gotten one run in and a guy on third base. They were in a good position to take the lead.

"Nice hit, but I'm about to wake you up from that dream, son."

And he was right. Up next walked Brenda, a stout Mexican girl who had shown no athletic prowess up to that point. Her previous plate appearances consisted of four strikeouts and a pop up to the catcher. She was also their right fielder.

"Oh see, you don't even know, Santa. Brenda is our ringer. Aren't you, Brenda?"

Brenda promptly set the bat down and flipped Chase off.

"See, look at that fire in her eyes. She's ready to tear that ball a new one." Chase continued before Carol stepped forward and took off her mask and motioned for silence.

"That's enough. We've got a game to finish. Then we've got a wonderful dinner to go attend. I know

Marge is cooking up something really good for you. If you behave, I may just tell you what it is."

Oh joy.

"Batter up!" Carol stepped back behind the catcher and pulled the crazy metal contraption she'd rigged together back over her face.

Chase stood there, a million thoughts going through his head. There was no way Brenda was going to do anything but strikeout. How were they ever going to win if they couldn't advance the runner? It was a losing battle.

"Hey, first!" shouted Liz from the bench. "Don't forget, you have to shake our hand even if you're upset over losing."

That was it. He wasn't going to lose. And just like that, Brenda swung and missed. He looked down at the dirt, just wanting anything to happen to help him out. He would be the winning run. The run that everyone huddled around home plate and celebrated with. The one that made them all winners. The hero.

He was going to need assistance, and that assistance was standing in the batter's box, looking perplexed towards the pitcher. Chase yelled some words of encouragement, trying to get her thinking positively, but the glare she gave him didn't put him at peace. He needed to try something else.

"Hey Santa, I bet you feel real good about yourself, taking out the poor girl who's never played a day in her life. Real big man." Chase was hoping Santiago would acknowledge him but instead he just pitched the ball, sending it towards the plate to a loud:

"Ball!"

They still had a shot.

"Come on, Brenda. You've got this!" Chase didn't believe she had it. At all. And he wasn't so sure any positive reinforcement would help as she glared daggers through him from the batter's box. It didn't look like anything would have help at that point. Then it occurred to him.

Chase tried being as casual as possible as he stood on first base, trying to act completely aloof to the game around him. The moment Santa started his movement towards the plate, Chase was off to the races. He accelerated towards second, not even paying any attention to Santa's motion to the plate. He didn't care. He just needed to be safe. He could see Liz running to cover second, so he knew the throw was coming in hot. He slid towards the bag, just waiting to see Liz's glove go down and tag him out. Instead she stood up and Chase went to the bag with ease. Looking back towards home plate, he could see Tim, the catcher, with the ball still in his hand and looking perplexed. Apparently he hadn't been expecting a steal. It was only the second of the game.

"Dirty pool, you thief." Liz playfully hit him on the shoulder and moved back to her area between first and second. "Don't think that's gonna work on us twice."

"You think you know the answers and I just keep rewriting the questions." Chase knocked the dirt from his shoes against the base, cockily.

Liz rolled her eyes and got into position. There was still work to be done.

Chase, now standing on second, wasn't sure how much better off they really were. He may have been the tying run but he was still stranded on second without anyone at the plate capable of advancing him.

He stood there, expecting his great steal to have been for naught, with Brenda racking up the final out. And then it happened.

With a pop of the bat, she smacked the ball out into the sky. It just seemed to go, and go, and Chase couldn't believe she actually hit it, let alone got it out of the infield. His smile disappeared as he noticed it dropping and dropping, going right towards a lone right fielder. He was perfectly placed under the ball, his glove raised high, ready to catch the pop out with ease.

Chase wasn't sure if the sun got in his eyes or if a gust of wind picked up at that exact moment but whatever it was, the easy pop out in to right field, turned into the ball dropping just to the side of the outfielder. He couldn't believe it. By the time the right fielder recovered, Chase was almost to third base with no signs of stopping. He was going to make it home.

He rounded third so fast that he knew he wouldn't be able to retreat back, he was all-in for the run. Lucas had just scored from third and was waiting behind, yelling at Chase to run. He could see Tim at home plate, just waiting for the throw in from right. It didn't matter, the ball wasn't going to make it there in time. Chase had it in the bag. His feet dug into the field with every step, as he drew closer and closer to the win.

A few yards from the plate, Chase started to slide, wanting to avoid tackling Tim to the ground. It was then he saw a white flash and suddenly the catcher had the ball in his mitt. Just barely ducking under Tim's glove, Chase's foot skidded across the white of home plate. He'd made it. He was safe.

"You're out!" Carol exclaimed.

Chase couldn't believe it. How could that even be possible. He saw it with his own to eyes, the glove didn't even come close to him. Was Carol blind? How could she not see what was so clearly right in front of her. He could fill the anger filling him from his toes to his fingertips. He didn't often lose his cool. Often.

"Are you fucking kidding me right now? Maybc if you didn't have your head shoved so far up your own ass, you would've had no problem seeing that he missed me by a mile." He hadn't even realized how much he wanted the win until it was so quickly taken away from him. He had enough.

"Woah, that's enough of that." Another camper chimed in and immediately received a death stare from Chase.

"Shut the fuck up, Timmy."

"That's enough of that language out here," Carol asserted. "You need to treat this loss with a smile. It's what's good for you. Humility builds character."

"No what's good for me is you act like a partial adult and treat this game fairly."

Both benches had emptied and were stepping closer and closer to the festivities, circling them and looking on in glee.

"What are you *implying*, Mr. Watson?" The venom in Carol's voice was pungent.

"I'm not implying anything. You're a weak person that just gets her jollies off by treating others like crap. You don't care about any of us. You just want us to be like you. Well that's not going to ever happen because, spoiler alert, everybody here hates your fucking guts, Carol."

For a second, Chase wasn't sure if he was about to get slapped or not. Given that she was a woman, he doubted he'd be able to do much legally but if anything it'd be a pleasant surprise. A reminder that she actually had the backbone to do something. As he suspected, she just stared at him, shaking her head and exhaling loudly, making her annoyance as obvious as possible. He could see a vein in her neck repeatedly throbbing as her face just became redder and redder.

"I've had enough." Carol adjusted her breathing, trying to remain calm. "Enough of all the back talk and all the insubordination. You have just a couple days left to behave and you can't even do that. You know, my brother used to have an attitude problem like you. Daddy decided that he wasn't going to stand for it anymore. So every day he made my brother go out and walk along the property line. Six whole miles. He was to walk and think about the kind of person that he wanted to become. And you know what? He walked. And walked. Until he finally became the man that he was supposed to. And you know what that kind of man was?"

"A killer power walker?"

"A *respectable* man." Carol's implication was clear. "So that's how we're finally going to break through to you."

"You're going to make me walk your father's property?"

"Always the joker, eh Mr. Watson?"

Chase couldn't help it. The entire situation was ridiculous and her vendetta against him was increasingly obnoxious. It was easier for him to just to laugh it off.

"We'll see if you're still laughing after you've walked the Hooper path. All of it." She continued. "Six-point-two miles long. Almost the exact distance my brother walked. We'll see if it makes you into a better man too."

"You're kidding me right?" Chase couldn't believe that this was even up as being a punishment. Given that there was so little time left, he wasn't sure if that meant Carol's usual punishments just wouldn't suffice or what it entailed. At that point, he just wanted to get away from her as quickly as possible before he did something he regretted.

"Unlike you, Mr. Watson, I am not a jokester. Now you better get going." She looked down at her watch. "If you hurry, you'll be able to get it done before it gets dark."

And just like that he was off. He didn't want to argue with Carol any further and he certainly didn't want to be walking in the pitch black. Liz had told him about the Hooper path, and that it got pretty narrow at parts, so the idea of traversing it at night wasn't entirely appealing. Let alone the bugs that seemed to multiply come nightfall.

The trail ran along the back of the baseball diamond so Chase walked off towards it. By that time, most of the other campers had left, heading back to the mess hall for dinner. Liz was still hanging around the diamond and gave him a little wave before he disappeared into the forest. It took several minutes before Chase could get the image of her smiling at him out of his head.

It was nice to get away from everything that had been going on at the camp and Chase was soon enjoying his walk through the woods. What started as a punishment, turned into something that Chase enjoyed more and more as he ventured further into the forest. There was something calming about not being around a single soul. He took a moment to smell the air, taking in a mixture of grass and something freshly rank.

So much for a lovely walk.

Chase couldn't believe his luck. Sitting on the downed tree next to him was a giant brown bull frog. He fought back the reflex to gag, imagining it exploding into a million pieces right in front of his eyes. At least he'd avoided doing it around Liz. Instead it just sat there, staring at him. He couldn't hold it back any longer and he fell to his knees, vomiting onto the sticks and dirt beneath him. With a *ribbit*, the frog was off and out of sight.

He rolled back onto his bottom and shook his head, laughing a little. Only he would see a frog and immediately throw up; at least he'd avoided doing it around Liz. It took a couple moments but finally his stomach settled and he felt a little more relaxed.

Then something moved.

Chase wasn't sure what it was for a moment, thinking the wind must have blown something over or a squirrel was scurrying around nearby. He looked around, trying to see what critter may have caused it but all he saw was forest. The foliage was so thick that it would have been a miracle had Chase actually spotted the source quickly—or at all.

"Hello? Is anybody—" Chase stopped himself before he became a walking cliché. He knew better than to say such things. If it was someone playing a joke on him, they were no doubt having difficulty not laughing after he played right into their hands with his 'scared victim' routine. He wasn't going to give them the satisfaction.

The feeling crept up his spine—that feeling of being watched. Something drew his attention to the space around him, suspicious of everything. He was unsure as to why this feeling crept over him. There was no reason for anybody to be watching, at least none that Chase could surmise. Still that feeling lingered, and his uneasiness grew more and more.

He continued down the path, deciding that if anyone were out there, they were going to have to go even further to try and prank him. The trail on which he walked grew more and more narrow as he continued forward. Soon, the low hanging branches and small plants were brushing up against his sides, encompassing his body more and more.

"Ouch," exclaimed Chase, and a prickly bush he passed caught onto his shirt and cut through his arm. He stopped, examining the cut and wiping the blood that was starting to seep out. It was hardly more than a scratch but it still made Chase fume. Then he looked up and his stomach dropped.

Twenty feet further down the path, a masked man, clothed in black from head to toe, stood clutching a baseball bat. He stared down at Chase with a sideways look of curiosity.

Chase wasn't sure how long the man had been standing there, maybe the entire time given that his clothes that seemed to blend in with the forest. The mask looked almost made of bark, a dark green moss covering parts of it. There was no mouth slit but the two eye holes were just big enough to see the piercing eyes staring back.

"What the fuck is this about?" Chase wasn't in the mood to play games, especially with whatever camper thought this would be a funny joke.

Chase stood there, waiting for a response but receiving none. The only sound that emanated from the man was heavy breathing that sent shivers down Chase's spine. At least, Chase assumed it was a man, based on their stature. There wasn't really any way to tell one way or another without Chase getting closer. Still, he wasn't going to be punked by some idiot in a mask. Judging by the height, it was probably Santa. But on the off chance it was Liz, he wasn't going to be too rough. Though he had to give it to whoever it was, the mask was definitely not store bought.

"Okay fine, this is how you want to do it?" Chase started moving toward the man, who gripped the baseball bat tightly. "I am so not in the mood for this shit."

Just as Chase reached him, the masked man swung the aluminum with sudden viciousness, smacking Chase square in the chest and sending him crashing to the ground. He gasped for air, a sharp pain running down it chest. It was a pain unlike anything he'd ever experienced before. What was happening? How did this guy just expect to get away with this? This was well past any prank. Chase was in severe pain.

The man circled around him, standing just above Chase's head. He raised the bat high into the air and Chase's eyes went wide. It wasn't possible for him to explain it away further. This wasn't some joke; this man was meaning to take his life. He wasn't just a masked camper playing a prank.

He was a killer!

The killer brought the bat down towards the boy's head but Chase dodged to the side, the aluminum thudding in the dirt next to him. Chase kicked at him, trying to scurry backwards. It was at least three miles in the opposite direction and he needed to get away before he could do serious damage.

But before he knew it, the killer was on top of him, pushing their knee into his chest, making it hard for Chase to do anything but focus on breathing. As he gasped for air, they reached behind their back, and Chase knew what they were reaching for before he even saw it. A tear rolled down his cheek as the masked man brandished a hunting knife.

He could see his own reflection in it. The little boy staring back at him, too scared to even move. Just hoping for the best.

The killer placed the knife on his knee, twirling it back and forth, pressing harder and harder. Blood dripped out and down their pant leg, onto Chase's chest. Still, their gaze on Chase remained un-wavering, soulless eyes staring down at him. They were just toying with him. How calm they were. They knew they had him dead to rights.

But Chase refused to go down without a fight.

The masked man must have seen this renewed confidence because he immediately raised the knife up high and plummeted it downward. Chase shifted over and the knife ran against his hip and buried deep into the dirt next to him. He kicked the would-be killer off him and darted off down the path. His hip was throbbing with such veracity that he tried biting down on his tongue to focus the pain elsewhere but it hadn't really worked.

He thought he could hear shuffling in the woods behind him but he didn't want to turn around. All he could visualize was the killer throwing a knife at that exact moment and striking him between the eyes. The likelihood was slim but the scenario played over and over in his head to the point he avoided checking on anything behind him, no matter what the noise.

It had been ages since Chase had jogged long term and he was starting to feel the effects almost immediately. He had always considered himself more of a sprinter—a fact that he never regretted until that very moment. He wished for nothing more than better lungs and hamstrings.

Stupid genetics.

The minutes that passed felt like hours and he found his legs failing on him during the final stretch. He was moving slow enough that the mosquito's that patrolled the woods had enough time to get a significant feast before flying off into the night. But the sounds behind him appeared to die off. In the distance he saw the lights of the camp and felt a little relief. Their soft glow made them like a beacon; light at the end of the tunnel. It was dinner time and the mess hall was sure to be full.

Perfect.

He broke through the front door of the mess hall and almost ran over a pair of younger campers, still in line for dinner. He stumbled a bit, barely able to catch his breath as he looked around at the room full of campers. They stared at him, perplexed. He could only imagine what they were thinking, especially after he finally spoke.

"Someone just tried to kill me."

He let the words rest in the air for a moment and allow everyone to really take in what he had just said. They were sure to be worried. It was a situation unlike anything they had ever experienced. Chase was having a hard enough time believing it himself. But the concern he was expecting to come across their faces never did. Instead they shook their heads and whispered to one another.

"Jesus, he's really just starved for attention."

"Some people really don't get it."

"He must be an only child."

Chase couldn't believe it. Where was the empathy? He had almost just been murdered. If the killer had gotten his way then Chase's brain was going to be splattered all over the woods. Why didn't they understand how serious this was?

"Come on, Chase, let's go—" Louie tried to settle Chase down but he just pushed him off, eyes darting around. Crazy.

"What don't you people understand?" he fumed. "Some sick fuck just tried to murder me! They tried to end my life! Quit looking at me like I'm some kind of fucking idiot and react like normal human beings, you terrible pieces of shit."

He could tell by the looks in their eyes that no one believed him. They were looking at him like he was crazy or desperate for attention. Couldn't they tell by the look on his face? The cut on his hip? The massive lump forming on his chest? Did they really think that someone would just make a story like that up? How could they so quickly dismiss him?

If there was anyone that was going to believe her, it'd be Liz. He knew he could count on her. But instead she just stared at him blankly, like she would a stranger.

"I'm not lying. I don't understand why you people aren't doing anything." His voice squeaked and cracked, almost on the verge of loss.

"Mr. Watson, sit down." Carol's voice came from the doors behind him but Chase chose to ignore it.

"Liz, please believe me. You have to believe me!" Chase pleaded and pleaded but everyone still looked at him like he was nuts. Why would they not just listen?

"I've had enough, Mr. Watson." Carol pushed her way towards Chase. "You have been nothing but trouble since day one and, had I been in control sooner, you wouldn't have made it past the first week. I'm sick of how terribly you treat me and everyone else trying to keep the camp in order. You are a pox on society and I will no longer accept any of your disreputable behavior. You're gone."

Chase wasn't entirely sure what she meant by that last part, given that there was so little time left. Carol told Louie to keep watch while she disappeared into the front office.

It only took two hours for his Aunt Jeannie to arrive at the camp. She looked anything but happy.

Chapter 18
Marion

CAMP WATANKA IS CLOSING ITS DOORS.

The words brought such relief to Marion that she wasn't entirely sure if it was really happening. It had to be some kind of joke. But no, Al's will made it as clear as day: once he passed, the camp was to be donated to the local parks and recreation program. He had always made it seem like the camp would always be there, even after his passing, but clearly he had other plans.

Marion still couldn't fully process that Al was gone. While he was never the poster boy for great health, she never imagined him having a heart attack at such a relatively young age. She told herself that it must have been his recent relapse that finally took his heart to the brink, but she had difficulty believing it.

Part of her thought that Carol may have poisoned him, but that notion was nixed upon hearing the toxicology reports. No, Al had passed on and there was nothing she could do about it.

After being in the hospital for nearly ten days, Marion was itching to return to Watanka. She had wanted to come back earlier but her nurse said it would have been a waste of time since she was still needed for checkups on her leg. Had it been a simple break, it wouldn't have been a big issue but given that the bone had protruded from the skin, she had needed surgery. This took up more time than she'd have liked, knowing the camp was going to be in desperate need of her after Carol's reign of terror. By the time the doctors let her leave the hospital, Watanka was in its final days.

Her suspicions were realized when she stepped out of Louie's baby blue Buick and saw half of the camp had been painted, with every camper looking completely exhausted. During the car ride Louie had caught her up on everything Carol was doing to transform the camp into her own creation. There was already so much that had to be dealt with, having to break the news to Carol about Watanka closing was likely going to be the most volatile. The final few days were sure to be the toughest.

On top of all the chaos, it was getting to be the hottest part of the summer, making it hard not to sweat through every piece of clothing she put on. Then there was the cast. The dirt and sweat just made it itch even more, getting to the point where it would take up blocks of her mind. The cast had become more of a nuisance than she'd ever imagined. It was her first broken bone and she hadn't known it was even possible to want to itch something so much. It was all she wanted yet she was never able to, especially after an unfortunate pen accident where Diane had to help her get it out.

Everyone else was getting ready for a fun night and there sat Marion, just wanting it to all be over so she could go home. A night that was usually spent getting drunk around the campfire with the other counselors had turned into a lonely getaway in her cabin, hoping that Carol didn't barge in and interrupt her while she finished up *10 Little Indians*. That's what her night has been reduced to: sitting down and reading a book some of her campers had been assigned for summer reading.

I really need a drink, she thought for a second but knew better.

The doctors had very unfortunately advised against her drinking any kind of alcohol after they'd prescribed her a nifty set of pain meds. As much as she wanted to go against those orders, if only just for a night, she had a prior experience with alcohol and pain meds that made that desire shrink to nothing. Her time for crazy drugged up nights were long past. No, it would just be a night in for her while the rest of the camp had a great time.

Diane had stopped by for a couple minutes before she departed with the toddlers for the night. She seemed like she was doing better but it was hard to get past her complaints about Carol. But at that point, there was nothing Marion could do but sit and listen to the complaints, act like she had even the slightest say in what would happen going forth, and hopefully give them reassurance. Watanka was closing up for its final summer and getting into a power struggle with Carol felt malicious, given her most recent state.

The news of the camp's closing was something that Carol took very harshly, saying how she was going to take it over and that she'd find the money somewhere. Marion didn't care to argue with her, the camp was simply never going to be the same again. Even if Carol could somehow keep the camp afloat, she'd be the only returning member of the staff (minus Marge, who had no allegiance either way and just enjoyed cooking food) and she would need to report to the Reynold's County Parks and Recreation Department. Marion hadn't seen Carol all day and it worried her a little. She was likely off somewhere on the phone with a bank, trying to get whatever loan she could to take the camp over for herself.

Go right ahead, Carol. Let this place eat you alive.

By the time Diane left Marion's cabin, she could hear the campers outside going to the spot across the lake that would be home base for their party. Every camper would leave, whether it was across the lake or off with Diane, leaving an empty camp by sunset. After spending a week and a half in an isolated hospital room, Marion wasn't looking forward to the silence.

She heard rumbling outside her cabin, and immediately tensed up. Although she had been gone all day, she wasn't ready for Carol to be back, hoping for at least a couple more hours without an appearance. A group passed by the window and Marion hoped that was it but then the door of her cabin wiggled and before she knew it, it was opening.

"How's my favorite cripple doing?" Liz peeked her head around the door with a big smile on her face.

"Oh you know, just seeing what else I can break for excitement." Marion breathed a sigh of relief and propped herself on her bed. Liz walked over and sat on the mattress next to her, fiddling with the teddy bear on top of it.

"Yeah, I almost didn't stop by 'cause I figured you would just be so ridiculously busy with all the stuff you can do around here." Liz practically waited for the crickets to start chirping, shooting Marion a look that said as much.

"You know, some people would consider it cruel and unusual punishment to be treating a cripple so poorly."

"Yeah, but you've only been one for like a week, so the rest of your life outweighs it. I think that's how it works."

"Really? I must have missed that day of life."

"Yeah, I'm pretty sure that's definitely a rule somewhere. I think I learned it in Economics 101."

"Do you even know what economics are?" Marion questioned.

"Of course. It's math and stuff," Liz guessed.

Marion debated for a moment whether or not to continue the joke but she really just wanted to get to what she knew Liz was busy thinking about.

"So are you planning on getting ahold of Chase when all this is said and done?"

"Well we exchanged information but I was hoping to progress things along a little bit further. You know, tonight. But, of course, who else would get kicked out of camp right before Final Bash if not for the guy I'm into."

"Woah, woah, woah. Are you saying what I think you're saying?" Marion wasn't sure if she was going to have to go into "big sister mode."

"Wait, what do you think I'm saying?"

"Uh, this sounds like a sex talk."

"What? No!" Liz denied vehemently. "We haven't done anything. And I mean, *anything.* No dry grinds. No snuggles in the grass. Nothing. It's been completely innocent."

"Oh, I guess I thought you two were—"

"No, we kind of are." Liz thought it over for a moment. "I mean, we talk a lot and we're pretty much always around each other during group stuff. And I mean, I'm into him. I think he's into me. I just don't really know what that means. It's not exactly something that's happening every day for me, you know?"

"Wait, so you're really getting on with this guy and you haven't done anything? Props, girl. I can't say my heavily hormoned self would have done the same thing at your age—then again, I've gone out with guys where we haven't done anything outside of kiss. So maybe that isn't true. Though I'm not entirely sure if those ones weren't gay. . . so if this isn't the guy, don't sweat it."

"And if he *is* the guy?"

"Don't worry, he'll be back in your life if it's meant to be."

The words left Marion's mouth but she wasn't so sure if she even believed them herself. If this summer had proven anything it was that anything could happen at any time and that life was random. It did not matter how much preparation occurred, everything could come crashing down out of nowhere.

Still, she didn't want to break Liz's bubble. She already had a tough enough life.

"You seem to be really deep in thought," said Liz, practically reading her mind.

"Oh you know, just thinking of how riveting my night is going to be."

"Why don't you go out? I know Louie was looking for people to do absolutely anything. I think Nancy had to run him off so that he didn't follow them across the lake. I love Louie but dammit if he's not an uber-creep sometimes."

"As much fun as getting hit on by Louie all night sounds like, I'm thinking not. In fact, I think I'll be avoiding any and all forms of alcohol this evening."

"That makes one of us."

"Yeah? What do you have on the agenda?" Marion asked, knowing full well that Final Bash was usually the most fun night of the summer. "I hope Carol hasn't taken away every good part of this place."

"You know, surprisingly she's been really cool about it. Gave us all a big speech about responsibility and how she really hopes that we behave but that it was up to us to decide if we were going to be acting like mature and responsible adults. She was going to be spending time in her cabin and not interfering. So we were to go about our business as any adult would. Whatever that means. I assume you had a hand in it?"

"Actually no, that was all her, surprisingly. Old reliable Carol turned into shockingly understandable Carol. I think she may be a little too distracted with the thought of the final days of Watanka. Good on her for actually caring about it, although I'm sure she has some insane reasoning with herself for doing it."

"I was actually a little worried she'd be in here when I came by."

Marion laughed, wondering how much of the camp's decisions were based on where Carol happened to be. "I can't say I've seen her around here. Maybe she meant the office. I'm pretty sure she spends more time in there anyway. I wouldn't be surprised if she just considered it her cabin now."

"God knows with her." Liz rolled her eyes. "I don't know how anyone can deal with her bullshit. It's beyond exhausting. At least you got a little bit of a break from her—though through fucked up means—but still."

"That's one way of looking at it." Marion had already felt bad enough about what the camp had become. "I just wish this summer would end. It just keeps going and going and just when I think it can't get any worse, something else pops up. If I have to deal with one more fucked up thing happening, I may just snap."

She looked over at Liz, who had a look of worry on her face. Marion knew she probably sounded bitter but at this point it didn't matter. She just needed to get through the night.

"You know, maybe all of this happened for a reason."

"Oh yeah? Since when are you an optimist?" Marion wondered.

"You've always been saying how this place has always just been a safety net. Something familiar that was fun and easy. Well guess what, it's not fun and easy anymore. Sure, it's not like it had the best return rate but we still got people. Now even the counselors don't want to come back. And you don't either. Which is exactly what you wanted. Then Al straight up croaks and gives away the camp in his will? Come on, if that's not the universe telling you to get away from this place before it kills you, then I don't know what is. You wanted a reason to move on. Well guess what, I think this summer has given you just about a million reasons to."

Liz was right. This was all Marion had wanted for so long. To be able to finally be done with it all. To finally move on with her life. Her prior excuses of being there for Al and that he'd be lost without her guidance—those were gone. He was gone. The camp was gone. There were no more excuses.

"It's gonna be really weird not coming back next year."

"You're telling me," Liz sighed. "Though, can't say I'm mad that my decision was made for me. Makes things easier knowing that they couldn't have been any different."

"It took me about a week to stop thinking about that with my leg. Day after day there'd be some kind of bullshit scenario in my head that would tell me exactly what I did wrong. How exactly everything happened. How the cable could have possibly been worn enough to break. There were so many different things that would go through my head that I didn't sleep the first two nights. And to this day what do I know? Absolutely nothing. They don't know what happened. They don't know how on earth the rope snapped. And I'm just left wondering."

"Do you think it was Carol?"

The thought had crossed Marion's mind before but Carol was far from being a violent person, even refusing to kill any bugs that made their way in the cabin. She wasn't the devious type.

"Definitely not. As much as we hate her, she cried for two nights when Al had to kill that Fox that kept killing all those bunnies and leaving them on the volleyball courts. I don't think she has a violent bone in her body."

"Yeah, says you. You didn't see how she acted with Chase the other day. Bitch was vicious."

"So I've heard. . ." Though what she heard wasn't exactly positive regarding Chase either. It sounded like an immature little freak out on both sides and she had expected better from both of them. Marion didn't dare say any of this to Liz, fearing she wouldn't take kindly to any chastising of her new guy friend.

"It was all ridiculous," reasoned Liz. "Sure, Chase was raving a little bit but there was no reason for her to kick him out."

"Do you believe him?"

"That someone tried to kill him? I wish I could laugh it off but I don't know. Why would he make it up? It could have just been somebody pulling some kind of twisted prank, but if that were the case then they've been keeping their mouth tight about it."

"I'm sure that's all it was." Marion hoped it was true. "I wouldn't stress too much about it. Besides, that's not what today is all about. Go enjoy your night. Go have the last hurrah that you deserve."

Liz stood up, looking like she wanted nothing more than to stay. Marion couldn't do that to her though. She needed to go off and have fun.

"Well it looks like about that time. I'll probably be back around later once I try and socialize a little bit. Who knows, maybe I'll be back with a little smokey-smoke to end our last night at Watanka on the right note."

"Oh Lizzy, a woman after my own heart," Marion swooned.

"If only we were gay."

"You're not? Reality shattered."

They hugged and then Liz was off to have "one last hurrah" with the campers. Marion would surely just sit and stew the rest of the night, wanting to be anywhere but there. At least, that's how she assumed it would go. She sat for a moment, deciding whether or not to dive back into her book or to just go asleep. Fireworks off in the distance signaled her getting to sleep would have proved difficult. Instead she just laid there, staring up at the wooden ceiling, eyes scanning along every grain.

Now that the decision was made, Marion wasn't sure if she was ready to leave Watanka. As much difficulty as she'd had with it, it was always such a comforting spot. No matter what happened in her life it was something she could turn to. Those late night chats with Diane. The almost motherly dynamic she had with Al, someone thirty years her senior. The bonding time with Liz. Sure, she would likely see Liz again and maybe exchange texts with Diane but Al was gone. There was no bringing him back. And now that the camp was going too. What was she going to do?

She was fast asleep within minutes.

"Marion!"

Marion awoke abruptly, hitting her elbow on the nightstand next to her and sitting fully upright in her bed. It had since become nighttime and the room was completely dark. She reached over and turned the light on, expecting to see Carol fumbling around the room. Instead the cabin was completely empty. Maybe she had just imagined someone saying her name?

She rested her head back down on her pillow and tried getting back to sleep. It was the only way she was going to get through the night. But instead of drift so easily into dream world as she previously had, all of her focus went to her broken leg. Underneath the plaster and clothe, she could feel the skin begin to nag as an itch rose to the surface. She needed something to get down between the flesh and the cloth. She looked around and spotted a fly swatter, which she could easily use the handle to scratch with. The only problem was getting over there.

While moving around hadn't been an issue, her last few hours of sleep had made her body stiff and unwilling to stand. She pushed through and got to her feet, putting most of her weight on her healthy leg. Using the wall as support, she hopped across the cabin to the fly swatter. Wondering for a moment whether or not it would relieve anything at all, something in her peripheral vision moved.

She looked over and a small cupboard in the corner swayed, partway open. Marion would have thought she was just seeing things had it not been for the squeak of the hinge as it opened slightly. It didn't make her feel any better about it randomly opening, but quickly dismissed it as the wind. Still, she couldn't help but feel uneasy at the sight. So she stood up and hobbled over to it, quickly snapping it shut.

Hopping back towards her bed, she almost reached it when the cupboard behind her snapped back open.

"God fucking dammit!" She had, had enough. The voices, the weird noises, the cupboards that were deciding they didn't want to close. Whoever was messing with her, Marion was done with it all. The cupboard was just large enough for someone to fit in, and with the extra blankets Carol usually kept in there, there wasn't anything preventing it. Marion knew that someone had to be in there. They were responsible for everything weird. And it was going to stop now. Whoever it was, they were in that cabinet, and she was going to find out.

She walked over to the cupboard, ignoring the pain in her leg as she accidentally put a little too much weight on the wrong leg, and thrust it open, expecting to see whoever was hiding away. Instead her legs gave out from under her and she collapsed to the ground. It took everything in her not to vomit.

Carol's body, bloodied up beyond belief, sat awkwardly contorted inside the cupboard, her lifeless eyes staring forward.

All Marion could do was scream.

Chapter 19
Ralph

Hours earlier. . .

A SCREAM ECHOED OUT THROUGH THE DARKNESS. Followed by another. The scream was so loud and piercing, it was hard to imagine anyone within a five-mile radius being unable to hear it. Ralph couldn't blame them either; he'd be screaming too if he were in their shoes as it was truly a sight to behold: Steven Allerjo was running around naked, trying to get whatever poor lass was in his field of vision to go skinny dipping with him. His approach of sneaking up on girls while completely nude was not proving effective. Apparently Steven had gotten into the vodka a little early.

What had Ralph gotten himself into? Outside of the naked guy running around, he'd just walked past two couples deep into what looked to be an all-night make out session—sure to progress into something else at any moment—something Ralph wasn't wanting to be around for. Off near the lake two people were being held upside down, with a beer funnel being filled to the brim by a yelling drunkard. It was absolutely chaotic.

Ralph had to give it to the campers though, this was a nice little spot they had notched out for themselves on the opposite side of the lake. The ground had been worn and the grass already stamped down, various tents set up along the eastern edge next to the forest. They really had quite the set up. And with the amount of alcohol they had around, Ralph couldn't quite figure out how they got away with it.

Looking around, it appeared as if every camper except the "toddlers" had decided to take part. Sally appeared through the crowd and Ralph couldn't believe his eyes. She was dressed in a beautiful blue sun dress. She smiled, showing off her red lipstick that contrasted her white teeth.

Jesus fucking Christ.

"You look beautiful. I like the dress." The words had come out unexpectedly enough, even taking Ralph by surprise. It took him several seconds to realize it had even happened, mostly being cued by the look of shock on Sally's face. At least he hadn't said what he was actually thinking, Ralph assured himself. Sally must not have been expecting such a compliment, because she turned awkwardly away from him.

Dammit you shouldn't have said anything, you stupid moron. This is such a bad decision. Why did you even think that would ever possibly be a good idea?

"Well aren't you a charmer. Thank you." She turned back around and her cheeks had turned bright red. Maybe it wasn't such a bad idea. He still felt like an idiot.

"So I guess this is it then, aye?" Ralph looked around at the drunken party around him, expecting something a little different.

"This is it?" Liz had been talking to Alice in a group behind them and had just noticed Ralph's arrival. "Come on. You have to admit, this is pretty impressive."

"I guess I just don't understand how this is even possible."

"Okay, well Al used to do this thing where he took the counselors and one lucky camper out at the end of the year for some big dinner. The other campers would remain behind and play games with one unlucky counselor. Usually the counselor that was left behind was so annoyed that they didn't care what the campers were up to, so the lack of supervision turned the games into those of the drunken variety. By the time Al stopped taking the counselors out, the tradition was cemented. Counselors liked having the last night to themselves and Al liked being able to punish people throughout the summer by taking it away. It was pretty much a win-win outside of the obvious legal repercussions if it were to get out. But Al took the 'ignorance is bliss' approach so we kept having it."

"It just all seems a little surreal. I'm suddenly understanding why everyone made such a big deal out of this thing." Although Ralph wasn't so sure if it wasn't the prospect of copious amounts of alcohol that intrigued most of the other campers. He just enjoyed the excitement of it all. He'd never been a big drinker, making that the furthest thing from his mind. Still, he only had only response when Sally walked up with some of the "special punch."

"Of course." Ralph almost gagged the moment the drink touched his tongue. It burned and was almost impossible for him to get down. This wasn't just punch. He struggled for a moment, trying to hide it on his face by looking away, eventually downing it in one big gulp.

A majority of the drink remained in the cup.

"*Eck!* Does this have alcohol in it?" Ralph continued to struggle through it.

"Oh damn, did you not want to drink? I'm sorry, I just assumed. . ."

"Someone just popped their vvvodka chcrrrrry," slurred Nancy as she stumbled past them, bottle of hard iced tea in hand.

"Yeah, I guess I'm not much of a drinker." Ralph was uncomfortable and wanted the subject to change but she was right back to it.

"Why don't you drink?" Nancy asked the question while simultaneously downing her tea.

"Why does it matter?" Sally interjected.

"It doesn't, I was juss a-asking. Usually someone decides that they aren't gonna drink and has a reason or somethun."

"That or you're just an uppity prick who thinks you're better than us." Alice, much more sober than her sister, joined in on the fun.

The reasons kept going through his head but he didn't want to acknowledge any of them. Why did they want to know anyway? Why couldn't it just be something they accepted? He supposed that was asking too much from a bunch of teenagers though. Particularly a bunch that were drinking more than their weight in alcohol.

"Maybe he doesn't like it because it's illegal," Sally answered for him. While she didn't know the actual reason, Ralph just couldn't find the words to support himself.

"Yeah, well I'm pretty sure I've seen him do illegal things this summer, including a pretty gnarly B and E."

"That doesn't mean—" Sally started but was swiftly interrupted.

"Oh shut up, Sally. Why doesn't he speak for himself?" Alice turned and addressed only Ralph. "Hello? Can you hear me?"

"I don't understand why it's such a fascination for you." Now even Santa was chiming in, trying to play mediator for a bunch of crazy people. He seemed to be the only one that was just casually sipping his beer.

"It's a fascination with me because the ones that don't drink are the ones that snitch. So is that what it is, Mr. Ralphie? Are you a snitcher? Planning on just going out and getting us all busted?" Alice shook her drink at him with the accusation. He finally had enough.

"Look, I don't drink because I've been around it enough. Simple as that. If you don't like that then I guess you can go fuck yourself. If you can even remember this conversation tomorrow." Ralph's sudden outburst stunned those surrounding the table into complete silence. Alice searched her head for all the expletives at her disposal and seemed ready to flow forth with them at any second, as her face contorted in anger.

"I feel like it's a little crowded here. Wanna head out?" asked Sally, before Alice could begin.

Head out? Where would we head to? Anywhere was sure to be better than that exact place next to the fire, which was becoming increasingly uncomfortable with every passing second.

"Umm yeah, sure," Ralph answered, his voice squeaked from either nerves or puberty.

Wanting to get away from the party as fast as possible, Sally and Ralph walked off down the path that headed back towards the cabins. The woods were a welcome serenity from the out of control party behind them. Ralph was sure he could hear Alice swearing up a storm, but by the time she had started her tirade, they were already long gone.

"Sorry about that," Sally started. "Those guys can be really immature."

"You're tellin' me. I just wish I had my own female bodyguard so that I could have her attack people like that." Ralph just wanted to move past the situation with some humor and Sally graciously accepted.

"Female bodyguard?"

"Well, duh, I don't want some kind of lawsuit. Can't be beating up girls, now can I?"

"Oh yeah? You think you can beat me up?" Sally raised her fists playfully, getting into a fighting stance.

"Don't even try me. I will whoop your ass straight back to Boston, little girl."

"Them's fighting words." Sally charged at him and Ralph grabbed her by the arms, stopping her from knocking him over. He swung her around and held her close to him to prevent her from swinging.

"Are you gonna calm down or am I gonna have to go all Bruce Lee on you?"

"Psh, you wish. I am the ultimate escape artist. Watch this." With a grunt, Sally tried contorting around, to get out of Ralph's grip and be free, but she failed miserably, just getting more wrapped up in his arms.

"Your escaping doesn't really seem to be going so well there, Miss O'Neill. Want to give up?"

"Never!" she proclaimed, wriggling around in his arms, leaning down trying to get any leverage on him. He just followed her motions and kept her close to him. She had no chance of escaping.

"Fine, you win," she sighed.

"Hurrah!" exclaimed Ralph, releasing her and raising his hands high in celebration. She turned around, remaining almost as close as when he held her, a smile adoring her face. Her lips looked so soft. And those eyes. So big and blue. It was hard not to get completely lost in them.

This was finally the moment. He had imagined it all summer. They both leaned in, their eyes closed and each anticipated the magic that was sure to follow. The moment could not have been more perfect.

"I have a girlfriend."

Ralph couldn't believe it. He opened his eyes to make sure he wasn't just imagining it but the look on Sally's face said it all: her eyes filling with tears as her face grew redder and redder. It had been eating at him for a month and he couldn't take it anymore. Ralph's stomach had dropped completely, anticipating the worst.

And the worst was what he received as Sally slapped him across the face as hard as she could. He couldn't blame her.

"You fucking asshole!"

Sally turned away from Ralph and walked off down the path, back towards the camp, away from the party. Ralph stood there, debating with himself whether he should chase after her, but before he knew it, she was down the path and out of sight.

She's not going to want to be near you. You completely blew it. She was going to find out eventually. At least you didn't take advantage of her. Or maybe you did. God dammit, Ralph. You have to do something.

Why had he decided to grow a conscience right then? Was there really any reason to be honest with her at that very moment? He could have done it at any time. Or, better yet, he could have not said anything to her at all. It wasn't like she was going to find out some way anyhow. They were going to be gone from the camp in the morning and they lived hours away from each other. It wasn't going to go any further. So why did he have to go blabbing and ruin it all? Why couldn't he have just let himself have that one kiss first?

Stupid conscience.

Ralph stared off into the woods, down at the path from which she disappeared. He kept hoping she'd come back and just let him explain. That's all that she needed to do, just sit and listen. Surely he could explain everything and it would all be okay. But what if it wasn't? What if that was the last they spoke? What if she just ignored him for the next 24 hours and was out of his life forever? He needed to do something before the moment was gone forever.

Ralph sprinted off down the path, deciding he needed to catch up with her. To explain it to her. He knew she would be mad but could he really blame her? For all she thought, he had been leading her on all summer when that couldn't have been further from the truth. He tried to tell her so many times, and had told himself over and over that he was going to break up with Ashley. She didn't mean anything to him. He just needed to make sure Sally knew that. If she just knew that, then everything would work out.

After a few minutes, he spotted something off in the distance. He wasn't sure if it was her at first but then he recognized the blue sun dress peeking through the night. She was laying down by some tree, likely crying her eyes out. But when he drew closer, he heard no sobbing. Maybe she was drunker than he thought she was? Why else would she have passed out in the woods? He continued towards her.

"I know you hate me right now but listen, I can explain." Ralph made it up the path and closed in on Sally. She finally came within full view and his mouth dropped in horror.

Sally was completely drenched in blood, an axe buried deep into her chest. She hadn't been dead for long, the blooding still dripping down her open chesty cavity.

Ralph stumbled backwards, holding his hand to his face and trying his best not vomit. He couldn't take his eyes off of her. What had been such a beautiful sight only moments prior was now the most terrifying thing he'd ever laid eyes on. The pain in her eyes had spread across every muscle in her cheeks.

Tears rolled down Ralph's face as he dropped to his knees and buried his face in the grass, his sobs barely muffled.

Who could possibly do this? The wind blew against his face and a shiver went down his spine. All he could feel besides the intense wind were the goosebumps creeping up along his skin. He needed to run. To get out of there as fast as he could. Sally's killer couldn't be far. He needed to get help. Anything.

As fast as his feet would take him, he started off down the path, trying to stop from hyperventilating as he made it through the forest, the night air biting at his lungs. All he needed to do was make it to the cabins. Then he could get Carol and she would call the cops. This would all be over and the sick bastard that killed Sally would pay. Ralph knew it.

Ralph burst from the forest and could hardly recognize his surroundings, his eyes had become so teared up. He wiped them and looked around, making out the big red bullseye spray painted on a bale of hay. He was on the archery range. He turned and looked towards the main office cabin, its light still on.

Before Ralph could even shout for help, he heard a *thwip*, followed by a sharp pain in his leg. He looked down and saw an arrow protruding from his calf. Adrenaline had kicked in and he could hardly feel his lower body, but that changed as another arrow zipped across the field and landed in his thigh, taking him to the ground. He screamed in pain and grabbed desperately at his leg.

He narrowly avoided another arrow as he crawled towards a bale of hay, trying to take refuge behind it. Whoever was shooting at him had taken up at the head of the archery range and were unlikely to run out of arrows any time soon. Ralph looked down at his leg and grabbed it tightly, trying to stop the blood from pouring out. He knew he needed to take it out but he wasn't sure how long he had till the archer had another shot on him. He leaned his head against the hay, his eyes darting from side to side, trying to get a view of Sally's killer.

Thwip!

The arrow entered through the hay bale and buried itself into the back of Ralph's head. Nearly losing consciousness, he fell to his knees, pulling himself from the arrow and unleashing a geyser of blood on the hay behind him. The only thought that went through his head was how weird it looked, seeing the blood shooting out like that. His blood. It gushed and gushed, like an oil drum being pierced by a pick-axe.

Barely conscious, he felt the warmth of his own blood pouring down his back like a shower. He could taste it in the air. *Pennies*, he thought as he dabbed at his wound with a finger. Another arrow shot out from the darkness hitting him in the back and collapsing him to the ground. He crawled to the bale, pushing his shoulders up against the hay to try and stop the bleeding, but he knew it was already too late. He'd seen enough movies to know what was next.

He looked up, trying to see his assailant but all he saw was a black shape moving towards him. It was hardly distinguishable from the night that shrouded it. Even by the time it was standing right next to him, Ralph could hardly identify a single feature, his vision blurring with every passing second.

With several blinks, he shook his head, trying to make out what stood before him. This time he could see it: the mossy black mask covered up everything but the eyes. Those terrifying white eyes. The figure raised something up, but at that point it was too much effort for Ralph to even look. All he could think of was how it could ever come to the point where he'd completely given up. He always imagined himself being such a fighter. But this was the time. It was over and he knew it. He couldn't stop it, even if he tried.

Ralph looked up one last time, just to see the final arrow unsheathe from the bow and pierce into his neck. His last thought was of Sally and how he hoped it was quick for her.

Chapter 20
Louie

LOUIE WAS DESPERATE for any form of connection and every passing hour he felt like he was getting further and further from achieving that goal. Every attempt to try and change his luck resulted in further embarrassment and made his night a total blur. He had even gone as far as to have Barry hang out and chit-chat for a bit. It didn't last long after an argument concerning Diane prompted Barry to quickly leave. He said he was going to be hanging out in his cabin but Louie hadn't seen him go into it. Instead he headed off down the road. He figured Barry didn't know anyone was looking, the way he'd crept off.

Probably off meeting with some girl. Lucky bastard.

Then Louie tried tagging along with Diane and helping her with the younger kids, but she wasn't having it.

"I'm sorry Louie, I really can't. Those kids are already enough to deal with and yes, I know you think it'll help, but it'll just be a pissing contest between the boys then. They're always trying to impress the guys. It's the same reason I told Barry he couldn't come. Sorry, Louie."

He wasn't sure if he believed her or not. Seemed more like she didn't want Louie around. Or perhaps that's where Barry was heading off to. It's not like it would have been the first time either of them had lied to him. Maybe he was just being paranoid.

Even the party going on across the lake, that he had supplied the alcohol for, was off limits. Buying for them was one thing, but he didn't need to get busted drinking with them. He could only imagine what Marion would have said if she found out. That would be worse than any citation the cops would give him. But he knew deep down that Alice wouldn't say anything. She may have been a little shit sometimes, but she kept her word.

So instead Louie just sat at the campfire, staring across the lake at the raging party going on a mere half-mile away. It wasn't exactly how he had imagined his night going.

The last few Final Bash's had resulted in some pretty epic bonding moments between Louie and some of the other counselors. One time Marion had gotten so drunk that she was slurring every syllable and Diane decided to put on a performance from her favorite Shakespeare play, *Romeo and Juliet*. One of the former counselors, Dan, taught Louie how properly shotgun a beer without spilling a single drop. Sure, most of the times were drunken but they were still great.

Louie missed those times. The camp just didn't feel the same anymore. Keith leaving abruptly and Al's death put a sour taste in his mouth. Even with Al's dislike towards him, it was clear just how big of a gap his absence left. He'd gladly welcome being talked down to if it meant Al would be back, and things could get back to how it was. But it would never happen. The camp was going down the drain and now everything was over. He was in the final days of being a counselor there.

Oh how quickly things have changed.

He wondered what would happen to the space that the former camp sat on. Al's will stipulated it was to be given to the "Parks and Rec Department of Reynolds" but he highly doubted they'd do anything with it. They hardly had enough people in the town to keep it operating, much less deal with a large patch of property 10 miles outside of their city limits. He also doubted that Al really thought it through when placing it in his will. If only he'd dictated that the land would go to Louie instead.

Ha. Like that would have ever happened.

Al's disdain towards Louie was quite obvious but it was still fun for him to think about what he'd do if he had the place to himself. He'd definitely clearly a nice spot in the woods for a marijuana farm and sell to the local high school kids. That would have been enough to pay the property taxes. The rest of the time he'd just lounge by the lake and enjoy the weather. Even with that ridiculous dream, he still felt a certain element was missing.

Louie kept staring at the bonfire, the light flickering across the lake and the teenagers running around in its wake. He could practically taste the alcohol they were sure to be drinking. And he wanted some. Even if it was just cheap vodka that was sure to give him a terrible hangover the next morning, he just needed to ingest some form of alcohol to make his night better.

Louie sat with his thoughts for a moment, debating whether they'd even have alcohol left over at the fires. He hadn't purchased very much for them and there were some pretty big guys over there. He bet Santa could drink a whole case himself. He also wondered whether Carol would pop out of her cabin and put a stop to everything at a moments notice. But stare as he did, she never came out. No matter how many times he expected her to emerge from the office and rule with an iron fist, the office remained undisturbed. But her light remained off. If she did care at all, she was too busy sleeping for it to have any effect. She wasn't going to do anything. What could she do anyway? Her time with authority was just about up.

"Screw it."

He stumbled out past the showers and looked at the campfire in the distance. He heard the music and saw some shadows, all seeming like a bunch of fun. That's what he wanted. That's what he needed. He deserved it. In fact, he deserved a lot more than that and he was going to get it.

Lately when he'd walk into his cabin, he'd been overwhelmed with sadness, feeling guilt over Keith leaving. So it was a nice change when he walked in and was simply excited. Sure, the circumstances may not have been the best, but happiness was happiness. He walked to the suitcase at the edge of his bunk and opened it up. He felt like he was opening up something legendary, like the Holy Grail or Ark of the Covenant. The moment felt so grand. There he was, knelt down before an old love and he was being invited back.

He grabbed the 750mL bottle of Svedka Vodka and poured its contents down his throat. He'd taken down a third of the bottle before he finally stopped. His skin tingled and grew warmer, his entire body feeling lighter. It was like a fifty-pound weight had been removed from his shoulders. Why hadn't he succumbed sooner? Everything in him had been saying to do this, and now he just felt dumb for not going back earlier. He was weak without it. He was a lesser person.

He'd almost taken down the entire bottle of vodka when he started feeling better. He thought about Keith and how there was no way his leaving could have been Louie's fault. If Keith wanted to go, he was gonna go. Louie not drinking wasn't going to stop any of that. In fact, his drinking didn't affect anyone but himself, so why should he even bother with what other people thought of his drinking? He always saw the looks of disgust when they were getting their drink on by the bonfires, and Louie would be way ahead of them in drinks. They'd be jealous and mad that he was better at drinking than them. That's all it was.

He quickly realized that he was missing out on his whole reason for drinking: the party across the lake. Pulling on a new sweatshirt—one that smelled much less like vodka—Louie set off from his cabin, heading towards the volleyball court, the swishing remnants of the Svedka bottle in hand.

Louie passed through the sand of the courts, almost tripping twice but still maintaining his balance, until he reached the forest's edge, where he searched for the trail that would lead him around to the party on the other side. Out of nowhere, Barry appeared from the darkness, clothed completely in black and barely even visible.

"Holy shit, Ninja!" Louie yelled.

"You scared the hell out of me, Louie!" Barry was right, he nearly jumped out of his shoes, clearly perturbed by something.

"Well if it isn't Mr. Barney Pepper."

"I see you're done with your whole 'no drinking' charade." Barry started moving past him, but Louie grabbed onto his arm and swung him around.

"What's that s-supposed to mean?" Louie couldn't believe he'd make such a comment.

"Nothing, Louie. Sorry I said anything," Barry quickly moved on. "Have you seen Diane?"

"What-a-you talkin' about? Diane's with the toddlers."

"I went down there and Marge had been sent in to take over by either Marion or Carol, she didn't say. I guess Diane actually got the night off so I figured she had made it to that party but I had no luck finding her."

"Well maybe she doesnwannabe found by you, Barry. You ever t-think about that?"

"Okay, Louie. You've been a lot of help." Barry pushed past him and headed towards the cabins, huffing and puffing as he did.

"Yeah, no problem! Maybe I'll just go find me some Dian*err* myself."

Louie turned and entered the forest where he saw Barry exit from. Even though he spent the last few summers at the camp, Louie hadn't taken much to walking or jogging in the forest, so his knowledge of the paths were limited.

"Uh, hello? Is someone leaking that can direct me in the right direction, directly?"

He hoped for a response but received nothing but the howl of the wind through the trees. He turned around, trying to gain any footing of where he was. He thought he saw some kind of shimmer so he moved towards it, trying to make sense of what he was seeing. As he drew closer, he could finally make out its big whitish shape: the moon reflecting off the lake. That would be his way to the party.

It made enough sense to him: once he reached the edge he would see the fires going on across the lake, and that was where he wanted to be, so if he were to follow along the shore of the lake, he'd eventually get there. It was all easy enough. Unfortunately, the portion of the shore that separated him from the party was not exactly "walk-friendly."

He stomped his way through the thick sticks and branches, everything crunching loudly around him as he did. He enjoyed this as he felt like a giant, trampling over a tiny town. Memories of Saturday mornings as a kid, watching *Power Rangers* reverberated in his mind. Each time a twig broke, he imagined a car crushing beneath his weight.

But then he stomped and completely lost his footing, not expecting the resistance his foot was met with. He tumbled, falling into dried vines and low hanging branches. The fall hurt like hell and he could feel the various scratches he received from the branches, but the alcohol had dulled any pain that would have sprung up from it. He dusted himself off and started moving towards the lake again when he stopped and looked at what he had fallen over:

A leg, completely removed from the thigh down.

Louie wasn't sure if he was seeing things but as his eyes adjusted he was able to make out even more of the carnage, and his stomach turned, releasing all of its contents onto the ground beneath him.

"Diane. . ."

Each stroke of blood adorning a tree trunk or body part strewn about wrote of the vicious tale that had happened there. Diane had been completely chopped up, mostly likely by an axe, and in more pieces than Louie cared to count. He started retreating backwards, the twigs snapping beneath him but he stopped, wanting to pay respects to Diane.

But the crunching noise of the twigs breaking continued. And it was right behind him.

Louie turned and knew he was dead before the first blow was even dealt. It wasn't the moss covered mask, its color black as midnight. And it wasn't the blood that covered their body. Nor was it the huge hunting knife in their right hand, its cold steel having only malicious purpose. It was their eyes. Those cold eyes, staring at him with a knife held high up, with only one intention: murder.

They buried the knife into Louie's chest over and over, each time digging a little bit deeper into the flesh. Each swing brought its own level of undeniable pain as the killer just laid into him, absolutely losing it. They swung the blade down, taking out gigantic chunks of flesh with each cut. He could hardly feel anything from the neck down, his body in a total state of shock, unable to move beneath all the weight. The killer took the knife and twisted it up against Ralph's neck, gentle at first, seeing how he'd react to the cold steel. If he was still cognitive. As his eyes opened wide in terror, they jammed the blade deep into his neck, breaking an artery and gushing a steady stream of bright red blood to the forest bed.

Louie stared up at the mask. The material helped it blend in with the harsh night but their eyes still pierced through the darkness. And it's all he could stare at in his final moments. Those eyes were wide as an open book and they truly hated every bit of who he was. How could anyone have so much anger in them that they'd want to do this to him? Or poor Diane?

Who?

Chapter 21

Liz

IT WAS JUST AFTER MIDNIGHT and the party had already slowed down drastically. Many of the people had left and gone back to the camp, wanting to sleep in their own bunks. There was a tent at the far end where three campers had passed out, sleeping it off for the night. Nancy and Lucas had gone off to one of the other tents and hadn't returned, likely engaging in some intense finger-banging and short coitus. Those still awake and not succumbing to their hormones left just Santa, Alice, Steve, and Liz.

Popping open a beer, Liz felt relief wash over her as the cold beverage made its way down her throat. She wasn't much of a drinker but how was she going to not take part in the festivities? Besides, she knew the Belar's would give her a litany of shit if she hadn't, especially after all the "work" that went into acquiring it. Nancy joked that Alice had to blow Louie to get him to buy all the alcohol, but Liz wasn't sure how much of a joke it really was. It wouldn't be the first time Alice had hooked up with a counselor but she figured Alice had more morals than that. At least she hoped. She dismissed the thought with a laugh.

"Don't you wish Chase were here?"

And suddenly Liz's plan of 'not thinking about Chase all night' was ruined. It was a stupid question to even be asked. Of course she wanted Chase to be there. It was the last night and they had practically been dating. What kind of a stupid question was that? Were they just trying to make her mad? Liz didn't have to think on this long as Alice simulated a penis going into a vagina with her hands. Liz promptly responded. "Just because it was going to be our last night together, doesn't mean I was going to sleep with him. Why does it always have to be about sex with you?"

But it would have been nice to have the option, Liz thought to herself.

"Alright, chill out, Liz-zilla. I can practically see you fuming from the ears." Alice put her arm around Liz and led her towards the drinks. "You need harder alcohol in you to settle that fire burning in you, dear."

"Pretty sure alcohol fuels fire."

"No, this does." Steve poured gasoline from a red container onto the bonfire and it roared to life.

"Yay, let's watch Steve catch his own ass on fire," Santa half-heartedly hoorayed and shook his head at Steve's stupidity. He proceeded to back away from the fire so as to avoid involving himself in any stray flames Steve sent his way. Steve furthered his stupidity by tossing the gasoline container carelessly next to their stockpile of firewood.

"Regardless, y-you need to deerrink more, betch." Alice was sloppy and definitely needed to have included herself in the group of camper's back at camp sleeping. Pouring herself a mostly rum filled Captain and Coke, Alice was starting to make Liz a little nervous. Liz hadn't seen alcohol poisoning in person, but she could sense that Alice was only a few steps away.

"I'm good on that. Think maybe you're done with drinking this evening too?" Liz tried to be as gentle with it as possible but Alice cut through the bullshit and snorted.

"I think I'm doing perfectly fine, thank you very much," she said, almost stumbling as she wagged her finger at Liz.

"I'm just trying to look out for what's best for you. I'm not trying to pick a fight."

Steve just sat there, not wanting to get involved in the inevitable catfight that was brewing. Liz just rolled her eyes at his neutrality.

"Of course not. Why would you? You're just a sad little girl that can't stop pouting over her dumb boyfriend. Oh boo-hoo, the one guy that was actually willing to fuck you in this place isn't here anymore. Big fucking whoop. Your cherry isn't going to be popped this summer, *Lizzaayy*. Get over it." Alice shoved Liz and Santa immediately stepped in between them, having looked on from the side. Steve still just sat there, shaking his head and refused to intervene.

"Alrighty then. Maybe it's about time we all head to bed." Santa guided Alice towards the empty tent at the rear of the clearing, next to Nancy and Lucas's tent.

"Good idea," Alice said, walking over to Steve and grabbing him by the collar. "Let's go into our tent and fuck. Since we actually hit puberty." She said this last part especially loud, wanting to make sure Liz could hear it.

Alice seemed to think she got the better of Liz with this last insult, huffing and stepping away with a huge smile on her face. Steve sighed and helped her over to the red tent next to the lake. Liz just stood there, stunned that she even resulted to such childish antics. She wanted to yell at her, even run over and hit her in the face. She could use a good punch or two. Maybe actually knock some sense into her.

But she was better than that. She knew sinking to her level would provide nothing but momentary satisfaction. Before Alice could rethink things and decide to bitch Liz out again, Liz decided to head back. It wasn't worth all of the drama.

So instead she slunk off into the forest, making her way down the trail from which she came. When she reached its end, she would walk to her cabin and go to sleep at Watanka one last time. It was the last night she'd ever see Alice or any of those idiots ever again. She was done.

At first, the moonlight shone through the trees and provided a nice little luminesce to guide her but that disappeared as clouds rolled in, covering up the moon, and leaving the forest nearly pitch black. Liz was thankful she'd worn pants as she tried her best to stay on the path, occasionally straying into an unkempt bush or grazing up against a low hanging limb that would have surely cut up her bare legs.

Liz had been walking for several minutes down the path before she realized that someone was following her. It wasn't noticeable at first but after a brief stop at a path split, she could hear them moving in the distance behind her. She stopped, trying to use her peripherals the best she could but all the forest provided was a black and grey blur. It was too dark to distinguish anything not directly in her vicinity. She looked around at what she could of the forest around her, and turned around in one swift motion, nearly jumping out of her shoes when she saw him.

"Sorry, didn't mean to startle you." Santa stepped out of the night, his eyes scanning the area around her, suspiciously.

"Look, I get that pretty much everyone back there got paired up and that they're all off having sex or giving blowies or whatever but that's definitely not going to be happening. I'm sorry for your night." And with that she turned away, setting off down the path, making her point.

"Flattered but no," Santa interjected. "I've got a girl back home actually. Think I've just been avoiding sending the wrong idea all summer for no reason at all? As much as I look like the polyamorous type, I like to stick with good ole fashioned monogamy." His smile put her more at ease. He didn't seem to have ill intentions. But what did she know?

"A genuinely nice guy? And to think, I thought those didn't exist at Camp Watanka." And her mind was back on Chase. How could he not be there? He was gone, just like everyone else at the stupid camp ever seemed to be. In and out of her life in a flash.

"Come on, you can't be mad at Chase." Santa was more intuitive than he appeared. "I was about one bad call from punching Carol in the face after the last week. Some of us just haven't had the shitty experience that reminds not to do those things. This is where Chase learns his lesson."

"Yeah, well maybe I'm sick of guys like him letting me down and always just being told that they'll grow."

"You have some very deep rooted Daddy issues, don't you?"

"Oh, Santa, you charmer you," Liz laughed, a mix of nerves and genuine need. "You know, I still can't get over the whole Santa thing. I mean, I get it. I bet you know plenty of Santiago's but still. It's just not a nickname I'd expect from you. Are you sure you're not trying to kidnap me and take me to the north pole?"

"Well. . . that, sure. But I also figured you could use a nice gentleman without shitty intentions to help walk you back. Especially after your little blow up back there—not saying you weren't in the right, mind you."

"I just. . . why can't girls just be fucking normal for once? Why does everything always have to be some kind of contest about whose life is better than whose. I'm so sick of all of that bullshit. I'm sick of them. They won't ever change and I hope that they fucking die."

"Those girls are terrible. That's just who they are. They were raised that way, they'll die that way. You just have to hold your head up high and know you're gonna be better than them. And would you actually kill them?"

"What?"

"Would you kill them?" Santa asked with a sudden sternness. "If someone put a gun in your hand and placed those girls right in front of you, no questions asked before or after. Would you do it?"

Santa's tone had taken a turn for sinister with this line of questioning. Liz tried to break the moment with a smile, hoping he'd comply, but his intensity remained, waiting for some kind of response.

"Okay, obviously I don't want them dead. God, why don't you just guilt trip me more, why don' chya?"

"Sorry," he laughed, breaking the tension. "Just wanted to put things into a bit of perspective. They're rich girls who don't know any better. They'll have life-changing epiphanies eventually."

"Dammit."

"What?" Santa yawned.

"Well now I have to go back." Liz turned around and started back towards the bonfire.

"Wait, wait, how'd you come to that?" he asked, following after her.

"Hey, don't blame me, you're the one that made this happen. Guilting me and all of that. Now I'm viewing her as an actual person and shit. I can just let Steve have his way with her."

"It's been like five minutes. They're probably all done."

"For my own conscience then."

Santa agreed with a sigh and they started their way back down the path. They reached the bonfire fairly quickly and to Santa's relief, Alice and Steve were back around the fire, arguing about something—Nancy and Lucas having joined them. Sex no longer appeared to be in Steve's immediate future.

"At least we don't have to hear that," Santa whispered to Liz as they reclaimed their seats around the fire. Nancy and Lucas didn't seem to care about them joining but Alice stared daggers through them. Steve just sat there.

"Alice. I'm sorry I—" Liz was promptly interrupted.

"Did you two have a good fuck?" Alice asked, redirecting her anger towards the two having just reappeared.

"Technically we could ask you the same question," said Santa, a little amused with himself. "But given the amount of time we were gone, I'm thinking I should ask Nancy and Luke that question instead."

"You just think you're so funny, don't you, Santa? Well—" And that was all Nancy was able to say before an axe was planted deep into her head from the forest at her back. Her body fell limp, dead on contact. As quickly as the axe appeared form nowhere, a knife protruded out of Lucas' throat from behind. He gurgled up the blood, choking on it as a figure rose up behind him and yanked the blade across Lucas' throat, spilling his esophagus onto the ground. They stepped forward, somewhat shielded by the darkness but the light of the embers bounced off their mask, helping their eyes remain visible from afar. Those eyes, filled with murderous intent.

The killer thrashed around like a shark going in for the kill, trying to zone in on their next target. They yanked the axe from Nancy's head and a gush of blood squirted out and covered the killer's mossy mask with a crimson red. Santa tried to push forward and tackle them but he was met with the blunt end of the axe, sending him careening to the ground. He tried getting up but was met with the knob of the axe, knocking him backwards and landing next to the bonfire, motionless.

Liz tried backing away, falling out of her chair. She stared forward, unable to believe her own eyes. She felt like she was sinking into wet cement as her body failed to respond to any of the commands her brain sent it. The only signal her body could interpret was fear as her eyes remained wide, unable to turn away from the carnage.

The killer swung around and grabbed onto Steve, who tried to grab a stick to defend himself with but ultimately grabbed only air. Using Steve's own momentum, the vicious monster swung him around and onto the bonfire, catching his clothes on fire almost immediately and giving it new life. He rolled off of the massive flames, screaming in agony, batting at them but doing nothing to stifle their intensity. He tried rolling to suffocate the flames but nothing worked. Steve rolled and rolled, unknowingly making his way over to the firewood. A brand new pyre.

"Please, no!" Alice screamed, trying to back away from the killer but only running into branch after of branch. She had nowhere to go.

"Hey, dickhead!" Liz yelled at the killer, trying to get their attention.

It worked, for a moment, as the murderous bastard's white eyes transfixed on her. Her stomach turned and she did her best to keep the stale beer inside from disturbing the crime scene around her. But all she felt was fear. As selfish as it was, she didn't want Alice to die because she didn't want to be the only one left. She didn't want to be alone with this maniac.

But the monster had other plans, as they turned away from Liz and charged at Alice. Grabbing her by the throat, the killer flung Alice backwards, sending her into low hanging branches. The wood pierced her flesh and drove it deeper and deeper as the monster pushed her body further and further into it. Alice screamed a blood curdling scream, one that was sure to stick with Liz for whatever amount of life she had remaining. Because it didn't just signal Alice's death. It meant Liz was all alone.

What the fuck is going on? It's the only thought that could go through Liz's head. She wanted to move, to run as quick as her feet would take her, but she just stood there. S*eriously, what the fuck is going on?* It was like she was in some kind of sick and twisted horror movie. How could this even be real? Was she dreaming? Was all this some hallucination from her crazy mushroom trip? This had to be a dream.

All she knew was that she needed to get out of there.

So she ran. As fast as her legs would take her, she was into the forest, her surroundings becoming a mixture of green and black. She kept moving, her legs starting to pulse from the intense adrenaline rush. Her head became light as she ran further and further, not expecting to have to run a marathon after the beers she had ingested earlier. It all became too much and she stopped, almost collapsing in a heap on the forest bed, resting her hand on a tree.

As she pressed her back up against its large oak trunk, gripping tightly onto the bark, she stared across the forest to a tree. Its massive vines wrapping around the ancient oak from top to bottom. Her eyes scanned along, wondering if they were strong enough to hold her weight. Would it be worth the climb. Then she noticed the eyes.

Through the vines and leaves, a pair of eyes were just barely visible in the darkness. It took everything in her not to scream when she saw them, to just dart off into the forest and as far away from them as her legs would take her. But those eyes didn't move. They just stared ahead, blankly. As the skies parted, the moonlight came down across the vines and the area brightened. She could see the full body now, their face scrunched up and the pure terror that adorned it. Liz wanted the clouds to return and for the darkness to hide what was taking everything in her to not barf. Their face had been battered beyond recognition and had been split in half from pelvis to sternum, the insides spilled out over the vines and moss.

Who the—

The killer appeared from nowhere, popping out from behind a tree trunk mere feet from Liz and brandishing a large axe caked in blood. She didn't know what to do. It took everything in her not to freak out, paralyzing all over again with fear. They had reclaimed the axe and were holding it tightly. She kept waiting for them to turn around, swinging the axe with as much force as she'd just witnessed, but it never happened. The killer just stood there, scanning the forest. Taking a deep breath, the psycho moved slowly away from her, back turned. They hadn't seen her amongst the thick foliage.

Liz waited a moment before moving again. She wanted to make sure that the killer wasn't just playing some sick game with her and waiting for her to show herself. So after several minutes she stepped out and moved through the brush, the density of which seemed to increase with each step she took. Vines and sticks whipped across her body as she tried to move through as quickly as possible. Small cuts covered her legs, making it feel like she was constantly being shocked.

Her eyes scanned the forest but all she could see was black. She'd move her sightline and just barely be able to make out long vertical streaks—*must be trees*—but even then, she couldn't tell what they were. Her eyes just refused to adjust. Finally, just calmed herself, closing her eyes and taking a deep breath.

Liz opened them and screamed with everything in her; they stood several feet in front of her, gripping tightly onto their axe. She quickly darted, turning around and hoping her speed would be an advantage, but looking back, the figure was on top of her like a shadow. She wouldn't be able to outrun them. It was impossible. She scanned her immediate area, trying to find a tree to climb, but the lowest branch was nearly seven feet in the air. So she did the only thing she could: she stopped and turned towards the maniac.

The killer was on her immediately, raising their axe up high and swinging it down at Liz's head.

This won't be the end.

Liz dodged to the side and avoided the axe as it crashed into the trunk of the massive tree, burying itself deep within the bark. It was completely stuck. She slammed her foot into the killer's knee and she heard a sickening crunch. It was her chance. She sprinted at the massive tree trunk and ran nearly five feet up it, using the embedded axe to propel herself up toward the lowest hanging branch.

She pulled herself up the tree but the killer was already standing to their feet, yanking the axe out of the bark, and looking up at Liz, fire in their eyes. Liz pulled herself up a couple more branches but then stopped, knowing the killer wouldn't be able to get up the tree.

"I think you may need to work on your core a little, dude." The humor settled Liz's nerves but she wasn't sure if it was a good idea, with the monster below her lunging at her with an even greater intensity. She had made them mad.

She hurried up each and every branch, trying her best to escape the monster beneath her. There was a thud below and she looked back to see axe, embedded in the tree just inches underneath her left foot. Before they could pull the axe out and try again, Liz decided on keeping both her feet. So she stopped, lowering herself a little, and grabbed onto the limbs around her for leverage. With one big swipe, she kicked her foot down, implanting it on the killer's hand. They screamed out but did not fall. Instead they looked up at her with cold eyes. The maniac tried lunging upward but Liz was too fast, kicking down at them. With one last stomp, her shoe connected with the killer's face, sending them tumbling towards the ground and landing with a *thud!*

It all happened so quickly, and she didn't see them land, but the impact was loud enough that she was positive that they couldn't have survived it. There was no way. Her eyes scanned the ground, trying to gain some reassurance. Instead she saw the killer, prone against the ground, staring up at the sky. They weren't dead. At least not yet.

She needed to end this.

Liz lowered herself down another branch, now approximately twenty feet above the ground. The maniac hadn't move an inch, but still stared up at the night sky. *Maybe they're paralyzed?* Liz theorized. It felt as though they were looking directly at Liz as she made her way down the tree but it could have easily just been paranoia settling in.

Steadying herself onto a large branch, Liz grabbed onto the axe with both hands and yanked back with all of her might. But it refused to move and remained completely embedded in the trunk of the tree. Repositioning herself, she put her foot up against the tree for leverage and pulled again, this time dislodging it from its spot on the tree but almost flying out of her hands in the process. As she recovered, her eyes moved back down to where the killer fell.

They were gone.

Liz looked all around her, trying to catch any glimpse of where they could have possibly gone off to. The moon provided less useful as the night sky became cloudier and cloudier, inconsistent as ever. She thought she saw something moving in the distance but couldn't be sure. She'd have to get out of the tree to investigate regardless. But what if that was what the killer was expecting?

"You know what, fine. I'm just gonna stay up in this tree all night and there's not a damn thing you can do about it."

A frog croaked amongst the howling wind, but otherwise she was met with only silence. But she still couldn't shake the feeling of being watched from somewhere out in the darkness.

"I know you're out there. You're not fooling anyone."

All she felt was selfish and alone. If she were to stay up there, sure, she could possibly survive till morning but who else would die because she didn't take action? Or was there even anyone left? This maniac surely wouldn't have gone after everyone. There were little kids in that camp. The thought cchocd in hei head over and over until she could no longer stand it. She needed to move. She needed to get out of the tree and get assistance. It didn't matter that the killer could very well be waiting for her to descend. She needed to help.

Then she heard the noise. It started out soft at first, but it was soon discernable as footsteps. Something was moving in the forest and coming directly towards her. She clutched the axe tightly, unsure of what she would do with it, but knowing it was her only means of protection. And that's when she saw the last thing she expected:

Chase exited the brush, a bloody hunting knife in hand and his cold, calculating eyes staring right up at her.

Chapter 22

Chase

"STAY THE FUCK AWAY FROM ME!" Liz screamed down at Chase, holding an axe in her hand. He wished she weren't holding it so clumsily. Being nearly twenty feet up in a tree meant that if it slipped out of her hand, Chase was going to have a much bigger issue to contend with. But at that moment, he really needed to get her out of that tree.

"Liz, I'm here to help you," Chase tried to sound as genuine as possible, maybe even forcing it a little, but they didn't have the time.

"You're the killer." Liz's words stung.

It's not like he could blame her for the accusation but it didn't make it hurt any less. If he had seen a bunch of people murdered and then come across someone he thought was sent home from camp, he'd have his suspicions too. Still, the idea of this girl thinking he was going to try and kill her at any moment wasn't exactly comforting. It was clear she didn't trust him, her eyes scanning his body looking for any hint of truth to the words he spoke.

Again, he couldn't fault her for not believing him. He could hardly believe it himself and he'd been repeating the events over and over in his head.

Chase had spent the entire car ride to the cheap hotel Jeannie had rented trying to convince her he wasn't lying. She just nodded along and seemed to be at least a little understanding to his problems. In fact, it seemed like she was going to turn the car around at any moment. Instead she just kept driving until she reached the hotel. Chase continued to plead with her as they went to their room but Jeannie stopped him, telling him he needed to grow up and stop seeking attention. "The divorce was eight years ago, you need to stop acting like a selfish little bastard. Your poor mother. . ."

Chase wasn't anywhere close to convincing her to go back. She just let him speak his peace while having no real intention of changing her mind. She let him go through what she clearly assumed was a prepared spiel and eventually locked him in the hotel room while she went to get a drink at the bar. Luckily for Chase, he'd spent his greater youth smoking in the abandoned motel next door and knew precisely where to hit the window to pop it out the frame. Given that the window was a different model than he was used to, it took a couple minutes longer than he thought it would but eventually he pried it off and darted down the road. Knowing it wouldn't be the best idea to confront a killer weaponless, he grabbed a road flare from his Aunt's emergency kit and hoped it'd come in handy. At the very least he figured he could signal for help.

Mostly sticking to the ditch and ducking when he saw headlights, Chase still felt uneasy walking along so closely to the forest. He knew there was no way he could be watched at that exact moment but the feeling still lingered on. Something about that forest didn't sit right with him. But cutting through it was his best chance to get to the camp in time. So he darted into the forest and never looked back, swallowing whatever fear sprung up inside.

Before he could even reach the main camp itself, he started hearing screams. They were deep and terrifying, but so far away that Chase couldn't figure out where they were coming from. The camp was in one direction, and the screams seemed to come from another. He debated whether or not it would even be worth it to follow or just go directly to the camp; save as many people as possible. But he couldn't. Leaving someone behind wasn't in his nature. He was there for a reason.

So he ran and he ran, chasing after the terrifying howls of what was likely a vicious murder. Chase passed over what he thought was the jogging path and continued past it, taking note of how he could get back to the camp. He had to be coming to the lake soon but the screams had died out long ago. The only noise were his own footsteps as he sprinted through the forest. Then he heard water.

He slowed down as he reached the water's edge, sloshing in the mud. His eyes darted around, looking for the source of the screams but there was no one. He could see the bonfire a little way down on the lake, and it appeared there were still plenty campers still up and partying. It couldn't have come from there. But it was still the most likely place he would find Liz.

Continuing down the shoreline, he figured he'd reach the party within fifteen minutes but the many branches and deep mud were starting to get in the way of that goal. Arriving at a particularly muddy spot, he decided he could no longer brave the shore and stepped back onto the dryer land to make it through the forest the rest of the way. His eyes raised and all of his fears were realized.

Louie's lifeless corpse laid several feet away with some other body parts all over the place, but Chase couldn't really get a match. They appeared to be female. Walking up to Louie, he knelt next to his body, which looked to be in immense pain right before finally succumbing to his wounds. Louie didn't deserve that. No one deserved any of this. And whoever had done this, Chase was going to make sure that they paid.

He clutched onto the hunting knife still embedded in Louie's chest and tried pulling it out but it refused to budge. Chase tried twisting the blade to get it free but had to stop, thinking about the damage he was doing to Louie's arm by twisting it. He never thought taking a knife out of someone would be so hard. They always seemed to go in easy enough. With one final tug, Chase pulled the knife free and then screams rang out in the distance.

Chase dashed through the forest, running towards where he thought the bonfire would be. He stopped and tried to locate the source of the screams but the moment he could pick out the distinct notes of

Liz's voice, his mind went into full panic mode. He needed to find her before it was too late. He couldn't lose her. He darted through the forest, hoping he was right about the direction of the voice.

When he finally came across the large oak tree, the ground beneath it looked like it'd had a scuffle. Then he saw her: perched up in a tree, nearly twenty feet high, Liz clung tightly to a large wooden axe, a look of a fear on her face unlike any Chase had ever seen before. She had been through hell. But she wasn't dead. She was still breathing and that was all that mattered. He hadn't even realized the bloody knife still clutched in his hand.

"Woah, woah, woah. This is not what it looks like," said Chase, who dropped the knife and moved away, his hands raised high. "I found Louie. And. . . someone else, I'm not sure who. But he had that buried in his chest by some psychopath. I needed something for self-defense so I. . . took it."

"You *took* it? You mean you pulled it out of his chest?"

It was a fair question. The idea probably wouldn't have come to most people, given how deeply embedded it was, but Chase had no choice. His survival instinct kicked in and he was forced to do the unthinkable. He tried to reason with her, "You have to know that this is just protection from whoever the hell is doing this."

"*You're* doing this!" she screamed, making Chase more uneasy at the sight of the swaying axe that she had held tightly in her grasp.

"Come on, Liz. You have to believe me. I'm not capable of anything like this and you know that. I'm just as scared as you are."

"The killer just disappeared and then you come walking out of the woods like some kind of savior? Wouldn't you be a tad suspicious if you were in my shoes?"

"What do you mean, 'just disappeared?'" Chase asked, suddenly very aware of his surroundings. If they had just disappeared, they could easily still be nearby. His eyes darted around the forest, no longer bothering to look up at Liz, who he knew was out of harm's way.

"I. . . why should I trust you?"

"If you really think I'm capable of doing anything like what I've seen this sicko do, I'd rather you just stay up there. Eventually the cops will come and save you because I'll have gotten them here. I swear to you, the only reason I came back is to get you out of here alive."

"I just. . ." she looked around as the wind howled through the trees, tears forming under her eyes. "Everyone is dead."

"But not us."

Liz seemed to be debating it but Chase couldn't wait any longer. He needed to get her down there. They needed to get moving. And as much as he didn't want to make a drastic decision, he grew wary of the darkness that crept in around him.

"I'm going to close my eyes now," Chase said, proceeding to doing so. "And you can swing that axe as hard as you want at my head. I promise I won't open my eyes. Because I trust you. And I know that you and I are both meant to get out of this alive."

Chase stood there, eyes shut tight. The darkness of the night wasn't much of a difference to his eyes being shut. His imagination kicked into gear as he could see Liz lowering herself down the tree. He could hear her shuffling about, her shoes scraping up against the bark. At least he hoped it was her. There seemed to be a thud in front of him and he wanted to peek, but made sure to keep his eyes shut tight. He pictured her standing in front of him, the giant axe in her hand as she raised it high into the air, wondering for a second what it would feel like as the heavy metal crashed down upon his skull. The moments that followed were some of the longest of his life, never being more uncertain as to what those next seconds held.

Then he felt it: Liz hugged him harder than he'd ever been hugged before. He opened his eyes and hugged her back, wanting to let her know that he was there for her. There to make everything better. That they'd get through it together. But she didn't allow the moment to last long. "We need to go. He knows I'm here."

"He?" asked Chase. "How do you know it's a guy?"

"You should have seen what he did at the bonfire. I'm willing to take the loss if I'm wrong but it all seems pretty male-oriented to me."

"We definitely both need protection so take this," he handed her the road flare, which she looked at questioningly.

"You're kidding me, right? What am I supposed to do, signal him to death?"

"Hey, those flares burn at fourteen hundred degrees. Fucking burn his ass. Unless you want this." Chase held up the hunting knife.

Another scream rang out in the distance.

"Let's go. Now."

Chase grabbed Liz's hand and led her through the woods. They tried running as much as they could, but the forest made it harder and harder as they couldn't seem to find a path. They just hoped they were going in the right direction. Then they heard a familiar noise, behind them. It was still quite a distance away but still, clear as day, the noise of sirens echoed through the night. Someone had called for help. Someone was coming to save them.

Then a figure stepped out just in front of them, cutting them off from their salvation. The man wore all black and had blended in with the darkness so well that they only noticed him when he was several feet in front of them, but his face was easy enough to make out in the moonlight.

"Get away from him, Liz!" Barry exclaimed. "You have no idea what he's capable of."

Liz stepped away from Chase, standing in the middle between he and Barry, just far enough away from both.

"What's he talking about, Chase?" asked Liz, falling right into Barry's trap.

"Please, let's not go through this again. Am I the guy that just came out of the forest in all black?! No. I'm the guy that just risked getting an axe in the face over his trust in you. You know I wouldn't do hurt anyone."

"You're holding a goddamn butcher knife!" screamed Barry.

"Yeah, for protection—from you!" Chase pointed the knife at Barry, in complete disbelief at what was happening. Barry was very clearly the guy behind everything. How had Liz not seen it before?

"I'm telling you, Chase killed all those people. He killed Diane. He killed all those poor people at the bonfire. He killed them all. I just keep coming across body after body, just too late to stop him but not this time. I got to him before he could get you, Liz. Now get behind me."

Liz looked back at Chase, then over at Barry. Was she really questioning him right now? What was he going to do if she walked towards Barry? Would he be able to stop her before Barry was able to make his move and kill her? All of his worrisome thinking was for naught as Liz stepped backwards and in line with Chase, stared ahead at Barry with a fierce hatred. His lies weren't convincing anyone.

"Liz, you're going to regret—"

An arrow penetrated through Barry's skull with such veracity that it poked out through his eye on the other side. His body twitched for a moment, but with his brain stem completely severed, his death was imminent. His body fell dead at Liz's feet as she looked behind him at the killer's silhouette, bow in hand, only twenty feet from her. They seemed to be assessing the situation, figuring out which way would be best to dispatch them with. The death and chaos was never ending.

And Chase had, had enough.

He knew this was his chance to end it all. So he wielded the knife and charge towards the killer. They had almost had another arrow restrung when Chase reached them, tackling them backwards into a giant tree trunk. He rolled on top of them and raised the knife high into the air, ready to end all of this carnage.

But the killer was too fast, shifting their weight and slamming their elbow into Chase's bruised ribs, redirecting the blade directly into Chase's shoulder. They rolled on top of him, using his own weight to send the knife deeper and deeper into his flesh. Chase had always wondered what it was like to be stabbed and the excruciating pain didn't begin to cover it. The burning was so intense that he just waited for the blade to dig deeper into his muscle and eventually take out an artery. All he could taste was blood.

Then everything went black.

Chapter 23

Liz

LIZ, COVERED IN EVERYONE'S BLOOD but her own, viciously swung the stick down but she wasn't quick enough, the psychotic murderer dug the blade fairly deep into Chase's shoulder. Still, she swung and swung down on his head until finally the killer rolled off Chase and cowered away from her. She thought she had the upper hand until she brought the stick down and he caught it in his hand, pulling it away from Liz in one fell swoop. The killer breathed heavily beneath that terrifying mask, staring intently at Liz, his eyes filled with vicious hate.

The maniac leapt forward at her but Liz was ready, kicking them in the face and sending them careening backwards. Liz looked towards Chase, his body motionless but chest appearing to rise and fall.

She wanted to run over to him, make sure he was alright and take him with her, but she didn't have the time. The killer stirred awake beside her and was slowly getting their faculties back. She needed to get moving.

Sprinting off into the forest, she tried following the sounds of the sirens as best she could, but had difficulty tracking them. She stopped for a moment but rapidly regained her movement as she heard shuffling in the woods behind her. The killer was looking to finish the job. She could only hope that they believed Chase was dead.

She had come across a giant oak tree and immediately knew she had gone in the wrong direction as she stood before a building she hadn't visited in many years: the old abandoned Shepard residence. Its presence sent goosebumps down her arms and neck. She never liked that damn house.

But she couldn't stop; the killer was only a few paces behind with only one purpose that she didn't really care to find out. She had to keep moving. So she ran up the porch and slammed the front door shut behind her. The house seemed to have less cobwebs than the last time she had been in there several years prior. It almost looked. . . lived in.

Great, am I in your goddamn secret lair, you evil bastard?

The thought creeped her out and made her realize what a huge disadvantage she was at if it were true. But it didn't matter now. She just needed to end it. Something crashed around in the house and immediately Liz knew: the killer had made it inside.

She walked through the old living room, the boards beneath her feet creaked with every step. She looked over at a large piece of cloth, draped across the old rotting couch. Maybe she could hide under it and catch them by surprise. Anything would have been better than just standing as she was then, out in the open and completely vulnerable. So she moved the sheet, deciding instead she was going to try and wrap the killer up in it, and her advantage came crashing down with one ill-timed scream.

Liz couldn't help it, seeing Keith's mutilated corpse beneath the cloth caught her by surprise and her emotions were too high to temper. Suddenly all the talk of Keith's sudden departure made more sense. Instead of playing basketball in Europe like they were led to believe, he had been rotting away in this old house for days, with no one the wiser. Who would have killed poor Keith? And more importantly, who would have had the power to cover it up without anyone being the wiser?

Before Liz could mentally go through her list of suspects, the masked killer appeared in the doorway behind her, axe at his side, ready to finish everything.

But so was Liz.

"How does it feel to know you're being taken down by a girl? Does that hurt your machismo?"

The dark, mossy mask of the killer tilted to the side, their white eyes staring directly into Liz's, like a curious dog. Then a laugh rang out, deep and terrifying, emanating from beneath that cold, black mask. Liz knew what she was doing. She could see the opening to the right side and the back door slapping open as the wind picked up. She had her escape route.

This was her moment and she needed to be quick.

She darted to the right and with one crack of the floorboard, her plan failed miserably as her foot had broken through the rotting wood, and pinned her in place. The killer just stared down at her, shaking his head as if he somehow felt bad for her. Or maybe he just wanted a challenge, as he started pacing back and forth, twirling the axe in his palm.

"Just do it, you coward," she shouted at the monster, twisting her ankle free from the floorboard.

The killer stepped forward and took one giant breath, so near to the end of it all. He raised the axe high over his head and swung it down in a fury. But Liz was ready. She threw the cloth at him, pulling the flare from her pocket and igniting it. The flame took to the cloth easily enough, spreading like wildfire and engulfed the monster beneath it. He swung the axe around blindly, trying his best to hit Liz but only managing to break apart the couch and corpse which laid upon it.

He swung more and more violently, trying with his last bit of life to end Liz's. But she kept her distance, watching the flames engulf him as they spread down his body, spitting off his back and onto the walls and ceiling. The flames were finally too much, dropping the killer to his knees, the axe in his hand falling to the floor next to him. The fire spread along the walls and down to the floor. Liz knew she had to escape before the flames became too much for the rotting structure.

Taking one last gasp of air, she sprinted forward, running past the killer and towards the doorway but before she reached it she found herself stopping, drawn to something behind her. She turned and looked at the killer, whose fingers twitched as they tried so hard to reach the axe only inches away from them.

"Let me help you with that." Liz couldn't resist.

She picked the axe up off the floor and swung it, like a golf club, down at the killer's head. She cracked the mask and the killer's skull, all in one sickening *smack*! She let the axe fall to the floor as she stared at the lifeless body of the maniac behind it all. After a summer unlike any other, it was finally over. The psycho was dead.

Suddenly Liz could feel the intense heat all around her as the flames began to engulf the house. She ran with all her might, bursting through the front door, breaking through the smoke and landing on the porch to safety. On all fours she crawled away from the rising inferno, only staring back at the blaze once she was sure nothing would collapse on top of her. All those years of collecting dust and cobwebs had made the house into pure kindling. The entire structure was sure to be gone in minutes.

The large particle board that covered the main window slowly burned away, giving an open view of the house and all she could see were flames. Liz hoped her eyes weren't playing tricks on her when she spotted that moss covered, stoic mask, melting away in the fire. Smoke billowed out of the house and sure to signal the nearby first responders. She would be saved soon. It was almost over.

The hand came out of nowhere, grabbing onto her shoulder and sending a jolt of energy through Liz's body as she forced her elbow backwards, into her attacker's face. It was going to end after all that she had been through.

"Owww!" Chased yelled, grabbing onto his nose, that was now surely broken.

Liz breathed a sigh of relief as she jumped on top of him and kissed him over and over. She had never been happier to see someone her entire life. Judging by the returned kisses, Chase felt the same.

Liz and Chase sat on the grass, leaning against each other for support. They stared out at the burning structure before them, the sun starting to lighten the sky from the horizon. A tear rolled down Liz's cheek as she watched it peek out through the tree-line, a sight she wasn't sure if she'd ever witness again. The sirens were growing closer and closer and she could see flashlights deeper in the tree-line. Help was on its way.

Her eyes went back to the house, the flames rising up, higher and higher into the dawning sky. With Al dead, and the final family residence burning to the ground, the only thing left for their legacy was Camp Watanka, a place that was sure to be a giant crime scene for some time to come. If it ever did become something else, the memory of what happened there would always linger on those grounds.

This place is fucked.

A bullfrog jumped up and landed on Chase's leg with a greeting of "*ribbet!*" Liz sat up, not quite knowing how Chase would react, and not desiring an inevitable flailing arm to the head. But instead he just sat there, staring down at the frog as it stared right back at him. Chase noticed her watching him and turned towards her, a giant smile spreading across his face.

"Suddenly frogs just don't seem like a big deal." And with that he laid his head back in the grass, wrapped his arm tightly around her, and pulled her in close. It was finally over.

By the time the cops arrived, having followed the billowing smoke that filled the night sky, the house was nothing more than ash. They searched the grounds for other survivors but Liz just wanted to get out of there. She could still feel the murderer's presence, despite him being turned to ash. It took them a little while to make it back to the main camp, but when they did, it was a sight unlike anything Liz had ever experienced. There were more emergency vehicles than she cared to count, their red and blue lights brightening the grounds. And there, standing in the middle of it all, being treated by two different paramedics, were Marion and Santa.

Liz sprinted for them immediately, making sure her eyes hadn't deceived her. She ignored the pain in her ankle as she nearly tackled Marion to the ground with a gigantic hug, giving one to Santa right after. After nearly five minutes of more crying and hugging than Santa was noticeably comfortable with,

"How are—I thought you were—" Liz could hardly catch her breath.

"Pretty sure we all thought the worst," Marion responded, giving Liz a sisterly kiss on the forehead. "Looks like you're needed."

They wanted her to talk about it, to go over all the events of the night in excruciating detail. But she didn't want to speak. She didn't want to do anything but sit there with Chase and fully take in everything that had happened. This wasn't just a normal night that she'd come back from the same. She had lost people and seen things that would only come to most people in movies. She had come face to face with a maniac and she survived.

They sat her into the back of one of the ambulances and covered her with a blanket, explaining that she was in shock. Liz hadn't felt like she was in shock but what did she know? She just knew that she wanted to go back with the others. But the detective in charge insisted it was important.

"I can only imagine what you've gone through," he began. "And I know this is one of the last things you want to be doing but time is of the essence and I don't want anyone else to have to go through what you have. No one deserves this. And we're trying to make sure that the maniac who did this is brought to justice. So is there anything you can tell us to help identify who did this? Even the smallest detail could help our investigation."

Liz sat on the question for a moment, first trying to imagine who could have possibly committed such horrible atrocities. How was any human being capable? The viciousness of their attacks quickly shifted her thoughts to how anyone she knew at the camp could possibly be the killer. It had to be a local, right? Or the killer from 1991? The thoughts all left her head in a flash as only one remained. . .

"Who cares who did it? He's dead."

∞

Liz was sure that the events of Camp Watanka would always stick with her but that didn't make her want to move past them any less. The constant barrage of questions from reporters, as well as those that acted like they were suddenly such good friends with her, had become more than she cared to deal with. She just wanted to go back to whatever kind of normal life was possible for her. That seemed to be getting less and less likely with each day that passed. Every aspect of that night became more vivid as other details were released by the police, enlisting the public's help to identify the killer.

The police found bodies throughout the property of Watanka. Ralph was skewered at the Archery range with nearly a dozen arrows through his body. The police found Marjory and the toddlers completely oblivious to the events of the previous night. They had spent most of their evening singing "Kumbayah" and playing with a large box of Legos that Marge had brought with her for entertainment. She nearly had a heart attack when the police told her what happened.

Diane, Louie, and Sally were all found in the forest, their deaths coming a variety of ways that Liz never cared to read into. They had done a full sweep of the camp grounds and still hadn't found all the bodies. But she had seen enough. The bonfire haunted her every day. It didn't matter how hard she tried moving past it, the images of them dying just stacked up over and over in her head. The only thing she could be grateful for was that Santa had survived the bonfire massacre, getting a bad concussion and second degree burns on his arms.

While there was some nerve damage that made him numb in certain areas of the chest and arm, Chase had been healing up nicely. His physical therapy took nearly eight weeks for him to complete, but once he was done he finally regained full movement with his arm. Liz had made sure to talk to him at least once a day once the both of them were back with their families. After all they had been through, Liz figured a long distance relationship was manageable.

Marion was also struggling deeply with that night. She'd found Carol's body and was the one to phone the police. She had done her best to alert the campers that had remained in their bunks for the night, but there was no way she could have gone through the forest to get the others. With her fractured leg, she was completely helpless. Broken bone aside, she was lucky enough to have never come across the maniac. Still, the guilt haunted her, even trying her hand at therapy to help alleviate some of it. Santa had simply dropped off the face of the earth. The last time Liz spoke to him he thanked her for all she had done for him. It felt like a goodbye but Liz hoped she was wrong.

While name after name had been seemingly crossed off the list as the police continued their manic search, Liz had trouble caring. The identity made no difference to her, nor would it have made any difference to the victim's families. Those murdered at Watanka were never coming back and the psycho who did it was nothing more than ash.

∞

Nine weeks after that horrible night, Liz sat on the couch in her mother's living room and picked anxiously at her nails. After nearly two months away from each other, she would finally be reunited with Chase. For the first time in months, rather than feeling like a victim, Liz just felt like a normal girl excited about a boy.

So when Chase finally pulled up, in his mother's hand me down car no less, she hadn't even given him enough time to exit the vehicle before she was out the front door and on top of him. All of her worries had washed away in an instant.

"What took you so long?" Liz asked, kissing Chase's lips as much as possible in between breaths.

"Media circus in front of the house—oww! Watch the shoulder, babe—someone must have tipped them off to where I was staying. So it's lookin' like it's time to find another family friend to stay with when I get back."

"You can always stay out here." Liz suggested, knowing he wouldn't go for it.

"I would if I could, darling. Now let's get inside. I have something I want to show you."

"Ohhh presents?!" Liz couldn't contain her excitement. She loved presents. And the big bag that Chase pulled from the back seat seemed to indicate she was right.

"Now what would ever give you that impression." Chase kissed her again as he teased opening the bag only to close it just before she could see any of the goods.

"Fine be that way, I guess that means you won't get your present either." Liz walked into the house and Chase followed, clearly glad to be in air conditioning after a long hot ride.

"Take a seat on the couch and I will be right back." She kissed his lips again and stayed for a moment, relieved he finally made it.

Quickly she was off, bounding up the stairs and running to her room on a mission to get Chase's gift. Her mind quickly went elsewhere when she saw the heap of mail on her bed. Apparently her mom had gotten sick of Liz continuously ignoring whatever stack of paper had been hanging around on the coffee table downstairs and thought her bed was a more appropriate place for it. Liz fingered through it quickly, hoping to find a driver's license in amongst the new mail. But instead it they were just letters from family members asking how she was doing, and an old brown package.

She ignored it and reached under her bed, grabbing Chase's gift from the spot she had placed it several weeks before when she happily wrapped it and imagined Chase's smile as he opened it. But as she got up, package in hand, she looked back at her bed, her curiosity setting in. *Who sent me that even?* She leaned in and picked it up, looking at the mailing address. It was addressed to her full name, so it was likely a family member, but she didn't recognize the return address. The college maybe? She didn't know anybody there so Liz found it all suspect. As much as she wanted to get back down to Chase, she really wanted to know what was in that little brown package.

She carefully sat Chase's gift down on the bed and grabbed the brown one. She opened it slowly, thinking it had to just be another box of chocolates meant to help her "get well soon." Instead confusion took her as she pulled the brown leather journal from the box. *Did someone get me a book?* She thought to herself, as she turned to its first page, wondering what it could possibly be about.

Her eyes opened wide in terror.

"Sweet, sweet Elizabeth. Half of me is surprised that you were the one but part of me always knew. I sure did my best to make sure that didn't happen but you're just a little spitfire, aren't you? So many others failed where you so eloquently succeeded. You were worthy. The camp didn't want me to take you and no matter how hard I tried, you kept persevering. I admire that. And so did Watanka. I should have known you were there to protect it.

I'm sure you've figured out by now who this is, in the general sense of the word—that big scary masked fella—but you still don't quite understand who I am in the more literal sense. And you deserve to know. You truly do. But only you, Elizabeth.

It didn't have to be like this. No, it didn't have to be like this at all. I just wanted what was absolute best for the camp. If anything my hand was forced by Al, those idiot counselors, and even the campers themselves. No one did as they were told. All they had to do was treat the camp with the respect it deserved. Instead they repeatedly sank it into the ground, and couldn't go about their business like they were supposed to. The point of the camp was to help mold these young people into the leaders of our future and somehow that got lost along the way. Somehow THEY lost touch.

But not me. I ALWAYS knew.

Things may not have happened how I envisioned them but the end point has always been the same: making Watanka into the camp it was destined to be.

Al just wouldn't see reason when I told him about poor Keith. But Keith deserved everything that happened to him and then some. He deserved the same fate as that stupid bitch that took him from me. That filthy Diane just couldn't keep her claws off of him. He was going to be my husband. We were going to run Camp Watanka together as the son and daughter that Al never had. I had dreams about it. But Al just refused to co-operate. All he wanted to do was to call the cops. Could never see the big picture. He forced my hand. Putting my hands around his throat was the hardest thing I have ever had to do, you must believe me. But once I took his life, I knew that ANYTHING was possible. Everyone forced my hand. If only you all had just listened to me then we could have made the camp what it was always meant to be. Instead you all just let it waste away and fought against it.

That's okay though. I rectified it. I made the camp more memorable than it would have ever been otherwise. No one will forget what happened at Watanka. And I don't want them to. Let them have their stories. The real truth is only meant for so many people, Elizabeth.

There are people that will call me psychotic but I know you understand that's not the case. My only real crime is caring too much. It's all of those "innocent victims", as the papers like to call them, that are the true sinners. No matter what I tried, they just wouldn't stop breaking the rules. Sex, drugs, no respect for authority whatsoever. These trespasses could no longer go unpunished. But you endured, didn't you, sweet Elizabeth? You really had such potential to go places. But now you've met me and there's no going back.

You and I are meant to be each other's end, Elizabeth. Our fates are intertwined and while you may have won the first round, we have oh so many more to go. And that's why I'm telling you this. I want you to know I'm coming. I want you to prepare for me. I want you to be at your absolute best so that when I stick my blade deep inside your flesh, you will know that I won and there is no coming back from it.

This was always meant to be a summer for the ages. Don't you see, Elizabeth? It was written in the stars. Sure, I was angry at first when the true endgame poked its little head out. I mean, I had worked so hard for this place. I always thought that it would be mine. But then it just became so obvious: it was never meant to be ruled. And good things must come to an end to truly be appreciated. Fate tried intervening in 1991 but Al didn't listen. Instead he just ran it into the ground. It's what he deserved so don't you dare feel sorry for him. He DESERVED it! Unfortunately, Al just wouldn't listen. He never really was much of a listener. But I am. I listen all the time and VERY intently. The signs were all around you. Maybe you should have just paid attention.

I hope your wounds are healing nicely, they certainly look to be. Mine have proven much more difficult than a simple stab wound. The mask may have broken most of the impact but that doesn't make getting hit in the face with an axe any less painful. But I'll heal up, sweet Elizabeth. Don't you worry about that. And when I do, it all starts again.

My mind is set on this, Elizabeth. Do you understand me? I want this to go as smoothly as possible. I don't want to have to chase you. But don't be fooled, I will. And when I catch up with you I'll make your suffering worse than even that stupid whore Diane. She deserved it more than anybody else. Moving in on Keith like that. She should have been ashamed of herself. What did I ever do to her to warrant such malicious behavior? She got what was coming to her. The story has been written for us and we're just left to live it out. The number of chapters is up to you but I promise you, it will always have the same finish.

There is no fairy tale ending where you save the day and ride off into the sunset with Chase. Anytime you think that you've beat me, I will come back more vicious than you ever imagined. This is a cycle. One that will repeat itself for the rest of our lives. If you want it to end, you must simply GIVE UP. Because now that I've found you I will never stop until I know what your insides look like.

Whatever I was before, died at that camp. Marion will have made sure of that with the police. Now all I am is legend. I'm the true

Camp Watanka killer. Not just some dumb counselor getting mad at his cheating whore. I made the name Watanka more famous than any of the Shepards ever dreamed. I brought the camp to its absolute peak. Just like I've always done with anything I've touched. Because I'm the counselor that did what was necessary when no one else would. And what will they say about me? Absolutely nothing. Which is what they always say about me. But do you know what went through my head every single time I killed one of those pathetic bastards? As I did fate's work and brought justice down upon them?

Old. Reliable. Carol.

See you real soon.

The End.

Epilogue

CHASE BOUNCED BACK AND FORTH on the couch, excited to even be there. He looked around the room at the framed pictures but hadn't seen many of Liz. It was mostly her mother, at various vacation spots, neglecting any representation of her family on the walls. He finally spotted one of Liz off towards the corner. It was from the last year of High School and he couldn't believe how adorable she looked in her blue dress and her makeup all done up. After what was essentially a summer outdoors, Chase hadn't really thought about how she could look even better than when he'd been around her. But there he was, staring at a beautiful angel who was now his girlfriend. He still couldn't even believe he could use that word but hell, he had even made the trip for her.

It ended up being a pretty long car ride but all he thought about was Liz the entire time. That made it go by all the quicker. They were both about to start school back up and he knew there wouldn't be much time after so the trip was necessary for them. They were going to have to resort to mostly skype calls and school breaks in order to see each other.

He hoped that would be enough, and while he knew that they would grow restless, they just needed to remind each other that it was only temporary. Eventually, they'd be able to get their own place and escape all the madness, together. They'd already made it this far together, how bad would a little further be?

Anxiety started to set in for Chase after a few minutes passed by and Liz still hadn't returned. While he was sure that it was nothing, something in his stomach was uneasy. After the summer he'd just been through, paranoia was a hard habit to be broken of. After another minute of waiting, Chase couldn't chance it anymore, and he raced for the stairs.

"Liz?" he shouted up to the second floor but received no response, the silence echoing in his head. "If you think you're being funny, you're really not."

Still, there was no answer and the worry began to creep into his nerves, putting him on edge. Something felt wrong. He sprinted up the stairs, trying to be as cautious as possible, but still trying to reach her fast. When he stepped onto the second floor, he looked around at the many doors, trying to see which was Liz's. Spotting the sign that read "Do Not Enter" posted upon the outside, he knew which one to check first. He burst in through the door, ready for anything but hoping for nothing.

"Liz, you are such a little—" Chased started but quickly realized he was talking to himself. The room was empty and even a little disheveled. He moved forward, goosebumps settling in as he approached the open book on her bed. It seemed so out of place with the rest of the stuff in Liz's room, he couldn't help but be drawn to it. Picking it up, it was easy to see why. His eyes widened in absolute horror as he realized exactly what it was: the killer's manifesto. A gory detail of all the events of the camp, written with so much childish glee that Chase's stomach turned over. But why did Liz have it?

He finished Carol's letter of insanity, and laid his head onto the bed, wanting to conjure up some tears to match the complete whirlwind that went on inside of him. But he was completely cried out. Too many tears had already been shed that even at that moment, his ducts remained dry. His face grew red and he just wondered to himself what he could have done differently. If he could have stopped her from going. If he could have convinced her that there was some other way. Chase was so distracted that he hardly noticed when a figure stepped in through the doorway in front of him.

Liz stood there, jacket on and fully-packed bag in hand.

"We have work to do."

A WORD FROM THE AUTHOR.

Thank you so much for taking the risk on my first book. I've been dreaming of releasing my very own professional novel ever since I was in the second grade, creating makeshift books out of construction paper. It was a very long journey to get to this point but it's done! It's an actual book that you are holding in your hands! (or a tablet if you bought the e-book.)

I wanted to create something that, while it featured a lot of the main slasher tropes, still took a more logical approach to the standard hack and slack affair. I labored over some of the logistics of the camp in order to avoid just having events occur to service the story. I wanted a good portion of the book to feel like going to camp with these characters, who were still developing as human beings in their formative years, and only interspersing a little bit of mystery/horror along the way. That way, when the shit hit the fan, it was a real shock to the system. You'll have to tell me if it worked.

If you're someone that is constantly feeling the need the create, don't just push it back. That nagging itch to create and populate a world with our own unique characters is there for a reason. So that an idea can flourish into something you never thought possible. This book is proof of that.

Thank you for reading.

ABOUT THE AUTHOR

Tyler Nichols was born in Battle Creek, Michigan in February 1991. He grew up mostly in Coldwater, becoming obsessed with great storytelling at a young age. After many years of writing short stories, he turned to screenwriting, completing many different scripts in different genres, though focusing mostly on horror.

After graduating from Ball State University, his obsession with storytelling finally took hold and he took to anything that would give him a creative outlet. His website, www.zombievictim.com features various projects of his, including videos and various writing.

His next book, an untitled horror/adventure, will be published in 2017, with the sequel to *The Crimson Summer* following in late 2017/early 2018.

Made in the USA
Lexington, KY
07 January 2018